Turn Left
at
Sanity

NANCY WARREN

Turn Left at Sanity

BRAVA

KENSINGTON PUBLISHING CORP.
http://www.kensingtonbooks.com

BRAVA BOOKS are published by

Kensington Publishing Corp.
850 Third Avenue
New York, NY 10022

ISBN 0-7582-0584-8

First Kensington Trade Paperback Printing: February 2005
10 9 8 7 6 5 4 3 2 1

Printed in the United States of America

Turn Left at Sanity

Chapter 1

"Do you remember George Murdoch?" asked Aunt Lydia around a mouthful of cucumber sandwich. "He was a regular customer. Sometimes he'd bring that fiddle of his and play to the girls." She smiled mistily. "He was a fine, fine man." At seventy-five, Aunt Lydia was an improbable redhead with a tendency to live in the past.

The dainty woman on the blue velvet settee, whose hair was white and float-away delicate, nodded. "He was hung."

"Really, dear? I thought they'd done away with capital punishment in Idaho," said Betsy Carmichael, who'd come in her Sunday best to take tea.

"More Earl Grey, ladies?" Emmylou Sargent walked among them with the heavy silver teapot she'd inherited along with the former brothel and some of the retired working girls. Afternoon tea at the Shady Lady bed and breakfast in Beaverton, Idaho, was a tradition Emmylou had started a year or so ago when she realized she was going to need a lot more business if she was going to make a go of running a B&B in a town where tourism had plenty of room to grow and the local industries were . . . unconventional.

After filling the bone china teacups, she passed around the cucumber sandwiches and the thin slices of lemon cake she'd baked from a recipe in a ten-year-old issue of *Gourmet*. She didn't figure, in a house that was over a hundred years old, its residents not much younger, that anyone would care if she used a recipe from the last decade. There were days she thought no one would notice if she served decade-old cake.

She had to admit that afternoon tea wasn't a roaring success. No one but the aunts who lived at the Shady Lady and their friends, who were too poor to pay, ever showed up, but it had become such a Sunday afternoon ritual that Emmylou kept it up anyway. It gave them something to do, a chance to dress up in the finery they all loved, and reminisce about their good old days.

By now Emmylou knew all the stories as well as if she'd been there when the Shady Lady had been upgraded from boom town brothel to become a vital part of the innovative Dr. Emmet Beaver's practice for healthful living, both mental and physical. The ladies gathered in the sitting room had been Intimate Healers.

Now they were old ladies, and Emmylou, who'd grown up here, was their collective granddaughter since her beloved Gran had passed on.

The sound of the doorbell shocked the assembled company of women into silence. The doorbell never rang. Anyone who lived in Beaverton would walk on in; the door was never locked.

"Could it be a guest?" Olive wondered aloud.

At the words, Lydia sat straighter and rearranged the folds of her red silk dress to its best advantage. Since she was self-conscious about her varicose veins, she crossed her legs and tucked them against the brocade sofa.

"I'll go and check," Emmylou said. She'd tried over and over to explain to Lydia that *guest* had a different connotation now that the Shady Lady was a B&B than it had forty years ago.

She didn't have any bookings coming in today. Heck, she didn't have any bookings all month—it wasn't hard to keep track. Probably, Geraldine Mullet had been watching *Gone with the Wind* again and was here to warn them all that the Yankees were at the door, ready to burn their barns and commandeer their plantation houses. When she was bound and determined to save Tara, Geraldine wasn't bad company. It was when she suggested burning the place themselves so those damned Yankees couldn't take them over that Emmylou had to draw on all her tact.

However, when Emmylou emerged from the parlor into the entrance foyer, it wasn't Geraldine standing there looking like Vivien Leigh might look today if she were still alive.

In her hall was a man she'd never set eyes on before.

A gorgeous man.

He was tall, with black hair that would have been completely straight but for the errant cowlick above his left eyebrow. His eyes were pewter gray, or maybe steel. He had the kind of face that made her remember that the heavy silver teapot she still held was sterling, and wish she'd hidden it before blundering out here.

If it had been Civil War times, he wouldn't have been gambling ne'er-do-well Rhett Butler, he'd have been a Union officer here to take what he could get, whatever her opinions on the matter. He didn't look to be a charmer or a gambler, this one; he looked like a hard-eyed predator.

She swallowed and said, "Can I help you?"

He turned those eyes on her and she felt a prickle of sensation climb her neck. Fear? Curiosity? She couldn't name it, but the feeling made her uneasy.

"Yes. I understand this is the only accommodation in town." His voice was crisp and completely unaccented, as though any kind of twang or lilt would be a waste of his precious time. No pleasantries, either, she noted, though his eyes gave her a very thorough once-over while she stood there staring.

"That's right," she said. Business was business and no matter how uncomfortable he made her feel, she was going to be nice to him. He was obviously a guy with enough money for the best clothes, like the casual but no doubt expensive charcoal slacks and black turtleneck sweater. His briefcase looked designed by NASA; he gave off the impression of having finished a business meeting in Manhattan and hopping on his Lear jet to get here. Clearly the Lear pilot had no sense of direction or he'd been drinking on the job, because Mr. Corporate had taken a wrong turn somewhere.

But, she reminded herself once again, business was business and he didn't look as though he'd have any trouble paying his bill. Although, when you lived in a town like Beaverton, you didn't give much credence to appearances.

"I can wait, if you're in the middle of something," he said, polite but cool, motioning to the silver pot.

"Oh, no, that's all right." Carefully, she set the pot on a marble-topped vanity that also held a bouquet of deep pink peonies in a crystal vase, their thin stems struggling to hold the overblown glory of the blooms.

She stepped behind the ornate reception desk that was built into the foyer and pulled out the leather-bound registration book she'd found in an antique shop. Flipping to a fresh page, she passed the book, and the fountain pen she kept specially, to her new guest.

Aunt Olive had tried to talk her into a computerized reservation system, but she liked the simple, old-fashioned book. It fit with the period of the Shady Lady and was well able to handle the few paying guests they received. Of course, she wasn't a complete Luddite. The Shady Lady had a very nice website, which Olive kept up. Emmylou also tried to be creative with a small advertising and marketing budget, and people who'd stayed here often recommended the Shady Lady to friends. Maybe they weren't running the busiest inn in the area, but they were making ends meet and Emmylou was optimistic enough to believe that once more people experienced Beaverton, which was like nowhere else on earth, tourism would grow.

She watched as the newest guest wrote his name in a bold but perfectly legible scrawl. Like his speaking voice, his penmanship displayed no extra flourishes, no wasted time, no wasted ink. No nonsense.

When he was done, she read over his entry. Joe Montcrief was his name, and she was pleased to find she'd guessed correctly. His address was in Manhattan.

"And how long will you be staying with us, Mr. Montcrief?" she asked in her best B&B proprietor's tone.

"It's Joe," he said. She got the impression that it wasn't informality that made him tell her that, more that he didn't want the extra time wasted with all those syllables. He'd even knocked the "seph" from Joseph. He should be glad his parents hadn't christened him Mortimer, or Horatio. "I'll definitely stay two nights, and possibly a third." No "if it's all right with you." No "if you have room."

"That's fine. The Blue Room is available," she said. In fact, all but the aunts' rooms were free. Four in all. But the Blue was both the priciest and the best she could offer. "It's got a queen-sized bed and a private bath. There's a small sitting area—"

"Is there a desk?"

"A rolltop."

A slight shudder seemed to pass across his face. "Tell me you have Internet access."

"Not in the rooms. There's a hookup in the library."

"All right."

This poor man was going to be so out of place here that despite her urge to divest him of some of his money, she told him, "You know, there's a Hilton only an hour's drive away. You might be more comfortable—"

He interrupted a second time. "No. This will be fine. Thank you."

Her conscience was clear. She smiled at him. "Our breakfasts are better, anyway."

"What time is breakfast?" He had the most amazing eyes. In the few minutes he'd been in her foyer, they'd changed shades. Not pewter now, more of a Paul Newman blue.

Since he was her only guest, breakfast was pretty much whenever he wanted it, though she decided to keep her lack of business to herself. "Seven to nine, but we can adjust with a day's notice."

"Seven's fine."

"I'll take your credit card imprint now, please."

She wasn't a bit surprised when he handed over a platinum card.

"Are you visiting family in town?" she asked.

"No. I've got business in the area."

"Really." She glanced up. She couldn't imagine what interest he could possibly have here. She knew every person and every business for miles and couldn't picture a single one of them being involved with a sharp-looking man from New York.

He sent her a bland smile but offered no further information. Whatever his business, she'd know it all soon enough. Beaverton was like that.

"Will you need help with your luggage?"

He glanced at her like she was nuts, and only then did she notice the navy blue overnight bag in the corner. "Right this way, then," she said, picking out one of the ornate brass keys from the board behind her and stepping around the counter.

She led the way and he followed. As they entered the hallway, she heard the muffled voices from the parlor. It wasn't tough to guess what the subject was. "We're serving afternoon tea at the moment," she said. "You're welcome to join us."

He didn't answer, so she guessed he wouldn't be swapping stories with Olive and Lydia over cucumber sandwiches. She breathed a quick sigh of relief. "We serve breakfast in the dining room," she said as they passed the big room she'd set up so prettily with antique and secondhand furniture finds. She'd collected small tables and chairs of different vintages, linen cloths, china and flatware that didn't match, and that was part of the charm.

She'd have to remember to freshen the flowers on all the tables. She'd also have an opportunity to add some variety to her morning menu. Since Aunt Olive only ate brown toast with raspberry jam and coffee, and Aunt Lydia had a bowl of oatmeal and stewed prunes every morning of her life, there was little scope for the imagination. Tomorrow, she'd put on a full breakfast—who cared if it was only for one man's enjoyment? Maybe he'd send all his Wall Street friends to Beaverton for their holidays. The thought made her smile as they got to the broad oak stairway and climbed.

For some reason, she felt suddenly self-conscious. Naturally, since he was behind her on the stairs, chances were that her customer was watching her back. Big deal. So why did she feel this hot, twitchy feeling as though her black skirt was too short and too tight?

She was glad when the endless stairway ended and she could show him his room. Its robin's egg blue and white striped wallpaper looked fresh, and yet fit with the late 1800s period when the Shady Lady had been built. The four-poster bed was original to the house, though the mattress was new. She wanted her guests to have the best night's sleep they could ever remember. It was, after all, what her great-great-grandmother had promised when she'd opened the brothel. Naturally, she'd had her own ways of ensuring her gentlemen guests slept well. Emmylou relied on top quality mattresses, Irish linen bedding, and her bucolic setting to do the job.

She ran a quick eye over everything, but there was no dust anywhere. The room looked as fresh as if the last guest had checked out this morning instead of three weeks ago.

The chintz duvet cover, in yellow with green-stemmed lilacs printed on it, was as fresh as springtime. The ceramic jug and basin gleamed on the old washstand; the rolltop desk, which had belonged to the great Dr. Emmet Beaver himself, had the rich patina of age; and the old Axminster on the floor held the grooves of a recent vacuuming.

Her guest didn't say anything, merely deposited his briefcase on the floor and placed his overnight bag on the easy chair she'd set by the window. Two other arm chairs flanked the fireplace.

"The fireplace works," she told him. "It's gas-powered." She showed him where the switch was located.

"Fine," he said again, sounding extremely uninterested in the fireplace. She supposed he wasn't here to curl up in front of the fire with a good book, or enjoy the view of her garden. Right, he was here to work. The room might be a little frou-frou for him, but then if you were going to stay in a former brothel turned bed and breakfast, surely you had a hint what you were getting into.

"I'll leave you to get settled, then."

"Thanks. Oh, do you have a list of restaurants in town?" She blinked at him.

"For dinner?"

"Right." Her mind raced. Where could she send him that wouldn't have him speeding back to New York before his first good night's sleep? A sleep, come to think of it, that he looked as though he could use.

A gleam of humor flashed across his face and she wanted to catch hold of it. How it transformed that cold, all-business countenance into something warm and teasing. "People do eat here?"

"Yes, of course," she said. "I'm trying to remember who's open on Sunday nights. I'll check and let you know."

"Thanks."

"Well, here you are then," she said, and stepped closer to hand him his key. As she reached him, he held out his hand, palm up. A strong hand. Clean, callus-free, and ringless. Once more she felt that curious prickling at the back of her neck like a premonition.

When she returned downstairs, she popped her head into the parlor long enough to say, "I'm going to make fresh tea." She could use a cup.

She entered the parlor with the fresh tea and a few more sandwiches, knowing they were all dying to hear about the new guest, when the object of their curiosity walked in. Since she hadn't dreamed he'd want to sit around drinking tea with old ladies, she was surprised. Even more so when she saw that he was carrying an overweight and rather smug-looking tortoiseshell cat.

"Does this cat belong to someone?" he asked in that crisp voice.

"Why, Mae West, what have you been doing?" Aunt Olive said. "We were napping together. When I came down here, she was still asleep."

"She seems to have woken," said their guest, though that wasn't entirely true. The cat purred lazily in his arms, its bright green eyes only half open. That cat knew darned well she wasn't allowed in the guest rooms. Maybe she was trying to fool them into thinking she'd been sleepwalking.

"I'm sorry," Emmylou said. "Mae West is curious." She was also man mad, hence her name. "I hope she didn't disturb you?"

"She was banging on my window and howling."

She held out her arms, but Mae West wasn't having any of it. She flopped to her back and turned so she could bury her head against that muscular chest. Emmylou wanted to laugh, but Joe Montcrief didn't look particularly amused. He was probably calculating his dry cleaning bill, since his cashmere was liberally covered with cat hair.

"I'm so sorry," she repeated, taking a firm hold of the cat, which meowed in protest. As she scooped up the animal, her fingers inadvertently dug into Joe's belly and she couldn't help but notice that he sported a nice hard set of abs. He smelled like something they didn't get a lot of at the Shady Lady. Like young, virile man. For a second she envied the cat, then gave herself a mental shake and dumped Mae West on the floor. With a *brrp*, the cat stalked to the couch and leaped to Aunt Olive's lap.

Joe was brushing cat hair off his sweater and the thighs of his slacks.

Lydia, watching him with interest, said, "You look like you've got a pretty nice package. What's the matter? Can't you get it up?"

Joe stopped brushing cat hair off his pants and glanced up at Lydia as though he couldn't have heard properly.

Aunt Olive, busy stroking Mae West, said, "Really, dear. Not in public."

Betsy merely looked interested.

"Tea!" Emmylou shrieked.

Joe raised his head and blinked at the assembled company. No doubt, they looked like something from a drawing room farce, but if he said one rude or insulting thing to her darling aunts, he'd be out on his ear and that was that.

"Thanks," he said. "I'd like some tea."

"I could bring some to your room, if you're working."

He looked over at Aunt Lydia, then at Olive and Betsy. "No. I'll have it here."

Well, she thought, as she poured him a cup in the best bone china with the pink roses, at least he'd forgotten about the unfortunate incident with Mae West.

"Joe Montcrief," she said, belatedly remembering her manners, "I'd like you to meet Lydia Smoltz and Olive Bennet, who live here, and Betsy Carmichael, who's come for tea." *And please let them behave.*

But Lydia, sadly, wasn't nearly finished. "Well, young man," she said, sitting straighter and giving him a glimpse of what a fine pair of legs a woman could still reveal at seventy-five years old, "you were wise to come to us. Did the doctor send you?"

"Doctor?" He held the delicate cup with no awkwardness, and still managed to look manly. Emmylou had a firm rule about getting involved with guests, but she could look, couldn't she?

"It's all right. We've helped many men like yourself over the years. An older woman can offer so much more than a clueless young woman. In our day, men didn't need any of those newfangled drugs. They had us, right, Olive?"

"That's right. We worked our magic the old-fashioned way. Too bad they couldn't bottle us back then."

"Sandwich, Aunt Lydia?" Emmylou asked desperately.

But her aunt waved her away. "What is your sexual problem? I'd be happy to help."

In her day, Lydia, along with Olive and Emmylou's grandmother, Patrice, had been what Dr. Emmet Beaver termed Intimate Healers. Lydia, however, hadn't grasped the concept of retirement.

"Sexual problem?" Joe echoed, looking dumbfounded, while three older women who all ought to have known better stared at his crotch.

Helpless to think what else she could do, Emmylou passed him his tea and placed a proprietary hand on his shoulder. In a case of desperate times and desperate measures, she said, "Sorry, Aunt Lydia. Joe is my client."

As her supposed client looked up and caught her gaze, the trickle of awareness she'd felt built up to a waterfall.

Those silver, gray, blue eyes were shot through with devilry. "Thank you, Emmylou," he said. "I think I'm going to need a lot of one-on-one work."

Uh-oh. She had a feeling there was trouble ahead.

Chapter 2

Joe was rarely surprised. A great deal of his success depended on knowing what he was getting into long before he got there. So he'd forgotten one simple fact about himself.

He loved surprises.

He didn't have the faintest clue what was going on in this faded, overstuffed, over-decorated room with its three old ladies and one very sexy young one, but he was going to sit back and enjoy himself until he found out.

Emmylou gave his shoulder a little squeeze, which he figured was thanks for not laughing in that sweet old gal's face—as if he would. He got offered sex all the time, so he rarely thought about it, but he'd never been offered sexual healing by someone old enough to be his grandmother.

The only sex problem he had was slipping out of a woman's bed as easily as he slipped in. From trial and error he'd discovered two fair playing fields. He dated women who were under thirty, before the biological clock hit the alarm button, or over forty, when they'd either already had their kids or decided they didn't want any. That way he could keep the relationships about sex rather than lifetime mating. It wasn't that he minded kids—hell, he'd probably have them someday—but he didn't like feeling as though he were trying out for the role of forever mate and daddy when all he wanted was some female companionship, a hot, willing body, and some laughs.

"Well," the same old gal said to Emmylou, "I don't see why you should get all the nice young men. I've had a lot more experience." She turned to him and asked, "So what is your problem, dear? Premature ejaculation? A reluctant member?" She glanced significantly at his lap. "Certain needs that aren't being fulfilled? Or—"

"Aunt Lydia! I should explain. You see—"

But he didn't want to hear some boring explanation.

"I'll bet you've helped a lot of men," he said to the woman Emmylou called Aunt Lydia.

"Oh yes, indeed. Dr. Emmet used to say I had a real feel for my work." She giggled, and he had the strong feeling it was an old joke being trotted out for his benefit. Half the fun was watching out of his peripheral vision the way Emmylou was frantically signaling the other two old gals, and the facial twisting and hand gesturing she was getting in reply. They wanted to shut "Aunt Lydia" up, but he wanted to hear what she had to say.

And then he intended to get back to the part where Emmylou had announced she'd taken him on as a client. She wasn't his usual type. Her address was Rosehip Lane, not Wall Street. She was a country girl, fresh and wholesome. She wore a starched apron, for God's sake. But under the apron she wore a hip-looking skirt that fit in all the right places. She smelled of cinnamon and ginger, but there was something far more intoxicating in her eyes.

She also looked to be well under thirty. Mid-twenties at a guess. Definitely not ready to obsess about motherhood. Yep. He could be interested in some sexual healing.

"We worked for the noted psychologist and philanthropist, Dr. Emmet Beaver," Lydia said.

"Dr. Beaver?" Was she putting him on?

"I'm sure you've heard of him."

"No."

"I suppose you're too young. His techniques were advanced. He had his own foundation here in town, you see. People came from all over with their problems."

"Sexual problems?"

"Not only those. Various maladies—"

"Nutbars. Lots of nutbars," Olive interrupted.

"And he treated them all. We were chosen as Intimate Healers, so we worked mainly with the sexual difficulties. We helped many a man, and many a marriage."

"Is that what you'd call a sex surrogate today?" he wondered aloud, intrigued.

"I prefer our term," she replied a mite huffily.

He bit back a smile. He supposed there was snobbishness in every profession.

"Dr. Beaver was such a fine physician, he cured everyone, you know."

An unladylike snort emerged from the saintly-looking woman with spun sugar hair. "Don't be a fool, Lydia." She turned to Joe and explained. "The foundation ran out of money so they told all the patients they were cured. They opened the doors of the sanitarium, released the patients, and then closed the place permanently."

Now he was interested. He suspected that long-empty sanitarium, and the acres of land it sat on, was the reason he was here.

"What happened to the—" He caught himself before he said "inmates" and substituted, "Former patients."

"Most of them still live around here," the spun-sugar-haired woman said. "They're all crazy as loons."

"They were all cured by the good doctor," the woman called Lydia insisted.

Olive sent him a sly smile. "She's as crazy as the rest of them. Hell, we all are, except for Emmylou, and if you ask me, she'd have more fun if she was a bit more crazy."

Oh, this was turning into a very interesting afternoon. Since the wiring was so old he couldn't plug in his laptop upstairs, he'd anticipated being bored witless, but that big old cat had done him a favor.

"Cucumber sandwich?" Emmylou asked him. She didn't

look embarrassed, simply resigned. It must be hell living with a bunch of retired sex healers.

There were places in Manhattan where you lined up for afternoon tea to get surly waiters and be jammed together so tight you knew what brand of deodorant the person next to you used. Or didn't.

This was much better. Not that he was a tea drinker, and it would take about a hundred and twenty of those doll-sized sandwiches to fill a man, but part of his object in coming to Beaverton was to gather information on the potential work-force for the new factory. It was obvious these women had lived here a long time and must know their town, so he could pump them for information while sipping tea out of a cup that was a direct threat to his masculinity. It seemed he *was* getting some work done this afternoon.

He was about to ask more about the esteemed Dr. Eager Beaver when a new distraction occurred. Two more old gals walked in. The first wore an ancient pink Chanel suit and a string of fat pearls he'd bet were real. Her purse and shoes matched. "I hope we're not too late for tea," she said in a cultured tone that sounded like Boston Brahmin. "Madame Dior and I suddenly decided we wanted one of your divine cakes, my dear." She walked to Emmylou and they air-kissed.

Madame Dior paused until the Chanel woman was well into the room before making her own entrance. And make an entrance she did. She swept in like a thirties actress onto the stage. Her short black hair bobbed as she walked, and she looked around with large, black-rimmed eyes. Her skin was white and her lipstick dark red. She wore black slacks and a silk blouse with abstract designs on it, and held a cigarette holder with a blue cocktail cigarette—unlit. The kind of cigarette holder that he'd only ever seen in old movies or at costume parties.

"Of course you're not too late. Come in," said Emmylou, rising.

"Miss Trevellen, Mme. Dior, I'd like to introduce Joe Montcrief."

He stood, as he'd been taught to do years ago in prep school when a lady entered the room. It wasn't the kind of thing you did these days, but with the over-seventy set it was still a popular move.

Miss Trevellen shook his hand and moved to the chair beside an étagère crammed with china and silver doodads that all looked as though they'd be at home in an antique store or museum.

"Wouldn't you like to sit here, closer to Aunt Olive?" Emmylou said, offering the older woman a place on the blue velvet settee.

"I'm fine here, dear. Thank you."

"I am zo 'appee to make your acquaintance," said the French woman in a smoky voice, choosing the seat nearest his and accepting a teacup from Emmylou, who was once more in hostess mode.

"My pleasure," he said. In fact, part of his pleasure was ruined because he doubted there'd be any more talk of intimate healers. However, the more old ladies he could interview, the more information he could gather on this town and its workforce. He was about to ask a leading question when a slight movement caught his eye, and he watched in astonishment as the ladylike Miss Trevellen, wearing pearls that had to be worth ten grand, slipped a little silver dish from the crowd of ornaments beside her and tucked it into her purse.

He glanced around to see if anyone else had noticed, but they were all talking, pouring tea, or choosing sandwiches.

Joe found himself in a dilemma. Should he point out that the old dear had pilfered from her hostess right before his eyes or should he keep his mouth shut?

He decided to keep his mouth shut when he caught sight of Emmylou, who'd paused in the middle of handing out tiny plates and tinier napkins and was gazing at Miss Trevellen with an expression of fond exasperation. He was fairly certain the old lady's purse now bulged in a second place and that yet another of the knickknacks was missing.

His gaze collided with Emmylou's for an instant and as clearly as though she'd spoken, he got the message. *Keep your mouth shut.* He did his best to send back, *I read you loud and clear.* And his message had an addendum: *I want you.*

She must have understood the entirety for she nodded imperceptibly, then her chest huffed a little and her blue, blue eyes opened wide. He didn't get, *I want you back.* He read something in her eyes, though. Not indifference—more the impression that she was attracted to him and didn't want to be.

Too bad. Maybe he could help her get over her reluctance. If he could spare the time from work.

Joe forced down three cups of tea as an excuse to stay; he wouldn't have missed his afternoon for anything. He had the chance to watch his very hot hostess, who wore a short black skirt and an apron and looked great in both of them. He'd never been much for the French maid fantasy, until now. Apart from the sexy Emmylou, were the entertaining older women. Emmylou managed to quell her aunts, to his sorrow, but Madame Dior sat beside him and told him how he reminded her of a boy she once knew in Nice. " 'Ee 'ad ze same beautiful eyes, and ze body. Ah, you make me feel young again."

His cell phone rang a couple of times, but he'd set it to vibrate and didn't feel like plugging in to the real world. He was picking up enough useful information from the tea party that his time was far from wasted.

"Well," Miss Trevellan said, looking to the French woman in a silent *Shall we go?*, when the front door opened and shut with a bang.

Emmylou started to rise, then sank back down when an angry female voice with a southern lilt could be heard ranting, "You will not believe what those mongrel curs have done this time."

Mongrel curs?

"I told them, 'This is the Beaverton Little Theatre Company, not Stratford on Avon,' and those interfering Pyes can take their play and . . ." By this time the owner of the voice had appeared. She was a faded, skinny woman in a flowered cotton dress that went to the floor. On a hippie chick it would have looked stylish. The woman saw him and stopped. "Oh," she said, and tilted her chin down so she could look at him through her eyelashes. Which she then batted. Unfortunately, at him. She fluttered her hand near her face and then giggled. "Well, I do declare, listen to me run on, and in front of company, too."

Once more he stood, then took the small hand held out to him. "I'm Geraldine," she said.

She gazed expectantly at him as though she expected him to kiss her hand, but he shook it firmly instead. "Joe Montcrief."

She sat down with a flutter of hands, lashes, and flowered dress, taking the tea Emmylou handed her with a soft "Thank you."

"Are you a theatrical agent?" the woman asked him.

"No."

"Oh. Well, that's just as well. They won't let me be Maria in this year's musical. Terrea Pye got the part, and you know that's only because she and her husband do everyone's hair."

"You would have been a wonderful Maria," Betsy said. "It wasn't right."

"I have to be a *sister*," the faded beauty said with a pout. "Can you imagine me? A *nun*?"

Olive guffawed, and it was an odd sound coming from such a dainty woman. "That's when I decided to be in this play, too."

"And me," Lydia said.

"Black is my color," Madame Dior stated.

Miss Trevellan sighed softly and said she'd always wanted to be a nun. Joe wasn't an every Sunday Catholic, but he felt that a woman who pilfered the silver during afternoon tea was not cut out to be a nun. Even a pretend one.

"I wouldn't have even been in this silly play if it weren't

for the fun we girls have rehearsing in the attic. I don't like practicing along with men." Geraldine turned the word "men" into two soft syllables and shot Joe another coquettish look from under her lashes. "Dr. Beaver always let the women and men practice separately. It's been just like the old times."

Ah, Joe thought. So the Beaverton Little Theatre Company was an offshoot of amateur theatricals in the loony bin. He'd have to get season's tickets.

"In those days, I believe the men and women put on different plays and performed them for each other," Emmylou said.

"Doesn't matter," Olive stated. "The play will flow seamlessly, you'll see. You will come, won't you, Joe? It's Friday night. You can go with Emmylou. She's not in it."

"If I'm still in town then, I'd love to come." It would be good for him to see the community in action. Not to mention spend some time with his hostess, who must be single if the old gals were fixing her up so blatantly.

"Olive!" Emmylou said, clearly mortified to have been set up by the older woman.

"It's settled then," Olive said, blithely ignoring Emmylou. "If you ask me, you could both use some fun."

Not long after that, the tea ladies took their leave. He felt like the groom in a reception line, as each took his hand and murmured pleasantries.

Betsy Carmichael told him he was a dear, sweet boy. Madame Dior clasped his hand tightly and told him to drop in and see her sometime. Geraldine Mullet kissed his cheek, and while her lips were near his ear whispered, "Until Friday, then." Miss Trevellen gave him her smooth, ladylike hand to shake and thanked him for the pleasure of his company at tea. Her face was delicately flushed as though she'd been for a brisk walk. Her bag bulged.

As far as he could tell, no money had changed hands to pay for the afternoon tea. What kind of way was that to run a business? And come to think of it, where were the other guests? The retired Intimate Healers lived here, and he doubted they were paying for room and board.

He had the sudden suspicion he was the only guest, which was tough for Emmylou and her business, but good news for the company that had sent him here.

When the three others had left, Emmylou began clearing away the dishes. The aunts made an effort to help, but she motioned them back into their chairs. "Your favorite show will be on soon. Relax."

"*Sixty Minutes?*" he guessed.

"*Temptation Island.*"

So Joe surprised himself by picking up the heavy teapot and stacking a few plates.

"You don't have to do that," she protested.

He didn't think he'd ever helped with dishes in a place where he was a paying guest, but then this wasn't like anywhere he'd ever stayed. He wanted to spend a little more time in Emmylou's company, and besides, he needed to report the theft he'd witnessed.

He followed the enticing sway of her apron and all the delectable parts of her that swayed along with it as she led him to her kitchen.

It was, he realized the minute he stepped through an oak swing door, exactly right for Emmylou. Old-fashioned mixed with modern. The kitchen was huge, with a black and white tiled floor, old oak cabinets with glass fronts, and a bay window with a view of the B&B's lush garden. In the bay was a round oak table and chairs that had obviously been there for a century. But the counters were granite, and the appliances stainless steel industrial.

"You must love cooking," he said, looking around him.

"I do," she said with a smile. "You shouldn't help me, you're a guest."

"Yeah, well. I wanted to talk to you privately."

She nodded. "About Miss Trevellen?"

"So you did see her. I thought so." He revisited that moment when he'd witnessed the woman tuck a silver dish into her bag. "She stole one of your"—he didn't quite know what to call all that junk—"your ornaments. In fact, she stole a couple."

"Yes. I know. She doesn't mean to, poor soul. She'll give my things back tomorrow."

"Give them back? In New York, pilfering the silver is petty larceny. I think that's a Class B misdemeanor."

Emmylou laughed softly. "This is Beaverton, Joe. I know it's wrong of her, but she can't help herself. Taking pretty things makes her so happy, and she always returns them. Come with me tomorrow if you like. See if I don't get my property back."

He shook his head in puzzlement. He really didn't have time to traipse all over town. He needed to view the potential property, and yet . . . "I can't resist. You're on. How do we do that exactly? Do we wear all black, throw stockings over our heads, and break in?"

She smiled mysteriously. "Wait and see."

God, she was cute. Her eyes were big and blue, her lashes ridiculously long and dark. Her hair was a tumble of dark honey, and her mouth looked like it talked straight all day and whispered dirty all night.

It had been a long time since a woman had intrigued him this way, even though she wore a starched apron and was surrounded by nutbars, some of whom had grave doubts about his sexual prowess.

His attraction surprised him. Partly it had to do with the way she smelled, like ginger and cinnamon. Like homemade cookies his grandmother would have made if his grandmother hadn't been so busy winning tennis championships at her country club. All he knew was that he wanted to spend some time with this woman, with her sex-obsessed aunts and her cucumber sandwiches.

When he went back into the parlor to collect more dishes, the other women were gone. He picked up Miss Trevellen's teacup and plate. She'd folded her napkin neatly and dropped not so much as a crumb, and yet she'd stolen from her hostess right before his eyes.

A sudden thought occurred to him on his way back to the kitchen. The spun-sugar-haired aunt had said they opened the doors and announced that everyone was cured when the sanatorium closed. "Was Miss Trevellen a patient of Dr. Beaver's?" he asked when he reentered the kitchen.

Emmylou paused in the act of placing crisp little cookies into an old-fashioned cookie jar. "The Beaverton sanatorium has been closed for a long time," she said at last, as though she thought her kleptomaniac neighbor's antics were somehow covered under doctor/neighbor privilege.

In a way he admired that kind of loyalty; besides, her very evasion had answered his question. "Does the local law enforcement know about Miss Trevellen's little hobby? Those pearls around her neck were worth a fortune."

She glanced up in surprise. "You know about women's jewelry?"

"I know a little bit about a lot of things. Well? Do they?"

"Look, Joe, Miss Trevellen's family was very well off. Those pearls have been in her family for generations. She's not a thief. You'll see."

"Just the local kleptomaniac who wasn't entirely cured when they closed up the loony bin?"

Her lips closed tight.

"No," he said. "Don't do that. Say whatever you want to say."

"You're a paying guest. I can't."

"Believe me, nothing you say is going to make me run off screaming into the night. I like this place. And I'm curious."

"All right. The sanitarium was not a 'loony bin' and that is an entirely insensitive term."

"Bet your Aunt Olive wouldn't think so. I definitely heard her refer to most of the townspeople as loons."

She turned around and planted her hands on her hips.

"Aunt Olive is eighty-three years old and was brought up in a less kindly age. She has an excuse. You should know better."

"Well, I wouldn't call it the loony bin to anyone but you."

"Fine." She started to turn away then seemed to change her mind. "Joe, Beaverton is a very special place. This is the kind of town that barely exists any more. People look out for each other and for the most part live happily and in harmony with each other and their world. We know our neighbors by name and we do our best to get along. But there are some . . . eccentrics here."

"So you're saying this entire town is populated by wackos?"

"Of course not. And what an impolite term that is. I'm saying that some of the residents are a little eccentric."

His eyes narrowed. "Define eccentric."

"All I'm suggesting is that you keep an open mind."

"Apart from you the only remotely normal person I've seen is that Frenchwoman."

"Mme. Dior?"

"Yes, the dark woman with the Parisian accent who came to tea with the klepto."

"Mme. Dior's real name is Dorothea Woodrow and the only French she speaks is what she's picked up from movies and Edith Piaf records. She saw Catherine Deneuve in a Dior commercial and decided she was French."

He began banging his head quietly against the wall.

"Really, it's not so bad. Before that she was Eva Gabor on *Green Acres*." She chuckled a little at the memory. "It was the obsessive use of 'darlink' that really got to us after a while."

"Okay," he said. "Tell me the worst. What nutbar gene is running through your blood?"

She colored slightly. "I wish you would find some more modern, appropriate, and politically correct terms."

"You're stalling. Let's see." He helped himself to an apple from the fruit bowl and munched. He was hungry and figured he'd expended more energy in chewing those minute sandwiches than he'd taken in. "Your granddaddy thought he was Napoleon and your grandmother decided she was France and surrendered to the emperor."

She rolled her eyes and went back to putting the food away.

"Oh no. I've got it. She was his nurse. Or maybe he was her nurse. I'm trying to be politically correct and all that," he said when she raised her gaze and looked as though she might smack him with her wooden spoon. "And . . . and . . ." How was he supposed to think when she looked at him like Eve must have looked at Adam, and still smelled of cinnamon and brown sugar. She was sex and comfort all rolled into one mouth-watering package. "They decided to play nurse?"

"Wrong again."

"But I'm getting warmer."

Finally she said, "My great-grandmother founded the town brothel. My grandmother ran it and added some extra services."

He stopped chewing to stare at her in amazement.

"Didn't you know this was the former brothel? It's in the brochure and on our website."

"My secretary told me this was the only place to stay in town. I never saw any brochure. So your grandmother was a—"

"I adored her. She taught me a lot."

Really? He wondered just what that might be. Decided he'd like to find out.

"I went away to college but came back to help her run this place."

"You ran a brothel?" Maybe she was a nutbar after all.

She sent him a "don't be any stupider than you can help" look. "It was a bed and breakfast by then. When Dr. Emmet stopped practicing there was no call for Intimate Healers anymore."

"How disappointing."

A sudden grin lit her face. "There's an attic full of old costumes and, um, things."

"Maybe you'll show me some time."

The grin hadn't completely faded, and now she sent him a provocative glance under her lashes that had to have been passed down in the Shady Lady gene pool.

There was a pause. He finished his apple and went to throw the core into the trash, but she stopped him and directed him to a small plastic bin decorated with flowers. It said *Compost* in fancy script on the side.

"Well," she said. "Thank you for your help."

"Did you think any more about those restaurants?" he asked her, not nearly ready to leave her company.

"I'm not sure . . ."

"I've got an idea. It's a nice evening. Why don't you walk me downtown and point out the best places." He moved a step closer. "Better still, why don't you have dinner with me?"

She turned all the way around until her back was against the counter, then she fiddled with her apron tie. "Dinner. With you."

He found himself smiling. "Yes."

"Like a date?"

"Exactly like a date." Not that he'd really thought of it in such quaint terms.

"Why?" She looked up at him with those big blues.

"Because you're a beautiful woman, I'm alone in town, and the bed and breakfast doesn't serve dinner."

A tiny dimple appeared at the corner of her mouth when she smiled a certain way. "All right." She must get asked out all the time, but he got the feeling she didn't say yes very often. She was intriguing him more by the minute.

Chapter 3

"You must be very hungry," Emmylou said beside him, sounding a little breathless. They were walking downtown for dinner.

"Not particularly."

"Do you always walk this fast?"

He turned to her and saw that she was nearly jogging to keep up with his stride. He had to remind himself this was Podunk, Idaho, on a Sunday. "Sorry," he said, making an effort to slow his pace.

"It's okay. Walking with you is like a workout with a personal trainer, and I can use the exercise." They continued walking, and he did his best to dawdle along, but he wasn't much good at it.

"Well, here we are on Main Street," she said a moment later.

"What the hell is that?" he asked, staring ahead at what looked like a rat rampant. It was carved out of wood and stood at least twelve feet high, dominating the boulevard running down Main. The creature stood on its hind paws, baring buck teeth which had been carved out of some much whiter wood. The whole effect was enough to put a man off his dinner.

"That's our town mascot. The beaver."

He blinked. "I'm surprised they didn't call this street Beaver Boulevard."

"Emmet Beaver vetoed the idea, I believe, out of modesty. There's a Beaver Boulevard out in our only suburb, though."

"He wasn't too modest for a twelve-foot carved beaver in the middle of town?"

She glanced up at him and he could see her blue eyes twinkling. "I guess not."

He stared at the world's biggest beaver for another moment and then shook his head, knowing there was not one single comment he could make that wouldn't get him into trouble. "So where is this restaurant?"

"Belle's Home Cooking is a couple of blocks down and then left."

"Belle's Home Cooking." Yep, he was in Podunk, all right, but her next words still surprised him.

"It's well named. It really is Belle's home. Ever since her kids moved out, she's missed them so much she keeps cooking big family meals and whoever wants to come for dinner shows up."

"What's on the menu?"

The street was all but deserted so he had no trouble hearing Emmylou or following where she led, which was straight down Main.

"Whatever she feels like cooking. For a while, after her youngest went off to college, she kept up the same weekly meals she'd served her family for decades. Roast on Sunday nights, leftovers on Mondays, Tuesdays was pork chops in mushroom sauce. Thursday was . . . um, spaghetti, I think. No, maybe it was chicken and mashed potatoes. Yes, that's right. Saturday was spaghetti. After a couple of years, people started to complain so now she's added some new stuff. I'm not going to fool you, though. It's plain home cooking."

"So this woman serves whatever the hell she feels like and people come and eat it."

"Yes, that's right. She's a very good cook. She sets her big table in the dining room and she's got a trestle table set up in the kitchen. Some people prefer that, because then they can chat to Belle while she's cooking. She's happy because she doesn't miss her kids so much, and anyone in town who's hungry for a simple home-cooked meal and doesn't feel like cooking themselves can go on down there."

"And you all share a table?"

"That's right."

He thought about Belle running her restaurant on a whim, and the woman he'd met at tea who'd decided one day to become French, and the old dear pocketing other people's treasures because she liked them. "Does everyone in this town just do whatever they feel like?"

She thought it over for a minute. "Pretty much. We frown on causing pain or harm. But that's about it."

"This is the craziest damn place I've ever seen."

"Happiest, too, I bet." She drew closer to him and he liked the sense of intimacy. "It's Sunday, so Belle will have a roast of some kind. That all right with you?"

"What are the other options?"

"Ernie's." So there were only two places to eat in town and one was somebody's home kitchen.

"Tell me about Ernie. And if he calls himself Colonel and serves fried chicken, I'm not interested."

"Honestly, Joe. You should try to keep an open mind." She shook her head at him and pointed across the street to a tavern with a neon Budweiser sign in the window that looked as though it needed a new bulb. "Ernie's wife got after him about his drinking, so he went out and opened his own bar."

"Why didn't somebody stop him? I thought you didn't cause each other pain in this place."

"Well, it's a funny thing. He's so busy tending bar that he doesn't have time for drinking anymore. And he needed Marge to take over the kitchen, which she did. I think it saved their marriage. Now they have something in common, he's taking pride in his work, she's too busy running the kitchen to nag, and things have worked out for them."

"Okay, I pick Ernie's. I want to see this for myself."

He'd like to see Belle at work serving up a roast dinner at her kitchen table, but he wouldn't get Emmylou to himself if he did that, so the bar would work for tonight.

Ernie's was the kind of place where you played pool in the back. It was a little on the divey side, but he figured if a woman who liked linen and lilacs on her dining table wasn't complaining, he wasn't either. The tables in Ernie's weren't covered in linen, but Formica. Faded red Formica rimmed with silver. The chairs were aluminum with vinyl seats that would have looked retro if he didn't suspect they were the real thing.

Considering he'd pretty much figured the entire town of Beaverton was populated by loonies, the patrons of Ernie's looked normal enough.

An older man in a ball cap nursed a beer at the bar; four kids who couldn't have been drinking age for long, and looked as though they'd worked at some kind of labor all day, wolfed burgers at a booth. Good, he thought. Those were the first people he'd seen in town that might be suitable hires for the new factory.

The guy sitting at the bar nodded to Emmylou, and the four boys said, "Hey."

He supposed Ernie must be the fifty-ish guy behind the bar, with a mustache that needed trimming and thinning gray hair.

"Hi, Emmylou," he said, "I'll be with you in a minute."

"Thanks, Ernie," she said. Joe watched the guy give him a thorough once-over. He felt like Ernie was her dad and he was taking her to the prom. That look said, *You'd better get her home by curfew and her panties better still be on.* In spite of himself he was amused. She hadn't been joking about people looking out for each other here.

He let her choose the table—this was her turf after all—

and she settled into a quiet corner. Julio Iglesias and Willie Nelson were wailing about all the girls they'd loved from a sound system that needed updating.

Plastic menus were propped between the rice-laced salt and the pepper. She handed him one and didn't bother taking one herself.

"The hamburgers are good. The bratwurst is okay if you like a lot of onion. Stay away from the fish and chips. It tastes like the fish crawled all the way inland before dying."

"So noted."

"The meatloaf is great and the pork cutlet's not bad."

He replaced the menu just as Ernie showed up at their table. "What do you want to drink?"

"Soda water for me," Emmylou said.

"I'll have whatever beer's on tap."

Ernie nodded. "And to eat?"

"Meatloaf," Emmylou said.

"Make it two."

After Ernie had left Joe tried to form some tactful question about the place and its residents when she forestalled him.

"You said you were conducting business in the area?"

Well, when she was his landlady checking him in to the bed and breakfast he could sidestep the question, but now that they were out on a date, it didn't seem fair. Besides, this was the kind of place where if you sneezed the entire population offered you a tissue. He might as well be up front.

"That's right. I'm looking at some property on behalf of a client."

"Really? What property?"

Did he tell her now or wait? She'd be delighted that he was here to bring a big factory and resulting prosperity to a town whose biggest attraction at the moment was a twelve-foot-tall carved beaver. On the other hand, he didn't want her getting her hopes up if he ended up advising his clients against the factory. And possibly, deep in his mind was the vestigial embarrassment that he was representing a company that manufactured such a foolish product.

He was saved having to decide when Ernie came up with their drinks. He'd barely taken his first sip of beer when a portly woman with her hair in a bun showed up with their dinner. He got the same once-over but the wife was more direct than her husband. "Who's your friend, Emmylou?"

"This is Joe Montcrief, Marge. He's a guest at the Shady Lady."

"That so?" Marge looked him up and down like he might only be pretending to be a guest at the Shady Lady, and she wanted him to know she had her eye on him.

He bit back a wiseass comeback. She looked like the sort who might take back his dinner if he gave her any lip, so he stuck to a safe, "Yes, ma'am."

Once she'd set two plates of steaming meatloaf, mashed potatoes, and peas in front of them he was glad he'd played nice. Emmylou was right, he decided after the first bite. The meatloaf was terrific.

The townspeople he wasn't so sure about.

"Every person who came into Ernie's tonight stopped to talk to you," Joe said as they walked back to the Shady Lady.

"This is a pretty small town. Everyone knows everyone else."

"Right. I get that, but you are something special. You make people feel comfortable." In fact, he suddenly realized, she'd be a great asset to making the deal happen. She was obviously well-respected in the town and he'd sensed that she was a power player, if Beaverton had such a thing.

"Oh. Thanks."

"Also, you are a killer pool player."

He was treated to a mischievous grin. "I hope I didn't bankrupt you."

"That six bucks is going to hurt. No question."

The quiet was almost eerie to a guy who'd spent the last seven years living in Manhattan. Without the sirens, the non-stop traffic, the yelling, cursing, and general noise of a big, crowded city, his eardrums seemed to be searching out something. Anything. Soon he'd believe he'd gone deaf.

He heard something at last, and only by straining his out-of-practice hearing. The rustle of undergrowth, so slight as to be almost unheard. The sound of their footsteps on the gravel shoulder beside the road that led to her place. For the first time in a very long while he could actually hear himself breathe.

Before he'd had time to get used to how much he was enjoying a quiet walk with this cookie-baking pool shark, they'd arrived back at the bed and breakfast.

"Thank you for dinner," she said when they got to the door, letting him know that the date stopped here.

"Let's not go in quite yet," he said. Once they were inside that door, she was the innkeeper once more and he was a customer. Out here they were still a man and a woman on their first date, and he hadn't said half the things he'd wanted to, hadn't asked her any of the million things he wanted to know about her town and her life.

Because he couldn't help himself, he reached out and picked up a lock of her hair, letting it sift through his fingertips. She didn't try to stop him, or rush inside, but a certain wariness entered her eyes.

"When do we get started?" he asked.

"Started on what?"

"On your program to cure my sexual problems."

She didn't blush or fluster as he'd half thought she might, she simply raised one skeptical eyebrow. "What *are* your sexual problems?"

"I've got one big one." He let his fingertips trail across her cheek and stepped in closer. "I want to make love to my landlady," he said softly.

"That's not a problem," she corrected. "It's an urge."

"It will be an awful problem if she turns me down."

"Good night, Joe," she said, and walked away.

"Wait. What about my problem?"

"Dr. Beaver was eccentric, certainly, but he did a lot of good. You should treat him with a little more respect. And me. I'm his great-granddaughter."

Oh, great. No wonder she'd been so uppity about the way he'd referred to the revered doc and his "sanitarium." In the middle of trying to get the woman into bed, he'd gone and insulted her grandpa. Nice move.

"I'm sorry. I didn't know."

"Now you do," she said with a smile and took another step away from him.

He didn't want her to go in; out here the air was soft and scented with all that flowery stuff from her garden. There was moonlight tipping leaves with silver and gilding the rustic wooden bench near where they were standing. A woman who created such a romantic setting must be a sucker for it, and yet he hadn't even had a chance to kiss her yet. Nor would he if he didn't think of something fast. She took another step away from him.

There was only one thing he could think of to make her stay. "Look, the truth is I do have a . . . an intimate problem."

"I'll bet." Sarcasm dripped off her tongue, but she did turn back, he noted. "You can't figure out how to have four women at once? The gals throw themselves at you so often you're exhausted? You're so big you—"

"I can't sleep when a woman's in bed beside me." Shit! Why had he gone and blabbed that? What the hell was the matter with him? He heard his own feet shifting on the gravel and dropped his gaze to a dark leafy bush he wouldn't have recognized in broad daylight, never mind nighttime.

She took a step toward him and moonlight made silver flutters of her hair. She looked like a mermaid emerging from the sea, the water sluicing off her body.

"Is this some foolish attempt to get me into bed? Because I'm not falling for it."

"No." He blew out a breath, wondering why the hell he'd blurted that out. "It's a stupid thing, but it's true."

"Why are you telling me?"

"Hell if I know. I didn't want you thinking I was making fun of you. I don't want you going inside with the impression that I'm a jerk." He blew out a breath. "And maybe I'm wondering, since the good doctor's blood runs in your veins, whether you might have some ideas?"

She must have believed him for she took a seat on the wooden bench and motioned for him to join her. As he sat down, she turned to him. "Is this recent or has it always been true?"

"Always. When I was younger I liked to make love all night anyway, so who cared? Now, if I'm at a woman's house I end up making lame excuses about an early meeting, which always pisses her off, or lying there awake all night. It's not so bad if they sleep over at my place; at least I can go watch TV or get some work done."

She looked at him as he imagined a caring shrink would, if she were practicing outside and at night. "Have you ever seen anyone about this problem?"

"No. It's not a problem. It's a quirk."

"It's a problem if you ever want a permanent relationship. You're what, thirty-five or six?"

"I'm thirty-two." Okay, so he was tired and he worked too hard, no wonder he looked older than his years.

"All right." A tiny furrow developed between her brows and he knew he had her full attention. But why the hell hadn't he made something up? Why tell this attractive stranger something that would make her think at least twice before jumping into bed with him?

Why tell her something he'd never told another soul?

Chapter 4

Emmylou gazed into the silver gray eyes of the man she'd had dinner with tonight. Her first date in nine months and she picked a man so terrified of women, intimacy, or God knew what that he couldn't relax enough to sleep.

And wouldn't her poor old grandfather be rolling in his grave if he knew that his progeny had turned out such a failure? If he knew that the woman who'd grown up on his theories of sexual release and emotional partnering as essential to mental health spent her life making a home, not for a husband and babies, but for retired Intimate Healers?

But, on the bright side, she had no trouble sleeping.

"I can't believe I told you that," he grumbled. In the silvery light it was impossible to see his face clearly, but she had a feeling he was blushing.

"Hey, it's good that you shared. That's the first step in overcoming this . . . quirk, don't you think?"

"Well, it's hardly going to encourage you to let me make love to you." The darkness was warm and intimate, like a blanket, so she felt tucked up in bed. The scent of roses was heavy in the air.

She touched his hand. "If it's any consolation, I wasn't planning on sleeping with . . ." She drew a sharp breath and grimaced. "Sorry, poor choice of wording. I mean, I wasn't planning on having sex with you anyway."

He turned his hand palm up and laced his fingers with hers. Little flutters of sensation played over her skin. "Why not?"

"A lot of reasons. The biggest being that I don't have sex with my guests."

"Okay, give me the smaller reasons."

"I'm not interested in casual sex."

"Any others?"

"I think that will do for now."

He smiled down at her smugly.

"What?"

"You never said you weren't attracted to me."

While she'd been throwing out reasons not to go to bed with the man, he'd moved much closer than she realized. And the hand that had laced with hers had danced its way up her arm, over her shoulder to her upper back.

The other came to rest at her hip. He was all the way inside her personal space, thank you very much, so near she could feel the heat of him against her, smell the sandalwood soap she kept specially for her guests. If she so much as raised her chin they'd be kissing.

He took the hand from her hip and slipped it under her jaw. His fingers were smooth but strong and she let him nudge her chin higher, closed her eyes against the starry night, and let him kiss her.

He touched his lips to hers as though she were breakable and had to be handled with care. He didn't ram his tongue down her throat, but used his lips only, tasting, testing her resiliency, letting her know he could be patient and slow.

This was nice, she decided. This was very nice. So she softened and leaned in for a moment. The second he felt her compliance, he pulled her against him. He was long and lean and, oh God, he felt so good.

Her hands wandered up to touch his chest, which was warm through his T-shirt and pulsing where his heart lay beneath. Then around his neck so she could pull him tighter, and then she opened her lips to him.

As his tongue entered her mouth she felt little fireworks explode in her head. *Just a kiss*, she told herself. *It's just a kiss*. But somehow it felt like more. He wasn't from around here, he wasn't the kind of man she usually saw or who made a pass at her. That's why she was reacting this way, she told herself, but herself wasn't listening.

The part of her that was Emmet and Louise's great-granddaughter took over. She pressed against him, running her hands through hair that felt both soft and a little spiky. Rubbed against him the way Mae West had earlier, thinking it was a purely feline response to want to rub against a desirable man.

He was exploring her mouth, inciting her to do some exploring of her own; if she weren't careful she was going to forget all the rules she'd set for herself and do her guest.

And that, she knew, was a really bad idea. So she pulled slowly away. "Wow," she said, licking lips that felt wet and swollen. "I didn't mean for that to get so out of hand."

"Come to bed with me."

She shook her head. "I already told you, I can't." She smiled up at him. "At least this way you'll sleep well." She rose from the bench and turned toward the house.

"You know that's not true. There's already a woman waiting for me in bed."

"What?" She stepped back, aghast, and caught her sleeve on the thorny stem of a rose.

"Mae West," he said in some amusement as she tried to free her right sleeve using her left hand. Ambidextrous she was not, but she didn't want to snag the nicest cotton sweater she owned. Fool to have worn it out with Mr. Big City.

"Damn it," she muttered as the thorn, instead of retreating, dug deeper and scratched her arm.

"Here, let me."

She didn't want him handling her, him with his sandalwood smell and intoxicating kisses. Before she could tell him so, however, he took her arm and, with surprising dexterity, freed her from the rose bush.

"Thanks. Darn thing needs pruning."

"My pleasure." He didn't let her go, but raised her wrist to his lips and kissed it. His lips left an imprint of sensation. If she reacted that strongly to a kiss on the wrist, imagine what he could do to the rest of her.

Unfortunately, at the moment she couldn't think of anything else.

Kitty litter. Why hadn't he told Emmylou he was here in the name of feline toilet paper? While Joe stared at the ceiling, wishing he had Emmylou rather than Mae West curled up beside him, he decided cat litter was the perfect product for this crazy town. Apart from being pretty, the area was an economic no-show, except for some penny-ante farming and a dab of tourism. However, scratch the surface, almost literally, and you hit phosphate. He was here to put together a deal to mine the phosphate that was abundant in the area—a key ingredient in cat litter—and check out a site suitable for building a factory to turn out Feline So Fresh—the number two kitty litter product on the market.

Joe's first instinct had been to turn down the job. He was a player. He put together big property deals, helped buy and sell companies that were household names—or soon would be. Putting together a land deal and factory for a kitty litter manufacturer had excited him about as much as it would Mae West. The original or her namesake.

A preliminary bit of research had quickly changed his mind. There was a heck of a market for cat poo absorption and not so many places where you could easily mine the phosphate necessary to manufacture the stuff.

What his clients, the Gellman brothers, also wanted, however, was a likely spot to build a plant. The old sanitarium seemed ideal. The building appeared solid; it was in a private

location and so far behind in taxes that it had been foreclosed on. He was certain he could negotiate a bargain price.
He'd even been initially optimistic that there was an employ-
able workforce in the area.

Now he'd met some of the townspeople, he wasn't so sure.
However, he'd barely started exploring the surrounding
towns, so maybe he'd find there were plenty of normal, em-
ployable people in and around Beaverton. It was possible.

He'd be here a few days, and in that time he decided it was
also possible that he might encourage Emmylou to soften her
policy on sexual relations with the guests.

Trying to ignore the snoring in his ear and the tuna breath
wafting over his face, he finally slept.

Joe was the only guest at breakfast when he strolled into
the dining room a few minutes before seven, not totally to his
surprise since he seemed to be the only guest in the Shady
Lady. In fact, the way people had stared at him last night, he
seemed to be the only unfamiliar face in town. He sat at the
dining table, where a carafe of mouth-wateringly fresh coffee
sat, with a folded newspaper beside it.

He poured his first cup of caffeine and flipped open the
paper—*The Beaverton Bugle.*

What they were bugling about here in Beaverton was a little different than what he read most days in the *Times* or the
Wall Street Journal.

"It's good to know that Mrs. Parton's twins were safely
delivered," he said as he heard the door swing behind him.

"They were high risk," Emmylou said.

"Yes," he agreed, folding the paper and putting it aside. "I
know. Also that she was in labor for fourteen hours, that her
husband Reg cut the umbilical cords, and added together the
babies don't weigh as much as one of Farmer John's squeal-
ing baby porkers, born the same day. Though not, I hope, at
the same facility."

Emmylou wore a blue half-apron this morning, with some

little flowers embroidered on it, but her denim sleeveless shirt and beige capris reminded him of the luscious body he'd held in his arms last night.

He couldn't look at her and not remember the intense kiss they'd shared, and from the way a delicate pink washed over her cheeks when their gazes met, she was obviously thinking the same thing.

"Good morning," she said. "Did you sleep well?"

Why had he told her that stupid thing? "I did fine until Mae West walked across my head on her way to the window."

"Oh no." Her eyes were even bluer when she wore blue, he noticed. He couldn't wait to kiss her again, and a lot more. "Were you able to get back to sleep?"

"I had to get up anyway to open the window. It wasn't wide enough for her. I bet she outweighs Farmer John's porkers."

"I can keep her out of your room if she bothers you."

"No. It's okay. I got some work done."

As she leaned over him to offer a one-page printed menu, he caught the scent of nutmeg and the yeasty scent of fresh baked bread.

He ignored the menu. "Just the coffee and toast, thanks."

She looked so disappointed, he checked out the menu even though he wasn't hungry. And suddenly his appetite roared to life.

"Okay, maybe I'll have the omelet to go with the toast," he said. She looked so pleased, he was glad he'd changed his mind. Gladder still when he tasted her cooking. The omelet was big and fluffy, packed with cheese and mushrooms and fresh herbs that he bet she'd picked mere minutes ago.

"Do you need directions anywhere?" she asked.

"No thanks," he said. He was certain she was being the courteous innkeeper, not trying to pry into his business. Still, he ought to go ahead and tell her the good news. She'd love what the Gellmans were planning for the town. But when he swallowed the last bite of omelet and opened his mouth to speak, the words "cat litter" seemed to catch somewhere. Even as he castigated himself for being such a snob, he remained quiet about his plans. He already had a map that the realtor had faxed his office a week ago. When the property met his approval would be time enough to tell her why he was here.

At nine A.M. sharp he pulled up to imposing wrought iron gates. They were shut, and a rusty chain and padlock kept visitors out—even visitors like him, who had an appointment. He had to wait ten minutes for the realtor, which annoyed the hell out of him, especially as his cell phone had no reception out here.

He was getting ready to check the perimeter of the property and see if there was a place where he could scale the fence, when at last a dusty blue Crown Victoria pulled up and a fortyish woman with a lanky body and overprocessed blond hair got out. She wore a navy pantsuit and too much lipstick.

"I'm sorry to keep you waiting. The traffic was snarled something awful," she said with a big smile.

The padlock opened on her second try and he unwound the rusty chain for her. With a smile of thanks she let him tug open the gates, which screeched menacingly, letting him know they hadn't been open in a while.

Maybe nobody had come through the front gate, but it was clear when they got onto the property that visitors hadn't been scarce. Empty beer cans and liquor bottles, the blackened remains of a few fires, and assorted litter were scattered around the neglected gardens and scrubby lawn with more dead patches than living ones.

An avenue lined with overgrown oak trees led to a huge marble and brick building that looked more like an antebellum estate than a loony bin.

As gracious as it appeared from the end of the drive, he realized as he got closer that the entire place drooped with neglect. Unfortunately, that included the roof. Dollar signs started to flash in his mental calculator. Following his gaze, Ms. Pearson, the realtor, said, "You'll want a building inspection, of course, but this was a well-built place. I'm sure it's salvageable."

"Maybe."

Once they got inside, it was better. The marble floors must have cost a fortune, he mused as they walked through an entrance hall that belonged in a castle. Classical columns rose from the floor; between them was a large stone fountain in the shape of an open oyster shell with a white marble pearl at its center.

In the cavernous entryway he imagined the echo of water that hadn't flowed for years. The double staircase was a gracious sweep of marble, and when he was halfway up he noticed there was something distinctly phallic about the marble columns. A second glance at the fountain and he got it. Marble cocks and stone pussy fountains—the foyer was a gigantic garden of genitalia.

"The original owner of the property was a little eccentric," the realtor chirped behind him, "but he spared no expense on building this place."

Eccentric. He seemed to be hearing that word a lot lately. Translation: insane.

There was evidence of some leaking, and a suspicious rustle that suggested nature, which abhorred a vacuum, had sent in rodents to add some life to the place.

It didn't really matter. A cat litter factory didn't need marble floors or stone baths. They'd run the numbers, but he suspected pulling down the old sanitarium and building a new factory would be cheaper in the end than trying to refigure this old mausoleum.

There was plenty of good, level land, though. All he had to do was negotiate the right purchase price and nail down the mineral rights. Should be a simple matter.

Easy.

They'd be in business within twelve months.

He drove back to the Shady Lady, figuring he could make a few calls, start the ball rolling from down here but be back in his own office in a couple of days.

As he drove home he blinked, hit the brakes to slow, and blinked again.

Unless he'd hit his head on one of the many phallic out-croppings and was hallucinating, ahead of him, at the side of the road and mounted on horseback, was Napoleon.

The long-dead, self-proclaimed emperor of France was in full uniform, including a big sideways hat that arched like a bridge. He was deep in conversation with a guy in a baseball cap sitting on top of a John Deere ride-on tractor.

As Joe drove slowly by, feeling as though he were staring at a car wreck, he noticed that Napoleon's hair was bottle black over a deeply lined face. When he caught sight of Joe slowing down to crane his neck for a better look, the man nodded with dignity. Joe fought the urge to pull his forelock.

Oh, yeah. He'd be done here in a couple of days, tops. The sooner he was out of Kooksville, the better.

Chapter 5

"I need to send some e-mails," Joe said after a few frustrating attempts to check his cell phone messages in his room. "Mind if I use the office?"

"No, of course not," Emmylou said. "Make yourself at home."

He tried to pretend that business had brought him into Emmylou's kitchen, but really he'd been lured by the irresistible smell of baking.

He shook his head. "I thought New York was full of wackos, but I drove past Napoleon earlier today."

Emmylou continued taking cookies off a baking pan and slipping them onto a cooling rack.

As though she heard the saliva pooling in his mouth, she said, "Help yourself."

"Thanks." He did, and as he sunk his teeth into a ginger snap that was crunchy on the outside and still hot and chewy inside, he wondered why he'd ever eaten a cookie out of a box.

"That's Helmut Scholl," she said.

"I thought it was a ginger snap," he answered around another huge bite.

"Napoleon. His real name is Helmut Scholl."

He swallowed and swiped two more cookies. "He's German and he's pretending to be Napoleon? If he's got to pick a manifestation of his megalomania, why not dress up as Hitler?"

"Well . . ." She paused and turned to face him, the metal thing she'd used to lift the cookies still in her hand. "Helmut likes horses. You don't picture Hitler on a horse somehow."

"You don't picture Napoleon shouting ja wolt, either."

The fact that he was even having this conversation made him wonder if there was something in the water of Beaverton that made even supposedly sane people nuts. Him, for instance. He hadn't been released from Dr. Emmet's bankrupt sanitarium so that couldn't account for the fact that he'd gone half mad in the thirty or so hours he'd been here. Between lustful thoughts of his landlady, having his sleep stolen by an overweight cat with halitosis, and meeting the "eccentric" locals, he wasn't feeling exactly balanced. He'd have the water quietly checked out.

While he was contemplating whether Emmylou's good manners would prevent her slapping him if he took another cookie, Aunt Lydia walked in—no, not walked, staggered. Her legs were a good three feet apart and she winced with every step. Not knowing much about old ladies, he kept his mouth shut, but Emmylou immediately dropped everything and rushed forward. "Aunt Lydia, what is it?"

"Don't fuss, girl. I tried one of them thongs. I hear they're sexy. Hah! You tell me what's sexy about getting rope burn up your butt?"

"Where did you get a thong?" Emmylou asked.

Ignoring Emmylou, the old woman turned to him and snarled, "You think thongs are sexy?" as though it was his fault she was wearing the thing.

He supposed that his first instinctive response—"Depends who's wearing it"—wasn't the most tactful, so he settled on a noncommittal shrug. Now Emmylou, in nothing but one of those aprons and a thong, oh yeah. Sexy as hell.

"And where did you get a thong?" Aunt Olive came into the room, repeating Emmylou's question.

After glaring at him, clearly unhappy with his shrugged response, Lydia wobbled in a circle, her legs stiff and pushed out to the sides, like a woman with two broken legs in casts. "You're not the only one who's smart, you know. I got it on eBay. I wanted it for my costume for the play. But maybe not."

Olive and Emmylou exchanged glances. "What else did you get?"

A crafty grin met them. Old Lydia looked so pleased with herself, Joe was pretty sure he was the only one who was going to like her answer. "A couple lipsticks. That's all."

Emmylou held out her hand. "Let me see."

The old woman put a hand in her lime green velour track suit pocket and handed over a tube of lipstick. Emmylou uncapped it, then turned the screw part at the bottom. He heard a tiny buzzing, and as Emmylou jumped, Lydia laughed so hard tears ran down her face.

"You got a lipstick-vibrator and a thong. What else?"

He'd never seen a vibrator disguised as a lipstick before, so he craned his neck for a closer look.

"Nothing. I was going to get that rabbit vibrator I read about in a magazine, but after this thong I'm not so sure."

"You should be ashamed of yourself at your age. Do you want people to know you're buying these things?"

"No one'll know, honey. I used your name."

The old clock on the wall ticked loudly in the silence, then, to his surprise, Emmylou started to laugh and resumed putting cookies onto cooling racks and the old girls showed no more compunction than he had in snitching the things. It occurred to him that Emmylou was acting like the grandmother with her aprons and home-baked cookies, while the old ladies were the carefree ones, buying thongs and talking trash. She was acting their age, and they were acting hers.

"I love eBay," Lydia said, having swallowed a bite of cookie. "You can sell things, too."

Olive made a rude noise. "Honey, what you want to sell nobody's wanted to buy for years."

"Well, that's where you're wrong. I put myself on eBay."

The metal spatula clattered to the counter. Emmylou said, "You did what?"

"I'm giving away a night of love."

"But . . . but . . ."

"My talents are wasted in this town. All the years of experience and the extra training I got from Dr. Emmet, and all the young men who come here would rather get their therapy from a vestal virgin. So I'm branching out. I'm franchising."

Emmylou made a sound like a small animal in pain.

He was caught by the reference to vestal virgins. Interesting. Didn't Emmylou date much? She was so amazingly sexy he found it hard to believe. But then, around here, who was she going to date? Napoleon?

"Do you have any bidders?" Olive sounded interested in spite of herself.

"Sure do. I bet I'm going to go for a good price. I bet I'll get rich. I'm calling myself Human Viagra."

"Demented Nymphomaniac would be more accurate," Olive muttered.

"Go ahead and scoff, you dried-up old prune. If I get too many men for me to handle, maybe I'll start an auction for you."

"Oh, goodie. What are you going to call me? Human Syrup of Ipecac?"

"You're still jealous of me, face it. Just because I'm younger and I used to get all the best clients." Lydia wagged her index finger in Olive's face. The two older women looked like a couple of bantamweights ready to go a few rounds.

"Because the word *no* is not in your limited vocabulary."

Thrusting a few handfuls of her freshly baked cookies into a wicker basket with a linen napkin in it, Emmylou backed stealthily toward him. The two bickering aunts didn't even notice.

As she came level with him, she grabbed his hand and pulled him gently along. When they were standing by the front door, and he was thinking how nice her hand felt tucked into his, she removed it and whispered, "Sorry, but I had to get out of there. Any minute I would be called on to take sides. I hate that. I have to escape for a while."

"Okay."

"I'm going to visit Miss Trevellen and get my stuff back. You want to come?"

He had to check in with the office, review his e-mail, and work on two reports to clients while he was down here. On top of the cat litter factory, he had a cable TV company looking to buy up some profitable newspapers in smaller centers, a private pharmaceutical company wanting input on whether the time was right to go public, a European spa company looking to branch out to the U.S. market, and about a million other things on the go.

Of course he didn't have time to visit batty old thieves. On the other hand, he needed to get a better handle on this town. And on the third hand, he was crazy about spending time with Emmylou and more than a little curious as to how she was going to steal her things back.

"I'm in. Should I call my lawyer before we go in case we need bailing out of jail?"

"Don't be a chicken. Come on."

After thrusting the basket of cookies at him, she slipped off her apron, ran her fingers through her hair, and that was it. As far as he could recall, she was the first low-maintenance woman he'd ever seen who looked this good.

He motioned to the basket of cookies. "Are these for Miss T.?"

"Yes."

"You're going to reward the criminal with treats?" It seemed remarkably foolish to encourage larceny. Besides, he wanted to eat all the cookies himself.

"It will be fine. You'll see."

"Your car or mine?" he asked as they emerged into late afternoon sunlight.

"We'll walk. It's a gorgeous afternoon."

It *was* a gorgeous afternoon but he didn't have all day to waste. However, it was hard to argue with a woman who was already striding purposefully up the winding path that led to the road. And, in fairness, they arrived at a neat little bungalow painted pale lavender in less than a quarter hour.

"Emmylou, my dear. What a lovely surprise," Miss Trevellen said with her cultured accent. Her makeup was as perfect as it had been yesterday. She wore wide black pants that he suspected she'd bought in the forties and a jacket of similar vintage with padded shoulders. "And you brought your nice young man with you."

"Pleasure to see you again," he said, shaking her hand gently so the bones didn't break.

"I was showing Joe around town and we thought we'd drop in and say hi."

"How nice. Would you like coffee?"

"Love some. I brought cookies." And she handed over the basket like Little Red Riding Hood giving gifts to the wolf granny. This town was more cracked than he'd realized.

Miss Trevellen's eyes lit up when she peeked inside. "Ginger snaps. My favorite."

"I know. I baked them specially." If he didn't know better, he'd have thought they'd come by royal invitation for coffee, not that the old woman had stolen Emmylou's property so she was forced to come by here and steal it back.

Miss Trevellen ushered them into her small living room and Joe couldn't believe the place. It was more like an upscale antique shop than anybody's house—in fact, he'd been to several old houses turned antique stores like this on Cape Cod. Old houses, with display cases and cabinets, shelves, antique furniture all crammed with pretty, dainty, breakable, and thoroughly useless things.

He blinked as he glanced from blindingly glittering crystal to china dolls to silver, each piece polished to brilliance. One cabinet held nothing but thimbles, pillboxes, and snuffboxes. He walked over for a closer look.

"Ah, you like my collection, I see. I'm a great collector. Quite a pack rat." Quite a thief, Joe would have put it. "My father was the same." And if he were still alive, no doubt he was serving ten to twenty in the clink for grand theft.

As he turned to a set of silver cups and goblets, he was almost certain he recognized the little filigree dish she'd slipped in her purse yesterday. Of all the brazen, larcenous—

His thoughts were interrupted by Emmylou's voice. "Why, what a pretty little dish," she said, reaching past him to pick up the very item the woman had stolen yesterday.

"It is pretty, isn't it? Note the fine workmanship. Late eighteen hundreds, I'd say. Probably English."

And definitely hot.

"I just love it," Emmylou said. "Don't you, Joe?"

"Sure do. In fact, I saw one just like it yes—" Hard to keep talking with the pain in his ankle from where his bed and breakfast hostess had just kicked him a good one, so he shut up.

"Well then, if you really like it, I want you to have it," the old dear said, her eyes bright with happiness. "There's nothing I like more than to give pleasure to my friends."

He blinked, then limped over to the couch and sat down. Miss T. poured him coffee and he watched in fascination as Emmylou admired two more pieces that were obviously hers and had them graciously bestowed on her. Then they all had coffee and cookies and Joe wondered when he might scramble back up the rabbit hole.

"I wish you could have seen your own face in there." Emmylou laughed up at Joe, thinking how nice it was to have someone in town she could laugh with.

"You mean when I was racked with pain after you kicked me in the ankle?"

"Sorry about that. No. When you realized my things were on display."

"And she gave them back as soon as you gushed over them."

"She can't help herself. She doesn't mean to steal but she loves pretty things."

"Then she gets the guilts and this is her way of giving them back?"

"You know, I'm never certain if she really knows she's giving a person their own property back or whether she truly thinks it's a genuine gift. I can't help but adore her, though."

"She stole your property." He looked even better than he had yesterday, and now that she'd kissed him her body was reminding her that she'd been without a man for too long. If only he'd stay a while, then maybe . . .

"She borrowed them for a day. And she polished the silver. She won't give away her secret, but no one can polish silver the way she does."

Chapter 6

"Hello, Mr. Elbart," Emmylou said in her usual cheerful tone as they passed a tall older man with upright bearing and a neatly trimmed mustache.

They were walking down Main Street on their way home, at Joe's suggestion.

"Hello, young lady," the man replied, with the polite smile of a stranger.

"I thought everybody in town knew you," Joe said.

"Mr. Elbart does know me, but he doesn't remember that he knows me. He had some kind of accident in the war. No short-term memory."

"Wow. That's got to be tough."

"Well, look on the bright side. He can hide his own Easter eggs. He can see the same movie down here at the theatre every night and it's always brand-new."

"And dining at Belle's is always a fresh experience."

"Exactly," she said, pleased he was catching on.

"And I don't suppose he's a man to hold a grudge."

For a man she'd pegged as an all-business workaholic, Joe had a surprisingly fun side. Well, not a side really. More like a tiny corner of his mind that remained rebel territory. She hoped the rebels were able to overtake more real estate in his over-regulated brain before he ended up missing all the fun in life. "In Beaverton people pretty much learn to make every setback an opportunity. You'd be amazed how good life can be when you're not always in some kind of competition for more money, bigger houses and cars, fancier jobs."

"Yeah, yeah. The joys of the simple life. I've heard it all before."

"Don't knock it until you've tried it."

The glance he shot her suggested he'd been trying it for a day and the simple joys of Beaverton weren't knocking him out.

She peeked into the Kew-T-Pye hair salon. When Edgar Kew, the barber in town, and Terrea Pye, the only stylist, had wed, they couldn't resist. Terrea, under the mistaken impression she looked good in chartreuse, snipped away at Betsy Charmichael's hair.

When Terrea glanced up, she waved. Betsy looked over and waved, too, her cherubic face wreathed in happiness, her hair well on the way to its usual style.

"If you ever need a haircut while in Beaverton, let it grow," Emmylou said in an aside to Joe. "Really. I don't care if it grows so long it's hanging in your eyes, or it's down your back. The wild man of Borneo look is better than what they'd do to you."

Of course, he didn't need her warning; all he had to do was watch. Luckily, Betsy had gorgeous, thick hair. "Poor Betsy. She's been getting Old Lady Three for years."

"Old lady three?"

"The Kew-T-Pye is the salon equivalent of a burger place. Combo One—that's what Olive has. A permanent that leaves perfect rows of white sausages all over a person's head. Betsy has Combo Three. Short at the back and sides, brushed back off her forehead."

"Why do people come here if it's no good??"

"It's cheap, convenient, and no one wants to hurt their feelings."

"You obviously don't have your hair done here."

"Thanks for noticing." She bit her lip. "It's kind of a guilty secret." She darted a half-humorous glance at him.

"I'm not going to blab."

"I pretend I do my own hair, but really I drive into Spokane to get it cut and styled."

"It's one of the first things I noticed about you," he said, suddenly serious. "You have beautiful hair. Sexy."

She felt suddenly breathless from the intense expression in his eyes.

"Thank you." Because he looked as though he might say more, she suddenly speeded her pace. "I've kept you from your work for long enough."

One good thing about the Shady Lady was that Joe got great reception on his cell phone. If he stood outside in the middle of the back garden.

"How's it going down there?" Milton Gellman's voice boomed over the cell.

The lawn was not as easy to pace as the hardwood floors in his office; he'd forgotten his sunglasses so he blinked like a mole with sunstroke every time his pacing turned him to face west; and he didn't like operating without at least a skeletal office. A desk, a decent lamp, Internet access. How hard was that?

"Fine," he said, "fine. I viewed the property this morning. There's potential there."

"Eric's got the mineral rights nearly nailed down. We'll meet next week and—"

Joe damn near dropped the phone when he heard a go-dawful racket behind him and shouts of "*Fire, fire . . .*"

"Milton," he interrupted, "I've got to go. There's a fire."

Milton Gellman was still speaking when he broke the connection. His first thought was for Emmylou. She'd been in the kitchen last time he saw her. Didn't most fires start in kitchens?

"Fire, fire!" The same voice came closer now, and it sounded like a middle-aged man yelling. Then his heart slammed against his ribs when he heard Emmylou take up the chant. He sprinted across the lawn toward the kitchen, only to crash into her as she emerged from the kitchen door looking perfectly composed.

She gave him a big smile and then did the damnedest thing. She put a finger over her lips.

Before he could demand an explanation, a man who looked near sixty sprinted into the garden, out of breath and red of face. He wore jeans and a plaid shirt with a white T-shirt showing underneath, and on his head he wore a kid's red plastic firefighter's hat.

"Thank goodness you got here in time," Emmylou said, running forward. She dashed behind a rose bush and emerged with a green coil of garden hose with a water pistol thing at the end. She handed it to the guy in the plastic fireman's hat.

"Don't you worry, Emmylou, I'll put out the fire," he said, sounding important. "Move back, now."

Emmylou grabbed Joe's hand and pulled so they stepped back toward the kitchen door.

"Oh, look," she said, pointing to a patch of weedy-looking stuff. "I think it's bad over there." The nutbar with the hose obligingly doused the weeds that didn't flame, smolder, or smoke.

"My herbs needed some water anyway," Emmylou murmured.

"Right," Joe said, as his pounding heart finally dropped back to normal. "And a sprinkler would be too dull."

She smiled up at him, that sweet, sweet smile that made him wonder whether he'd soon be prancing about in a red plastic hat. "He doesn't hurt anyone, and my garden gets watered regularly."

He thought about that for a minute. "So if I come roaring into your bedroom in the middle of the night and yell 'horny,' will you put out my fire?"

She half rolled her eyes so she could look at him through her lashes. "Maybe." Then, while he stood there with his libido hanging out along with his tongue, she waved cheerfully to the overgrown toddler. "Thanks, Harold. Is it safe for me to go back inside now?"

"Sure thing. I'll finish up out here." And before Joe's bemused gaze, he doffed his plastic fireman's hat.

She disappeared back inside the kitchen and Joe followed. "What do you mean, maybe?"

The water was running in the sink and she was washing her hands. She glanced up. "I mean maybe."

"Last night you said no."

"That was last night. Today I'm saying maybe."

"I don't know what I did to go from no to maybe. And I sure as hell don't know how to get from maybe to yes."

Her smile was the kind that caused men to go to war, make fools of themselves, and pledge to fight dragons. "But that's what makes it interesting, don't you think?"

No, he damn well did not think. He liked signals. Plain, clear, "yes, I like you fine" and "I'm single and feel like sex" signals. Or, "No, I'm not interested," "have a boyfriend," "am in fact a lesbian" signals. Maybe didn't cut it.

"I'm the only sane person in this whole crazy town!" he shouted, frustrated.

"Are you?" Emmylou replied, as unfazed by his yelling as she was by the lunatics who surrounded her. Well, she must be one of them if she was questioning his status as most sane person in Beaverton. "Let's see. How many hours a week do you work?"

He felt thrown off balance by her odd question. "What's that got to do with anything?"

"Answer the question, please."

He tilted his head back a little so he could stare down his nose at her. It was a killer move for intimidating underlings, and it only made her open her eyes wider, waiting for his answer. "I don't know how many hours a week I work. I don't punch a time clock."

"All right. We'll guesstimate. You usually arrive in your office by . . . ?"

"Seven-thirty, eight o'clock," he said.

"Good. Do you take coffee breaks?"

"I'm not in a union shop."

"Lunch, then."

"Sure." He hesitated and added, "Most days."

"And what do you do on your lunch hour?"

"Eat."

"Picnic in Central park? Feed the ducks? Skateboard down Wall Street?"

"I meet people for lunch."

"Ah. Do you." She leaned back against the granite counter, obviously enjoying herself. "What kind of people?"

"I can see where you're going with this. Clients. I meet clients for lunch. So what?"

"So nothing. I'm just asking. And I think a business lunch with a client counts as work, don't you?"

He shrugged, wondering why he should feel guilty for working hard. "I suppose."

"All right. So you start at seven-thirty or eight o'clock, you don't stop for coffee, you meet clients for lunch, and you finish around . . . ?"

"I don't punch a clock. I told you." It was usually dark, though, when he left the building. Come to think of it, it was usually dark when he started his working day. "I finish around seven. Eight." *Midnight.* Sometimes he worked all night and snatched a couple of hours on the couch in his office. He kept extra clothes at work just in case.

She nodded, as though he'd said exactly what she'd expected him to say. "So you work between eleven and twelve and a half hours a day by your calculation. Who is the sane one, Joe? The man who believes he's a fireman a few times a week and waters the garden, which helps keep things growing, or the man who never sees the sun?"

"You can't get ahead by being lazy," he said, and only after he'd heard the words echo around in his head did he recognize them as his father's.

"Well, you're ahead, all right," she announced cheerfully, in the kind of tone she'd use if she were patting his cheek. "If life is a race, you should hit the finish line ahead of everybody." She said it with the kind of ironic intonation that made him suspect her idea of a finish line was a pine box. And him in it.

Not pine, of course. If there was one thing all his hard work had provided him, it was riches. He could afford an acre of marble mausoleum if he so desired.

Which gave the term cold comfort new meaning.

Chapter 7

Joe studied the oil painting hanging over the fireplace. It showed an attractive woman of means from the turn of the century, he guessed. Her clothing looked rich but respectable, the expression in her eyes anything but.

"My great-great-grandmother," Emmylou said.

"She looks a little like you."

"She was an incredible businesswoman," Emmylou said, turning to follow his gaze. "She built this place in the late eighteen hundreds. Of course, it was a brothel, but it made her rich and she ended up marrying one of the town fathers. I've always suspected he got tired of paying to come here. She moved with her husband to a big fancy home in town and everyone turned a blind eye to the fact that she still ran the Shady Lady. It's been passed down from daughter to daughter ever since. My grandmother was the madam here when Dr. Emmet Beaver came to town and built his sanitarium."

"Did he disapprove and try to hound her out of business?"

She laughed. "Not at all. He wasn't one of those prudish health nuts. He believed that sexual release is vital to human health. He was a bit of an eccentric genius, I think. He'd been trained as a medical doctor and specialized in the psychiatry of the day. He was also fascinated by electricity, and from what I can understand, he put the two together. He had this theory that the human body runs on a series of circuits. So long as you don't block a circuit or short it out, everything works smoothly."

"Electricity, huh?"

"I know it's a bit out there now, but back in his day he had a huge following. He believed the sexual system was particularly vulnerable to blockage, and that, of course, could mess up everything else. So he encouraged the free flow of impulses leading to a natural release."

"Orgasm."

"Exactly. A lot of women suffered from what they used to call hysteria. He was one of the pioneers in using vibrators to treat their conditions."

"You're telling me that the first vibrators were used by doctors to cure hysteria."

"Isn't it delicious?"

"And your great-grandfather was one of those quacks."

"He wasn't a quack. He did a service to women who were never taught about their own pleasure. I like to believe that after they were treated by the doctors, they learned to treat themselves."

"And now they show up in lipstick cases."

Hard to believe Joe was standing in the parlor of a bed and breakfast having a conversation like this with the inn's proprietor. Even more ludicrous was the fact that the conversation was turning him on. Although Emmylou could talk about home-canning tomatoes and that would turn him on, too, he suspected.

"I feel something very electric whenever I touch you or kiss you."

She drew in a quick breath and her face was suddenly vulnerable. Interesting. She could talk about sex and sexual theories, but the minute theory became personal and he tried to put it into practice, she backed off. Her blue eyes clouded and her brows pulled together.

He stepped forward and pulled her against him so fast she didn't have time to protest. Her heart tripped beneath her breasts, he could see it in the pulse at her throat. "Feel that current passing between us?"

"That's not electricity," she said, her voice suddenly breathless.

"What about this?" And he kissed her. Kissed her long and slowly, opening his mouth on hers so her lips parted, letting the amazing rush build. This didn't happen with other women. He couldn't decide if he was flirting with the forbidden in trying to seduce the innkeeper, or whether it was something about Emmylou and him together which he'd never found before. He sincerely hoped it was the former, because there was no future with this woman, not even in the short term. He'd be leaving soon and the very idea of asking her to leave Beaverton was ridiculous. He tried to picture her walking down Broadway on his arm and he felt—God, he felt a sense of calmness come over him, like she belonged on his arm and who the hell cared where that arm was so long as she was there?

Now that he'd startled himself as much as he had Emmylou, he pulled away slowly, leaving her looking dazed and stirred up.

"Oh," he said, running his index finger over her moist lower lip, "I think he was onto something, all right."

"Maybe."

"So, if the Shady Lady has been handed down from mother to daughter, what happened to your mother?"

"Well, she was brought up strictly in the Beaver method. Whatever feels good is okay so long as you don't hurt yourself or anyone else. She got the first part figured out fine, but once she discovered she was pregnant, she wasn't interested in staying around and being a mother."

She said it as though she were talking about someone else's life. He didn't hear any bitterness, but he felt a burning outrage on her behalf. "What did she do?"

"She left. She had me—named me Emmylou after Emmet and Louise—and then went off to live her life her own way."

He'd always assumed, from her name, that her mother

was a country and western fan, but once more he'd guessed wrong. "But didn't she inherit the Shady Lady?"

"No. Patrice left it to me. My mother didn't want it. She became an exotic dancer and made quite a name for herself. She has a trick with badminton birdies."

"I see." And he did see. Somehow, this incredible young and sexy woman had ended up stuck looking after a bunch of antiques—both human and architectural. He was conscious of an urge to rescue her from this humdrum existence in Bedlam aka Beaverton.

"I'm the first woman in my family in five generations to stay out of the sex trade. I'm the black sheep."

"So," he said, stepping closer. "How respectable are you?"

There was a disturbing twinkle lurking deep in his eyes that urged her to throw caution to the winds and act as disreputably as any ancestor she'd ever had.

Maybe there was more of her Intimate Healing ancestors in her than she'd realized, for the minute Joe had told her about his problem with sleeping, she'd been drawn to help him. And not entirely for altruistic reasons. She had a problem of her own.

She'd been without sex for too long.

Heat built slowly as he came closer. Rules, she reminded herself, were made to be broken, even her own "no sex with the guests" rule. Beaverton was, after all, a live and let live town.

A love and let love place.

And then his cell phone rang and Joe the wonder businessman took over. As he headed for the garden, she swore to herself that never in her life would she own a cell phone.

Emmylou was humming happily to herself as she prepared her world famous muffin batter, ready to bake her world famous carrot, zucchini, and walnut muffins for breakfast tomorrow. At least, they would be world famous if anyone in the world outside Beaverton, Idaho, ever tasted them.

Joe was going to love the muffins. She thought she had a certain combination of spices that no bakery could top. And from Joe it didn't seem such a big step to the rest of the known world.

She could hear the rumble of his voice in her office. The man managed to do business 24/7. He seemed vaguely surprised every time she dragged his attention away from his precious deals. Tonight she planned to snag his attention in a big way. A scented bath, a little silky excuse for a nightgown, and a whole night together. And if he wanted even to touch the hem of her nightgown, he was turning off the cell.

She was just adding the cinnamon when, out of the corner of her eye, she noticed stealthy movement at the kitchen window. She turned to see what was going on but the window was empty. However, she'd lived in Beaverton too long to believe things were ever what they seemed, so she walked over to the back door, opened it, and stuck her head out.

Sure enough, she saw a body crouched beneath her kitchen window, feet planted in the herb garden Emmylou had been babying.

"What are you doing?" she asked, half exasperated, half amused.

"Shhhhh" was the hissed reply. Madame Dior raised her head. She wore a silk scarf wrapped around her hair movie-star style, and even though it was evening she wore big sunglasses. "Where is he?" she whispered.

In a house of women, *he* could only mean Joe. "He's working. He's always working."

"Good. Sneak away as soon as you can and come to the bingo hall."

"Why? What's going on?" She doubted she was being recruited to play bingo—it would already be crowded with players. Beaverton only had the one place large enough to hold a crowd, so all town meetings—and there weren't that many—were held at the bingo hall. Except Mondays. "There's a bingo game tonight."

Madame Dior was so rattled she forgot to speak in a French accent and therefore was amazingly understandable. "Ernie's wife's cousin works at the real estate office and she phoned to tell Marge that *he*"—she motioned upstairs, presumably to let Emmylou in on the fact that she was referring to Joe without using his name—"is planning to buy the sanitarium."

"Really?" Her first thought was that this would be a good thing for the town, depending on what he was planning to do with it. "What's he planning to do with it?"

"I hear it's going to be a factory."

"A factory?" They were miles from nowhere out here. Apart from some farming and a little ranching, there wasn't much commerce or industry. "What will the factory make?" She wasn't at all sure how she felt about a factory in the old sanitarium. It was a part of the town's heritage—part of her heritage.

Dr. Emmet Beaver had willed the sanitarium to the town. Unfortunately, he hadn't left enough for the taxes on the property should the sanitarium one day close and the building remain empty for thirty years. She'd felt sad personally when the county foreclosed. The sanitarium had been in the hands of a realtor so long they'd all mostly forgotten it was for sale. She wondered if there'd be enough proceeds from the sale to build a community swimming pool—or at least fix the running track at the high school.

"That's the worst part. They're planning to dig up all the land around here to mine something or other. The factory's going to make cat litter. That's what he's here for."

"Mining? Cat litter?"

The other woman shushed her and then nodded. She glanced around, placed a finger over her lips. "Come as soon as you can," she whispered, and scuttled away until she melted into darkness.

Emmylou stood staring at the freshly trampled herbs without seeing them. Joe'd found time to kiss her senseless and indulge in conversation about the town and its residents, as well as her background. She'd been pleased that he was interested and mildly flattered that he was so curious about her life. Now she knew better.

He'd been pumping her for information and extremely reluctant to share with her what business had brought him to town. No wonder he didn't want to tell her. What was he planning to do? Strip-mine all of Beaverton?

She'd soon find out.

She tossed the rest of the ingredients in her mixing bowl, wishing she'd bought some awful store-brand mix, gave a perfunctory stir, and stuck the bowl in the refrigerator.

She'd have taken Lydia and Olive with her, but they were already at the bingo hall. They went almost every week—and if she knew her aunts, they weren't going to be too pleased if their game was interrupted for a town meeting.

She yanked off her apron, stuck it on a hook by the back door, and was about to slip out that way when she realized that Joe would be able to see her from the windows of her office. She might as well go through the front way and tell him she was going out.

Even though she was on her way to talk to him it was still a shock when she bumped into him—almost literally—in the hallway.

"I was coming to find you," he said, in that deep, rich voice she liked too well.

"Oh, I was on my way out. Do you need something?"

"No. But something's come up on another deal I'm working. I'll be leaving in the morning."

"Oh." The dismay she felt was all out of proportion to a guest leaving. Even a paying guest who hadn't asked for an AAA, frequent flyer, or library card discount on the room rate.

He must have heard the wistful note, for he moved a little closer. "I'd like to stay longer, but I've got other clients, other deals cooking, and I can do everything else from my office in

New York. I'll be back later, probably. Once things get rolling."

Her thoughts tumbled around so she couldn't grasp a single one. There was the sense of regret that the most intriguing man she'd met in a long while was leaving so soon, dismay that a fast-lane workaholic was bent on destroying Beaverton, and frustration that she was already regretting the end of an affair that hadn't even started.

When she got to the bingo hall, she noted an ominous buzz from inside—a hive of very anxious bees.

Forcing a calm smile to her face, she walked in. As she'd suspected, almost everyone in town seemed to be there. The buzzing amplified then died down as people recognized her. She nodded, hugged, patted shoulders, and kept going until she found a place at one of the long tables beside Olive and Lydia.

"What's going on?" she asked.

"I was almost going to win, that's what happened. All I need is B-17 and I've got bingo, but old busybody Napoleon stopped the game. I've got a mind to sue him, that's what."

Since winning cards paid all of two bucks, Emmylou figured the emperor must be shivering in his Hessian boots.

"All right, I think most everybody's here now. I call this town meeting to order," Ernie said into the microphone. Since he was the bingo caller, he'd naturally taken the role of MC for tonight's meeting. He looked very important, and Emmylou supposed that since the information came from his wife's cousin, he felt some responsibility in taking charge of the proceedings.

Napoleon, who usually ran things, seemed a bit perturbed, but then everyone was likely perturbed about the news.

"This ain't a town meeting, it's a bingo game," Lydia muttered, but not loud enough for anyone but those closest to hear.

Ernie went on. "Most of you have seen the stranger in

town. Young man putting up at the Shady Lady, name of Joe Montcrief."

A few people looked at Emmylou as though she might be surprised by the news that she had a guest staying at the B&B. She nodded.

He went on. "Joe was spotted this morning touring the sanitarium with a realtor. My inside sources tell me he's planning to buy the sanitarium."

There was a collective gasp of shock, but Emmylou controlled hers. How could Joe blow into town, see how special it was, and still plan to destroy it?

Ernie continued. "He's here representing a company called Feline Good. He's—"

"It's Feline So Happy," his wife corrected him in a stage whisper.

"Yeah, well. He's going after the mineral rights under our soil so this company can mine the phosphate that they use in the cat litter products. Ladies and gentlemen, our farms, our fields, our flower gardens, our parks and recreation areas are all at risk. My source—"

"It's Marge's cousin who's the source, we all know that," somebody yelled.

"Be that as it may, we have to stop this mining venture. After they've pulled up our land to mine the phosphate, they'll then desecrate the memory of the good doctor Emmet Beaver by turning the sanitarium that he willed to the people of this town into a factory to produce cat litter." He paused for dramatic effect. "We have to stop him."

"How?" a voice from near the back called. Emmylou didn't have to turn her head. She knew it was Wilton Norris, her nearest neighbor, who liked to bring her presents. Small things. A pretty rock he'd found in the garden, flowers, an avocado, whatever caught his fancy. He was a sweet, gentle man in his late sixties.

There was a long pause. Ernie said, "I don't know."

"Maybe we could bribe the young fellow to make sure the

deal falls through," said Edgar Kew, the barber. "That's how they do things in big cities, you know." He'd never been farther than Boise in his life.

"With what? We can't even afford to pay the taxes on the place, which is how it's getting sold out from under us in the first place," Ernie reminded them.

Napoleon rose, his hat adding height and turning the rather small man into an imposing figure. "Vee must organize an army, and rout ze oppressor!" he said, shaking his fist to heaven. Or in this case, the faded brown beams in the ceiling of the old hall.

"Bribery and violence," Olive muttered. "Just what we need. Can't you do something?"

Emmylou rose from her seat. "If we could come up with the tax money then maybe we could stop the sale." She'd been thinking about this since she first heard the news but that was about as far as she had been able to think.

The heads around her nodded, and there were lots of murmurs of agreement. But everyone was still looking to her for the answer.

"Or maybe we could come up with an alternative buyer for the property."

"The farming sucks. All this place ever had going for it was that it's quiet and has pretty scenery."

"What about tourism?"

Emmylou's bed and breakfast was the only accommodation, and she wasn't exactly turning eager travelers away from the door, but she agreed that tourism was an avenue better pursued than cat litter.

"We need a draw," Edgar Kew said.

"What, you mean like a lottery?"

"No, a tourism draw. Like the Grand Canyon, or the Eiffel Tower."

Somebody yelled from the back, "We've got the biggest beaver in the United States. World, probably. What if we advertise ourselves as Beaver Capital of the World!"

Emmylou put a hand over her eyes.

Ernie said, after a long pause, "I like the fact that people are coming up with some creative ideas. Maybe we could use the sanitarium to make money."

"But who'd want that old place?" Mme. Dior asked. "No one goes to places like that any more."

"It would make a great setting for porn movies," Gregory Randolph said.

"Good idea."

"Maybe we could have a reality show there," said Lydia. "We could have one of those *Survivor* shows."

From beside her, Emmylou heard: "*Survivor, Beaverton.* Can you stay in this town and still keep your wits?"

"Shh," Emmylou said to her aunt, trying not to laugh.

"Good thoughts," Ernie said, taking charge once more. "We'll form a committee to think about all these ideas and come up with some new ones. My wife's been taking notes, so all your suggestions are written down."

"That's great that you're going to have a committee, Ernie. But what about Joe?" Lydia asked.

"He's leaving tomorrow," Emmylou said.

"No. He can't leave yet. We need time."

"Yeah. We need to keep him here while we do our own deal."

"Right. How do we do that?"

"Kidnap him?"

"Hold him for ransom?"

"No, no," Olive said. "We don't want him to suspect we're keeping him here."

"Good point, Olive. Can't have his office getting suspicious."

"I can give him car trouble," Gregory Randolph said. Gregory was a brilliant mechanic. Like Emmylou, he was a product of the town. His parents had met in the sanitarium and later married and settled in the area. Apart from a tendency to break into opera at unlikely moments, his mother was a model parent. His father claimed he'd been abducted by aliens, had escaped, and that they would return for him since he knew their secrets. He built a shelter in the backyard and took his family into hiding during every full moon.

Gregory had grown up normal apart from being tone deaf and claustrophobic. When his dad died they buried him in the shelter and closed it up permanently. Greg lived with his mother, but everyone knew he had a thing for Jayleen Priddy at the grocery store.

"Great idea, Gregory. But how do we stop him taking a bus or something to get out of town?"

Lydia rose to her feet. "We've already figured that part out. Emmylou's going to sleep with Joe."

"God, give me patience," Emmylou muttered under her breath. She started counting slowly to ten, but Lydia wasn't finished yet.

"Joe's got a sex problem she's helping him with." She glanced around the assembly and then grinned. "Not that I couldn't have cured him a lot faster."

Emmylou smiled over gritted teeth, feeling every one in town stare at her. Lydia had trapped her in her own lie.

Surprisingly, Olive came to her aid. "She doesn't need to sleep with the man if she doesn't want to. He's so sweet on her, he'll stick around given half a chance. Don't you worry about that."

Emmylou shot her aunt a grateful smile, and talk moved to the committee which was forming to find another buyer for the sanitarium. Naturally, she was asked to join the committee and she agreed. She'd moved back here out of loyalty to her gran, but now that the town was threatened, she realized how much she loved it. Somehow, she was going to help save Beaverton.

The town's young doctor, who'd done a residency at the local hospital and liked Beaverton so much he decided to stay, was also appointed to the committee in his absence. Of all times for him to take a holiday, Emmylou thought, when they could really use his calm good sense. Maybe Dr. Gord Hartnett even had some ideas, or connections.

She barely listened to the rest of the meeting. She wondered how she was going to keep Joe hostage without his knowledge. Sure, he was going to have car trouble between now and Wednesday morning, but how on earth was she supposed to stop him from finding alternative transportation?

Her skin felt hot and cold as she relived the steamy kisses they'd shared. Maybe Lydia was right. She should seduce the man and keep him naked and so busy that he'd forget all about work.

Except she was nothing like her female ancestors. She'd never specialized in the erotic arts. When Lydia and Olive and the rest of them used to talk technique, she tuned them out. She was bored by sex long before she was old enough to think about doing it. Somehow, that boredom had never lifted. Oh, she liked sex fine, but you had to be careful or it could lead to huge complications. Messy, emotional ones she didn't want.

She had to admit, though, that there was something appealing about the idea of seducing Joe—or in letting him think *he* was seducing *her*. Yes, that was it. Maybe she could give him a little encouragement. Enough that he'd want to stay to get her into bed. He wouldn't be the first B&B guest who'd tried.

Since the interrupted bingo night continued once the meeting was over, Emmylou was able to talk to Gregory Randolph without anyone noticing. Once she'd obtained his promise to pay Joe's car a visit before five Wednesday morning, she walked home alone. The air was sweet-scented and quiet, the stars bright in the clear sky.

When she entered her own garden she savored the pleasant sense of coming home. What they were planning to do to Joe— make sure his car was disabled and so force him to stay—was wrong. She accepted that. But saving the town was right. Feeling unsettled, she strolled through her garden and let the scents of jasmine and rose soothe her. The Queen Elizabeth, a mass of soft pink smudges in the fading light, drew her in, so she had to lower her face and breathe in the fragrance. Beside it grew a very nice Honor, its blossoms white as the moon, its scent so light she had to close her eyes and concentrate. How much honor was she demonstrating, she wondered, stroking a satin petal, sabotaging one man's business in order to save her home?

Chapter 8

The light wasn't on in Joe's window, and Emmylou had a momentary pang that he'd gone to bed early in order to make a crack of dawn start in the morning. Then she realized that the office light was still shining and he was illuminated like a man on a TV screen. His face was drawn in concentration and he was pecking away at his computer keyboard.

That man needed desperately to loosen up.

She entered through the kitchen door and then went to the office.

As she'd suspected, Joe had his head bent over the computer. He was tapping away and simultaneously talking on his cell phone, thanks to a hands-free earpiece she'd only ever seen on TV. No one in Beaverton needed their hands free while they talked on the phone.

But then no one here was a big shot. No one here would want to dig up other people's property in the name of feline hygiene, either.

She'd planned to offer him some cocoa, but since he was already communicating in two places at once, she decided to go ahead and make it anyway. Maybe cocoa wasn't the fastest route to seduction, but she had to work within her comfort zone.

When she came back a few minutes later with two steaming mugs, he was still tapping away but mercifully no longer on the phone.

"Hi," she said from the doorway.

As he raised his head, she almost felt his effort to lift the weight. He was tired.

"Hi yourself," he said, closing the file and spinning her chair until he faced her. "Do you need your office back?"

"No. I brought you some cocoa."

"Thanks." He took the proffered mug from her, put it on the desktop, and rose to stretch.

Oh, he was nice. His shirt clung against elongated muscles and she found herself wanting to follow the lean lines with her fingertips.

Before he could look down and catch her ogling his body, she shifted her attention to look out the window. As though there were anything of interest out there. A dark garden, a couple of floodlights that she'd placed to illuminate the garden and the parking area.

One of the floodlights outlined the shape of Joe's car, the one he'd be driving off in tomorrow.

She saw a slight movement between the pink rhododendron bush and the wisteria. At first she thought it was Mae West rustling the branches, then a much larger, man-sized shape emerged.

Hell's bells, she'd arranged that Gregory Randolph was going to tamper with Joe's car, but did he have to do it now?

She'd assumed some quiet sortie in the middle of the night, not that he'd walk into her yard at 10:15 to vandalize a guest's vehicle. She should have been specific in her instructions, but really, didn't everyone know that car vandalizing was best accomplished between the hours of midnight and dawn? Probably, Gregory had an early start in the morning and wanted to be in bed at a reasonable time.

If Joe kept working in her office, he'd see Gregory. She'd never bothered with drapes in this room, and now she wished she had drapes, blackout curtains, California shutters, layers and layers of stuff to block the view. Well, she couldn't do that, so she'd have to get Joe away from the window.

"Why don't we take our cocoa into the front room? It's a lot more comfortable."

He sipped from his mug, then licked the line of chocolaty foam from his upper lip. "This is great. Thanks. But I'm waiting for an e-mail to come in. I should probably stay right here."

If he was trying to be polite and get rid of her, she was going to have to act as dumb as the man out there getting his vandalizing tools ready. He hadn't even bothered changing into all black clothes, but was tromping around in the white T-shirt and jeans he'd worn to the bingo hall.

Didn't the man have any respect for the profession he was temporarily entering? Or at least his victim? Never mind the victim's hostess, who was about to have a panic attack.

"Okay." She smiled brightly. "While you're waiting, maybe we could sit right here and get to know each other better."

And please, Gregory, be fast with that car before she had to resort to her pediatric dental history.

Joe was nobody's fool. His eyes narrowed. "I'm leaving tomorrow, Emmylou. Isn't it kind of late to be getting to know me?" He didn't say so, but his tone implied that she could have gotten to know him intimately if she'd gone to bed with him last night. Typical male.

She tried for an expression of hurt disbelief. "But you said you'd be back."

"It's hard to say. I hope to be."

Oh boy. Things must really be moving along if he felt ready to leave and not come back. Probably he had other harmonious, happy communities to destroy this week. Given a month, she bet he could devastate an entire state.

"Well, we could start getting better acquainted now. You never know when circumstances will throw us together again." Like a dead car tomorrow.

He glanced at her and raised his brows a little. "Okay. I've got a few minutes now. What do you want to talk about?"

"I don't know. But I enjoy your company. It's been nice having you in the house." She was grasping at straws here and she knew it. How long could she drag out a pointless conversation? She thought about Lydia and Olive and took hope.

The trouble with that theory, of course, was that both Olive and Lydia were female. Joe didn't preamble but got right to his point. "Look, Emmylou, you said you're not a casual sex type and I respect that. Since I'm leaving in the morning . . ."

She let her natural annoyance bubble. Okay, if he didn't want a pleasant conversation she could easily work up to a fight. No trouble at all. "So you're saying what? That a conversation with a woman is pointless unless it ends in sex?"

He pushed out his lips, stalling for time like a debater sensing a verbal trap. "No. I'm not saying that. Exactly. But when a woman's young and beautiful and I'm incredibly attracted to her, then every conversation leads closer to sex, sure."

"But that's absolutely ridiculous. What if I were your doctor or your accountant or some other professional?"

"I'd let you take my temperature and do my taxes, but unless you were married, I'd still be trying to have sex with you. It's life."

"What if I were a nun?"

Nothing on his face smiled, but his eyes did that wonderful crinkle thing at the corners. "Then we would not be having this conversation." He looked at her with a puzzled expression. "Don't you feel that way? I mean, assuming you find me attractive . . . ?"

She thought of the way she melted when he kissed her. "You know I do."

"Then don't you think we'll end up more frustrated if we keep talking and it doesn't go anywhere?"

"Well, last night would have been too soon, but now . . ."

Now, what? He came up with an answer for her. "Now I've passed the Miss Trevellen School of Larceny and Good Manners?"

She laughed aloud. Out of her peripheral vision she could see that Gregory Randolph had the hood up now on Joe's car. How long did this disabling business take? She was in a cold sweat, gulping her cocoa like it was courage-giving whiskey.

Greg was bent over the open hood of the car, his white T-shirt gleaming against the darkness. Please let him get the job done quickly.

A computerized ping broke the strained silence in the office, and Joe said, "Ah, my e-mail."

He started to turn his chair around to his computer, which faced the window, which looked out on a man screwing with his car.

She had to stop him. No time to think. She stuck her foot out and stopped the chair midtwirl.

"Emmylou, I need to get that," Joe said, an edge to his voice.

"But I need you," she said, hoping that her voice sounded husky with passion and not strained by panic.

He opened his mouth, no doubt to tell her to get a grip, or at least wait until he'd read his e-mail. She couldn't let that happen, so she launched herself at him, sloshing cocoa mug and all.

"Whaa—" he managed before her lips clamped over his.

Blindly, she managed to get her mug onto the desktop so her hands were free, then she plunged them into his hair, making a human vise to keep his head from turning. She opened her legs around his and snugged up tight onto his lap.

It was a move born of desperation, and if he pushed her off him, which she was pretty certain he'd do, she'd end up sprawled on her butt all over the rug, and when he turned around, he'd view more than his e-mail.

She expected to go sailing through the air and hit the rug

ass-first. She expected outrage when he caught sight of Greg out there messing with his car. What she hadn't expected was that after a startled second of total stillness, Joe would kiss her back.

Oh, not just kiss her, but make love to her mouth.

His passion exploded around her and in her, sparking her own. She nipped at his lips, grabbed the back of his head to pull him closer, felt his mouth so hungry on hers, on her skin, his hands in her hair, on her neck, racing over her back.

"... want you," he said and the echo of those words played over and over in her head. *Want you, want you, want you . . .*

Heat began to build in the three-point triangle of nipples and crotch. If Dr. Beaver was right, she had a dandy little electrical circuit running between those three hot spots.

He moaned with hunger, or maybe that was her—hard to tell over the pounding of her heart.

He pulled at the buttons on her shirt, fumbling open the top one and then the second, while she waited in a fever of impatience. She forgot why she was doing this, forgot everything but the fact that she needed this man and she needed him now. He got the rest of the buttons undone, not smoothly but fast, then pushed the sleeves down her arms to her wrists and stopped, so she ended up with her arms bound behind her, a circumstance he seemed to enjoy.

With some wriggling she could easily free her arms, but he looked so pleased with himself she let well enough alone.

"I like you in this posture," he explained with a devilish glint in his eyes. The fatigue had vanished and he pulsed with energy. "Your breasts thrust forward, and your busy hands still. No bread baking, flower arranging, cookie cooling. All you can do is sit there and let me touch you."

At his words, she shivered, and he grinned at her then ran his warm hands up her stomach, traced the front of her bra, and slid them around behind her to the fastening. In a second her breasts were free. Since her arms were stuck in her blouse, the silk and elastic of her bra ended up stretched across her upper chest, but Joe didn't seem to notice.

"Oh, honey," he said, gazing at her breasts for a long moment.

She felt naked, exposed, helpless. With her arms back like that, her chest was pushed forward, right into his face.

"*Annnnyyya*," she said, when he lifted a breast and brought his mouth down to kiss the tip. Her head fell back of its own accord so she would have overbalanced and fallen on her head if Joe hadn't slipped an arm around her back to steady her.

He sucked at the swollen nipple, flicked back and forth with his tongue, and generally teased her until her entire body felt lust-engorged and needy.

He sucked gently, and she pulled herself upright, anxious to press her torso more firmly against his wonderful, magical mouth.

When she did she let out a cry that had nothing to do with passion. Gregory had abandoned his tools and was standing there in front of the raised hood of Joe's car, staring at her with his mouth hanging open.

Since she remembered well enough watching Joe from the garden, and thinking he looked like someone on TV, she knew she must look like the star of a porno flick. but she hadn't planned on acting out *Emmylou Does Joe* for an audience of one.

Fool! Bad enough Greg was an utter failure as a criminal. Did he have to be a Peeping Tom?

Since she couldn't use her arms, she jerked her head frantically, hoping he could interpret *Get the job finished and get the hell off my property* from a couple of head jerks.

"Did I hurt you?" Joe raised his head from her breast and already she missed the gentle sucking that was driving her wild.

"No," she said. "I'm loving it," and to prevent any more conversation, she stuffed her nipple back into his mouth. By keeping her eyes closed, she was able to ignore the goings-on beyond the window and concentrate on the far more immediate goings-on in her nervous system.

His tongue was working magic on her and her bound hands only added to the intoxication. She wanted to touch him and couldn't, wanted to bring him pleasure as he was bringing her pleasure, but she was helpless. As she struggled to free her hands she only succeeded in wiggling her torso, which was thrust unnaturally forward.

There was a very nice bulge beneath her lap, and her hands itched to have access. Since that was denied her, she made do with rubbing against him—her splayed legs allowing her to nudge her neediest parts against the enticing ridge. Her skirt was up around her thighs, and her thin panties allowed her to feel everything: the denim of his jeans, the hard line of metal teeth, all of which got in the way of what she wanted to feel.

"Open your zipper," she begged.

He hesitated only a second then slipped a hand between them. She hoisted herself up onto her knees and heard the slide of zipper, felt him fumble a bit, and then felt the edge of his penis nudging at her. He guided it, rubbing at her through the silk panties. She sighed with pleasure as he rubbed back and forth over her clit, the silk scraping lightly between them.

Of course, this wasn't at all what she'd had in mind when she'd come in with an innocent cup of cocoa, but somehow she knew that the kisses between them would never have been enough.

Her breath was coming fast, her heart pounding. She was so close. She wanted to grind herself down on him. If her hands had been free, she'd have pulled her panties aside and impaled herself.

"Emmylou," he said with a huskiness that sounded incredibly sexy coming from crisp, waste-no-time, businesslike Joe. "We need to get upstairs and get a condom."

"Mmm." They needed to get upstairs anyway. Bingo would be over soon. But this was too incredible, frustrating, amazing, erotic.

"Honey," he whispered in her ear, kissing the lobe, playing his free hand through her hair. "You know I'm leaving tomorrow."

Oh no you're not. But still his words acted on her like an icy shower. What had she been thinking? She couldn't make love to the man she was manipulating so deceitfully. It wouldn't be right. She almost wailed with pent-up frustration. Maybe this was her punishment for her crimes, to be left with her whole body throbbing with need, so close to orgasm she could tumble into it as fast as she could tumble into Joe's bed.

But it wouldn't be fair.

She struggled to get herself under control. "Right. Of course you are. I'm sorry, I don't know what I was thinking." She tried to shrug her shirt back on, but all she succeeded in doing was gyrating her breasts in his face like a lap dancer.

He let out a breath that sounded more like a moan. "Maybe we can continue this when I come back."

"Yes." She could barely think, barely focus her eyes. She was approaching a bad case of sexual-frustration-induced hysteria and no vibrator was going to cure her. Not when the real thing was so enticingly close.

He cupped both her breasts and kissed each in turn rather sweetly before pulling her bra back in place, getting her shirt back on, and buttoning her with quiet competence.

Frustration thudded through her veins, but she knew he was right. Not because he'd be leaving tomorrow and she didn't want a one-nighter, but because he wouldn't be leaving tomorrow and she'd manipulated him into office-chair hanky-panky so he wouldn't see his car being vandalized. Somehow, such deceit didn't seem like the basis for a healthy sexual relationship. Even a short one.

She cast a quick glance outside but Gregory was gone, thank goodness, and Joe's rental car appeared untouched.

"I don't know what I was thinking," she said, scrambling off his lap so clumsily he winced.

"Sorry," she said, mortified, trying not to watch as he

tucked everything away and rezipped. She wanted to yell at him to stop. Maybe would have if she hadn't seen the aunts coming down the garden path toward the front door. She could hear them arguing even through the window.

The front door opened and then banged.

"I did not insult you in front of all your friends. I said I thought a reality show in Beaverton was a stupid idea because it is a stupid idea, not because you thought of it."

"Yeah. Well, you could star in it. They'd call it *The Blair Bitch Project.*"

"Ha, ha."

The two were so busy quarreling they stomped right by the office and disappeared into the kitchen.

"Nice to see the older generation setting such a good example for us young'uns," Joe said.

"Well," she said, giving her head a shake and trying to tamp down the lust raging through her body, "I guess the cocoa got a little out of hand." Inside her bra, her nipples were still damp from his kisses.

He gazed back at her with a sheepish expression. "Yeah. That stuff should come with a warning label."

Feeling increasingly foolish about the way she'd attacked her guest—even if it was for the good of the town—she backed out of the room. "I'll let you get back to your e-mail, then."

His eyes widened suddenly. "Right, the e-mail. I forgot." Since he didn't seem the type to forget about work ever, she let herself feel flattered.

"I'm making an early start in the morning, so I'll say good-bye, and thanks for everything."

"It was nice to, ah, meet you."

He looked as though he'd say something, or maybe try to talk her into bed, and she was half disappointed when he only nodded.

Feeling like a big idiot, she held out her hand.

With a wry grin, he rose and shook it solemnly. "It's been

a great pleasure meeting you, Emmylou. And it would have been an even greater pleasure to sleep with you."

"Or not sleep," she said, remembering his little problem.

"Sleep's overrated."

She nodded. "But it's better this way."

"Is it? Is it better to walk away because you can only have one night with someone or is it better to have great memories?" His eyes were still dark with passion, his breathing not quite back to normal any more than hers was. She understood what he was saying all too well, but still she had the knowledge he didn't that their time together extended beyond dawn tomorrow, whatever his plans. There'd be no single perfect night of love followed by him riding off into the sunrise. He'd be back eating her famous carrot-zucchini breakfast muffins and then the awkwardness would begin.

So she gave him the one-raised-eyebrow treatment and said, "That is a great line. Two ships passing in the night and all."

"It isn't a line," he said, stepping forward so he could rest his hands on her hips and look down at her. "But I can't make promises. I don't know when I'll be back. Or even if I'll be back."

"I understand," she said. He was here to wreck her town. Why bother returning to chart the destruction? It was like he'd organized the firing squad but wasn't going to hang around for the actual execution.

"Well," he said, still not releasing her, "how about a rain check?"

He had no idea how soon he could be collecting, or that his plans for Beaverton's destruction were about to be derailed, and him along with them. Before she got too carried away in sexual fantasy, she ought to remind herself that the man making her almost pass out with lust must know this fertilizer factory would devastate the community.

"Wait until you come back and we'll see."

"Emmylou?" Lydia's voice floated down the hall. She pulled out of Joe's arms, not because the aunts would mind—they'd be delighted—but because she didn't want anyone thinking she'd seduced Joe to keep him here.

Especially not Joe.

She decided to make a very special breakfast—maybe she'd add French toast to her world famous muffins, or something else with a lot of sweetness in it—since she anticipated one very grumpy guest.

Chapter 9

In the darkest-before-dawn blackness, Joe pulled out his keypad and flipped the locks on the rental car. As he hoisted his meager baggage into the trunk, he wished he were also bringing along better memories of last night than Mae West's tuna breath and the way she kept hogging his pillow.

A picture flashed through his mind of Emmylou with her head thrown back while he feasted on her breasts. Maybe he'd come back this way to see that wild attraction to its logical conclusion, but even as he had the thought he knew he wouldn't. There'd be other jobs, other women. He couldn't waste time on lost causes.

Five minutes later he realized he was doing exactly that. If the engine wouldn't turn over on the first or second or third try, the chances weren't good for the fifty-second. Cursing the car, the car maker, the rental company, this town, and the guys who'd hired him and sent him here, Joe finally gave up and hauled himself back out of the car.

The inside car lights came on fine, so he didn't think it was a dead battery. By holding the door open and squinting at a lot of buttons with ridiculous kid's stick figure drawings on them, he finally found the one that opened the hood of the car.

Back outside. He yanked up the hood and found the pole thing that would anchor it. The light from the security beam cast a vague glow in his direction, enough to see that his engine looked pretty much like every other car engine he'd ever seen. No obviously broken or loose hoses or wires sprang out at him. Not that his hopes had been high.

Since he'd taken advanced calculus in the same time block that automotive maintenance was offered in high school, and he'd never had the sort of home where a junker sat parked in the driveway and a teenaged Joe could pull it apart and tinker, he knew piss-all about cars except who to call if there was a problem.

But in Beaverton at 4:45 in the morning, he didn't have the faintest idea who to call.

He leaned under the hood and turned every thing that looked like it could be tightened, wiggled a couple of hoses on the premise that it could be some kind of loose connection, then stared at the engine hard for a minute.

Back in the driver's seat. "Come on," he whispered under his breath, and tried again. The engine made a brave attempt at a roar but once again it didn't catch.

Flipping open the glove compartment, he hauled out the rental paperwork and called the number on his cell phone. A chirpy recorded voice told him the rental desk at the airport would be open at nine A.M. and if his flight left before that, he could leave the keys in a drop box.

He responded savagely to the sweet-voiced message, even after the system booted him off and there was nothing but a dull buzzing in his ear. The rental company was too Podunk to have an 800 number.

Getting seriously pissed now, he glanced at his watch and contemplated his options.

They weren't attractive.

His flight left at seven-thirty and if he didn't get on the road now, he was going to miss that plane. Beaverton didn't look like it boasted a rental car agency or so much as a single taxi. But what the hell did people do here if they needed a ride? Jump on the back of Napoleon's horse?

If he waited around to get the car fixed, he was going to miss his plane. Could he wake Emmylou and ask to borrow her car? Her old Ford didn't look great and he hated the thought of waking her so early, but he really didn't have a choice.

Slipping back into the Shady Lady as quietly as he'd slipped out, he ran up the stairs and headed for her room. He hesitated outside, then knocked. He had to knock a second time before he heard a sleepy, "Just a second."

It was, in fact, not many seconds at all before Emmylou opened the door and blinked at him. She wore a robe of pale blue cotton that she hadn't bothered to belt; she hugged it around herself, and the way it clung to her body, he had the sudden conviction that his landlady slept in the nude.

All his circuits jumbled and all he could do was stare into her heavy-lidded, somnolent eyes, and want her.

"What is it?" she asked at last.

"Sorry to bother you. My car won't start. Could I borrow yours to get to the airport? I'll arrange to have yours returned and the rental picked up. The fools at the rental place are going to pay for this."

She blinked a few times and lifted a hand as though to push it through her tousled hair. The robe slipped and she hastily resumed her previous pose. "I don't have enough gas."

"I could get some."

"Not before the pumps open at nine," she explained.

"You mean there's nowhere to get gas between here and the airport?"

"Nor for fifty miles. Didn't you read the highway signs?"

Of course he hadn't. When he'd arrived in this place it hadn't occurred to him he could end up stranded.

"Is there a taxi?"

She shook her head.

"A bus?"

Another head shake.

"Is there any person in this town I could pay to drive me to the airport?" His whisper took on a frantic note.

Once more she shook her head. She didn't even have to stop and think first.

"Well, shit. The rental agency doesn't open until nine. And there probably isn't another plane out until tomorrow." He felt furious and stupid and helpless, all of which he hated. "Now what am I supposed to do?"

"Put the coffee on?" she suggested. "I'll get dressed and then I'll make you some breakfast."

He jingled the thoroughly useless rental car keys in his pocket. "Who runs the local garage? Or do you have a mechanic in Beaverton?"

"We do. His name is Gregory Randolph."

"Where does he live?"

"You can't wake him up at this hour," she said, aghast. Her sleep-befuddled brain hadn't caught on to the fact that he'd already woken her, proving it could be done.

"I'll make it worth his while," he said.

She shook her head at him as though he were missing something important. Well, she was right. If he couldn't get the bloody car on the road, he was missing his plane out of here.

He made her give him the directions he needed, then headed back down the stairs for a dawn-streaked plod downtown.

Emmylou made her special French toast. It was important to prepare a breakfast that was going to help calm an irate man, while at the same time not raise his suspicions that she'd known all along he'd be joining them for breakfast.

While she was cutting thick slices of her homemade cinnamon raisin bread, the phone rang and she picked it up.

"The Shady Lady," she said, having learned at a tourism seminar that she should always answer the phone as though a valuable customer was on the line, even when she knew that it was Greg Randolph calling.

"He just left," said Gregory, not bothering to identify himself. "I feel almost bad taking his money to fix a problem I caused myself."

"I saw you tow his car away. Did he try to get you to drive him to the airport?"

"Yeah. I told him I've got too many jobs today, and that no one else in town could drive him either."

"I know how you feel; I hate to charge him for another night's accommodation."

"We'll live with ourselves somehow."

She laughed. "I guess. Is he on his way back here?" She glanced out the window in case Joe should appear walking down her front path.

"No. After I told him I had to order in the part and it would take at least a week, he went off to see if he could hire a plane."

"Oh no." It hadn't occurred to her that he wouldn't wait for the next commercial flight out, which was tomorrow. "What did you do? Send him to Al Roper?"

"What would I do that for? Al's got the air ambulance. That's a good plane. I sent him over to Jem Bradley."

Her nerveless hands dropped a piece of bread into the egg mixture so it splashed over the side of the green pottery mixing bowl. She barely noticed. "You told Joe he'd have to ride in a crop duster?"

"Frankly, I think he's ready to rent a pogo stick to get out of here."

"I've got to get hold of Jem and make sure he thinks of an excuse not to take Joe up."

"Already taken care of. Jem got a bad case of the flu right after I called."

"Oh, here comes Joe now. I'll talk to you later."

Joe strode toward the B&B in the purposeful, straight-on way he did everything. If he was irate, he wasn't showing it in his outward demeanor; he seemed the same as always. Focused, efficient. Sexy as hell. She wasn't thrilled at the way all her female bits stood up and cheered at the sight of him. She understood perfectly, of course, the complex chemical and physiological patterns of attraction and arousal, but she did not love that they were happening around this man who'd gone from being the most interesting man she'd met in years to her adversary.

She'd have to have a talk with her girls.

Chapter 10

Joe walked into the Shady Lady and his jangling irritation eased. It was so quiet here, so peaceful. He breathed old house smells with an odd sense of nostalgia, since he'd believed he'd never again smell the unique combination of aged wood, beeswax furniture polish, the faded rose fragrance of potpourri.

As he walked down the hall in search of Emmylou, he welcomed the much fresher and extremely enticing smell of breakfast coming from the kitchen.

He put down his bag and headed for the kitchen. He paused at the swing door and listened. She was singing along to the radio. And if he wasn't mistaken, that was a Beach Boys song. For some reason, his sour mood lifted even more. He knocked and, hearing a "Come on in," pushed through. And there she was.

He shouldn't be glad to see her. He didn't want to be glad to see her. She'd thrown herself at him last night and then refused to see their attraction through to its logical conclusion. She was a sexually exciting woman who had, for some reason he couldn't figure out, denied them both one of life's great pleasures. If he were on his way to New York right now it wouldn't matter, but he was back here in her kitchen and about to spend another night under her roof. Was he in for more frustration or the promise of pleasure that hummed between them every time they came near each other?

She wore another grandmother apron today, and under it were pastel cotton shorts and a yellow and green sleeveless blouse. Her hair was tied back with a yellow scarf. She looked as cheerful as a spring flower and her smile was as warm as a June afternoon.

"Hi. I hope you like French toast. It's my special recipe."

He leaned against the counter and crossed his arms. "How did you know I'd be back?"

"Gregory Randolph called. He said he'd call later when he knows for sure what's wrong."

Joe felt his frown settle. "The rental company should take care of it."

"Oh, they will. Don't worry." Her back was facing him so he couldn't tell how she felt about spending another night under the same roof. She sounded a bit strained, though.

"I sure didn't get far." Not only in leaving Beaverton but in scoring with the town's hottest woman.

While he stood there, puzzled and slightly miffed, she flipped French toast with expert ease, sending a hiss of fragrance into the air. Cinnamon, nutmeg mixed with other more subtle scents he couldn't identify, and suddenly his taste buds were singing the "Hallelujah Chorus."

"Sorry about your car."

"Yeah." He rubbed a tired hand across his face. "I guess I'm stuck here another night . . ." Realizing belatedly how crass that sounded, he quickly said, "I mean, no disrespect to you or your very fine inn but . . ."

She laughed. "You haven't had coffee yet, have you?"

"I guess it's obvious."

"I just made a pot."

"Emmylou, walking into this kitchen is the best thing that's happened to me today."

"Well, it's only seven-fifteen. Who knows what delights are still in store?"

While the French toast sizzled, she sidestepped to the coffee-pot and poured him a mug. She picked up a carton of milk and added some to the coffee, slid open a drawer in which stainless sparkled like sterling and grabbed a spoon, stirred the brew, and handed him the mug.

"You remembered how I like my coffee." Efficiency like that impressed the hell out of him. Left him feeling absurdly flattered, too. She'd taken the trouble to memorize how he liked his coffee. Maybe she did that for every guest who walked through the doors of the Shady Lady, but he preferred to think he was special.

She smiled absently at him and opened the big wall oven and removed an empty plate.

"Sure that's cooked?" he said.

She rolled her eyes at his lame morning humor, but he didn't care. He was—okay, not glad to be here, since he ought to be getting ready to take off about now. He should be writing up his notes and figuring out what still needed doing on the Beaverton deal. And he needed to start putting some effort into finding a spa location to rival Baden-Baden. But right now, in the fragrant kitchen with a woman who was like home, the way Dom Perignon was like wine, he couldn't hang onto his irritation.

Then she eased two slices of perfect French toast onto the plate. "Your breakfast is ready if you'd like to go into the dining room."

"Where's your breakfast?"

"I'll have something later."

"Eat with me," he said, wondering what he was doing.

She blinked at him. "I usually eat in the kitchen."

"Great. I'll eat in here, too. It's weird being in the big dining room all by myself." He looked around. "And besides, I like it in here. It feels like home."

"Your home is like this?"

"No. Not my home." In fact, not like any place he'd ever lived. "I mean like some Hallmark movie-of-the-week version of home. Home, with a capital H as in 'home sweet home.' "

"Oh. That sounds like a compliment."

"Yes." He took the plate from her and placed it on the big round oak table by the window. Outside she'd hung a humming-bird feeder and a little guy was out there now, stabbing at the red plastic flower to reach the sugar water.

"But you're a guest."

"I know. We guests get ridiculous whims. Deal."

While she stood there, obviously thrown off her stride, he went around her to where he'd seen her open the cutlery drawer and pulled out knives and forks for two.

"Placemats and napkins are in the next drawer down," she said automatically.

He glanced up. "Should I be setting the table for the old gals?"

"No. They'll eat later."

"Right," he said, secretly relieved to be spared the lippy geriatrics, and wishing Emmylou was half as anxious to get him into bed as her aunt Lydia was.

"Eat, eat." She waved at him, but he shook his head. If there was one thing he'd learned from his society mother it was that you never started eating before the hostess.

She placed syrup and butter on the table, and opened the industrial fridge and emerged with a crystal bowl full of straw-berries.

Her breakfast was soon plated and she sat down opposite him, then hastily half rose to remove her apron, which she folded neatly and placed on the chair seat beside her.

"Well, I don't normally do this."

Probably she didn't normally roll around half naked in her office with her male guests either, but he decided not to men-tion that, guessing it would add some awkwardness to their cozy breakfast.

Still, it was tough to look across the breakfast table and not think that somewhere between them being half naked and breathing heavily in her office last night and gazing at each other over breakfast this morning, more should have happened.

He sipped his coffee and wondered where she got her coffee beans. Her brew was never bitter; it tasted the way he thought coffee ought to taste.

Then he bit into his French toast and felt the flavor burst. The texture was exactly right. "You know, there are restaurants and hotels all over the world that would kill to have you working for them."

"I know. I trained for that very career, in fact, but I chose this instead."

"And you're happy."

"Of course. Oh, there are times I'd love a bigger challenge, and I need to get away sometimes for a city fix, but this is where I belong."

He glanced across at Emmylou, who'd been singing in the kitchen, obnoxiously cheerful when he'd had a crap sleep. If she passed up men like him, what did the woman do for sex?

"Can I pass you something?" she asked, and he realized as he'd been puzzling about her sex life, he'd been staring.

"No. I was wondering if you're seeing anyone."

She took her time. Finished chewing as though she'd choke for sure if she didn't chew a thousand times on each side, then swallowed. Took a sip of coffee.

He waited for her answer in growing impatience.

She swallowed the coffee. Looked at him straight on. "Are *you* seeing anyone?"

"That's not fair. You haven't answered my question yet."

"And I won't, unless you go first."

"It's complicated," he said.

She nodded as though she understood all about complications.

Always he liked to be honest and up-front with women.

But Emmylou wasn't from his world. It was as though the stork had accidentally dropped a mega-babe in the middle of Hicksville, and somewhere in Manhattan was a young woman who eschewed Saks and mail-ordered to Lee Valley for her clothes—Eddie Bauer for formal wear.

"I had a girlfriend up until about six months ago. It wasn't really going anywhere, and she's looking to get married so she decided to cut loose. I still see her once in a while."

"She's your booty call."

He blinked, startled. Hearing Emmylou talk so casually about a booty call was like hearing Jessica Simpson chat about nuclear physics.

Emmylou must have read his mind reasonably well for she grinned at him. "We have cable."

Okay, she knew about casual sex, and she still hadn't answered his very simple question about whether or not she was seeing anybody. "So tell me about—"

His cell phone rang. With a curse of irritation and a muttered apology, he answered. "Sorry, I missed your call earlier," his assistant Anna said. "I was in the shower. Then I figured I'd get to the office before I phoned you. The Fellson Group are going ballistic about the merger and now they want out."

"What? Why?" Of all days for him not to be in his office. That merger was a coup that had taken him almost eight months to pull off on behalf of the Fellson Group, a telecommunications company that was looking to grow. He gulped coffee and grimaced as it burned on the way down.

"They want you in their office yesterday."

"Yeah. I know. But I can't be in their office yesterday. I can't be in their office today, and the way things are going, I won't make it tomorrow. Bring me up to speed, what's the latest?"

Her words were like machine gun fire and it took him a second to catch up with the speed and volume, as though he'd been speaking a foreign language and now he was read-justing to English. It wasn't that they spoke a different lan-guage in Idaho, of course, but they treated it more gently and the words rolled out at a slower pace.

"Look," he said, picking up his coffee, giving Emmylou a "Thanks for breakfast, gotta run" wave and heading out the door to the garden to improve the connection, "I've got my cell and e-mail. We'll get them through this. I'll be there by the day after tomorrow. E-mail me the details. I'll call the CEO as soon as I'm caught up."

From the merger, she moved on to give him status reports on three other active deals. He felt frustration throbbing all the way to his fingertips. This was nuts. He had too many deals on, and nobody he could turn anything over to. He needed to hire more staff, but then he never had time to train them properly.

He got off the phone, checked his e-mail, and the cell rang again. He lost track of time, and felt as though he were back in his office, once going so far as to bellow for Anna—only realizing his mistake when Emmylou ran into the room. "What are you hollering about?"

"Sorry. For a second there I thought I was in New York."

"Well, you're not."

There wasn't time to apologize; the phone rang again.

A sandwich appeared at his side and he glanced at his watch to see it was after one. He waved his thanks, reminding him-self he'd have to make sure Emmylou charged him extra since he was using her office and eating more than just breakfast.

An hour later, things had slowed a little and so he rose, stretched out his back, and took his empty plate back into the kitchen.

Emmylou was making bread. None of that bread-machine bread, either. She had her hands in the dough and was knead-ing with a rhythm that immediately soothed him—though he didn't know until that second he'd been jangled.

There was a novel on the counter, with a bookmark in it decorated with dried flowers. It looked like one of those women-in-book-clubs type of novels he never found time to read.

"Thanks for lunch," he said, and put the blue and white plate beside the sink.

She glanced up from her task and he could see that she was getting quite a workout from the bread. Her cheeks were a little flushed and her breathing quicker than normal.

"Not a—what is that thing hanging out of your ear?"

"Earpiece for my cell phone."

"Oh, how awful," she said as though it were a malignant growth.

"Yeah, well, it's how I do business."

"Hmm. How do you do life?" she muttered, but not so low that he didn't hear her. He could let it go, but he kind of liked watching her at her homely task. He'd never imagined a woman kneading bread could look sexy, but then Emmylou could make pretty much any activity crank up his libido.

"I beg your pardon?"

She looked up at him and he knew she knew he'd heard her fine the first time. "I said, 'How do you do life?'"

"Pretty damn well, thank you very much." What bug had crawled up her ass? He remembered suddenly the way he'd bellowed for her as though she'd been his employee and figured she was still pissed about that. "Um, sorry about earlier. I didn't mean to yell for you."

"Is that how you treat your assistant?"

"Anna's very happy in her job. She's not complaining." Well, why would she? She was extremely well-paid and had the ambition to match her talent. He was grooming her to go places and both of them knew it. If he occasionally forgot his manners around Anna, she also sometimes forgot hers around him. "You know, New York is a bit different than Beaverton."

She gazed at him, her blue, blue eyes so open and uncomplicated. Then she said a very strange thing. "What did you have for lunch, Joe?"

"That very nice sandwich you brought me. I believe I said thank you." He hoped he had. Had he forgotten the simplest of good manners when she'd done him an unexpected favor?

But that apparently wasn't what she was getting at. "What kind of sandwich was it?"

He blinked. Thought back to when she'd brought it to him. He could see her, the shape of her, and that had caught his attention. He remembered the plate with the sandwich on it. By concentrating, he thought he'd seen a frill of green lettuce peeking out the side. But what the hell kind of sandwich had he eaten? He'd been so busy with his business he hadn't even noticed.

Well, you didn't get ahead in life without balls and bluster and he liked to think he had plenty of both. Certainly enough to brazen out a name-the-sandwich contest with a woman whose idea of fun was kneading bread dough in the middle of the afternoon.

"Tuna fish," he said. And just so she knew he'd paid attention, he added, "With lettuce."

"Was the bread white or wheat?"

Well, duh. He hadn't hung around here for two days not to know she kept a healthy kitchen, so he said, "Wheat."

"Did you find the pickles too salty?"

"No. They were perfect. Thank you."

She pulled her hands out of the dough and went to the sink to wash up.

"The sandwich was made with deli beef on rye bread. I served it with carrot sticks, not pickles." She shot him a "you are so pathetic" look, and then said, "But you were right about the lettuce."

"I was busy," he confessed, feeling like a jerk. "I didn't notice."

"You think?"

He could tell her he'd managed to salvage a multimillion-buck deal today, for which he'd earn a fat fee, but until the merger was complete it wouldn't be true, and besides, not paying attention was bad, boasting was worse.

"Have you—" She cut herself off in midsentence as he waved his hand at her. He had a call coming in.

He turned away so he could concentrate, but not before he'd seen a pretty impressive eye-roll from the sexy bread-baker.

What? He felt like asking her. What the hell was he supposed to do? He hadn't asked to be stuck here. He had a job to do, and a pretty damned lucrative one. It did bother him a little, though, about the sandwich. How had he not even noticed what he was eating?

Had he lost touch with the simple things in life? No, of course not. He was busy, that's all. The next time she cooked for him, he'd make a point of oohing and aahing over every mouthful.

Since the reception was crap in her kitchen, and in most of her house, he found himself once more in the middle of the garden feeling like a dork. He was trying to make notes in his palm pilot, but what he really needed was his own office with all his equipment and Anna. God, he missed Anna. She was getting a raise that would knock her Gucci socks off when he got back.

"Where are you? On the plane?" Frank Gellman bellowed.

"No. I'm still in Beaverton. I'll be home tomorrow."

"Thought you were done down there."

For some reason he did not feel like sharing the fact that he'd been stranded in this town. It made him sound like he wasn't in control and that wouldn't do. Not with the Gellmans. "Yeah. Something came up. A snag. I'll tell you about it tomorrow."

Emmylou watched Joe pacing back and forth as though the green lawn was a boardroom floor; he trampled a tiny misplaced daisy and never even noticed.

He was so clueless about the basic, everyday aspects of life that he made her want to smack him. Hard. But even so, watching his long stride eat up the grass, sensing the energy that pulsed from him, she felt energized. Sure they were opposites in every way, but it was definitely a case of opposites attracting. A serious case. Besides, she could help Joe. She knew she could. If the man didn't let up, he was going to implode.

Okay, so she had some serious Intimate Healer blood flowing through her veins, and she couldn't help but feel that Joe was a sad case. How could a man who ate food without tasting it possibly appreciate the simple joys of making love? As she watched his very nice body walking away from her, she wondered what he'd be like in bed.

At a guess, she'd say he'd be competent and thorough—as focused on the task of getting and giving pleasure as he was in everything. She suspected no woman would leave his bed without at least one orgasm, because he would always want to close the deal. He was driven to succeed in everything he undertook, but she suspected there'd be little silliness between his sheets. Not a lot of lazy fooling around to no purpose.

She sighed. She didn't have the training of her aunts or grandmother, all she had was instincts.

She had damn good instincts.

Apart from the urge to help him was the knowledge that Joe would be in less of a hurry to leave Beaverton if he had a promising new affair on the go.

Or was she flattering herself?

Of course, prostitution hadn't been practiced under this roof for many years and she wasn't about to give her body for the sake of the town. Oh, no. The truth was, Joe appealed to her. She hadn't answered his earlier question about her sex life because his cell phone interrupted her, but when she thought about it, the answer was kind of pitiful.

She loved Beaverton, but finding a man with all his own

teeth and all his wits was close to impossible. She'd had a couple of love affairs in college, one of which lasted two years, but she'd wanted to come home and her relationship ended with no hard feelings.

She'd gone along quite happily, putting all her energy into getting the Shady Lady up and running as a bed and breakfast. Then, just when her body was reminding her that she was a young woman in her prime, along had come the new doctor to take over old Doc Gazinski's practice. Dr. Gordon Hartnett was blond, golden, gorgeous. Brad Pitt with a stethoscope. Unlike poor old Doc Gazinski, he was even competent. Even more unlikely, he was single.

She and the good doctor had enjoyed a very nice, and very discreet, relationship for a year and a half, when Miss Trevellen's niece came to visit and then came down with severe tonsillitis. Dr. Hartnett may have taken her tonsils, but in return he gave her his heart. They'd been married six months and Terri was expecting her first child. She was one of Emmylou's best friends and it was obvious that she and Gord were meant for each other, crazy in love.

Although Emmylou missed the sex, she found she didn't miss Gord. She'd decided some time ago that she was essentially a practical woman. Growing up as she had, sex held no mysteries for her and love made people plain crazy. She'd decided that while she enjoyed sex when it was available with a clean, decent man, she didn't miss it when it was off the menu. And as for love, she didn't need any more craziness in her life.

But lately she had been feeling a little twitchy. Time to take another lover twitchy, and her pickings were slim indeed. Enter Joe, who'd stumbled into her B&B like a storybook prince to the rescue. A modern hero who was hopefully packing more than a kiss.

Last night it would have felt wrong to have sex with the man since she knew he wouldn't be leaving the next day and he didn't.

Tonight was a different matter—if she could ever separate him from his damn cell phone for five minutes.

That phone was driving her nuts. And the way it was permanently stuck to his ear plain gave her the creeps. She never knew from one minute to the next whether he was talking to her or to some overworked minion in Manhattan.

An unfamiliar depression settled over her, in spite of the smell of baking bread, one of the best mood-lifters in the world. Joe's big deal, which involved constant communication with people who sounded unpleasant to her, must be the Beaverton factory. She couldn't imagine how devastated her friends and neighbors would be when their idyllic town with its pleasant fields was churned up to make cat litter.

It was such an insult.

If she could make Joe fall in love with the town as others before him had, then maybe he'd help them fight to keep it. But getting him to change allegiance from the bunch of billionaire corporate sharks who seemed to own him body and soul, to a small town full of people who appreciated a simple life and didn't yearn for more seemed beyond her.

She glanced out the window and there he was, back on that cell phone, gesticulating in tight circles with one hand as he talked, pacing a track through the wet grass. Did he see how pretty her garden was? Did he even notice his feet were getting wet?

On a sudden whim, she poured a glass of lemonade into one of the pink glass tumblers and took it out to him.

"Right. I get that," she heard him say. "Run the numbers again with the square footage cost estimates and get back to me."

He didn't say good-bye, but he rolled his shoulders and stopped talking so she assumed he was done. He hadn't even noticed her approach. "I brought you a drink," she said.

He gave her a tired smile and a curt, "Thanks."

The sun glistened off the fresh water she'd put in the stone birdbath, and the scent of the moss roses at their feet was as poignant as a lover's memory. She breathed deep.

Joe could have been in a boardroom for all the notice he took. He was fiddling with a palm-sized electronic device. She set down the lemonade and walked up behind him, then put her palms over his eyes.

"What are you doing?" he asked, his voice sharp with surprise and irritation. "I'm busy."

Even his eyelashes felt stiff with tension as they scratched against her palms.

If she hoped to make him human again, she was going to have her work cut out for her. "Name three flowers in my garden."

"I don't have time for games." Still, he didn't pull away and she was suddenly deeply aware that her breasts brushed his upper back. His muscles felt warm from the sun and she noticed a couple of silver hairs among the thick dark strands at the back of his head.

"Come on. Only three."

"I'm not a botanist."

"Okay, fair enough." She glanced around at the climbing roses resting their red cheeks drowsily against the lattice arbor, while fat bees buzzed their way from blossom to blossom. Joe was surrounded by deep blue hydrangeas and bright yellow day lilies, purple clematis and orange poppies. A person would have to be blind not to notice. "Name three colors of flowers in the garden."

He huffed. "This is ridiculous."

"How can you come out here and not enjoy it?"

"Red, yellow, blue," he snapped, reciting the primary colors.

"Congratulations," she said, and handed him his lemonade.

She walked back to the house.

"Hey," he said, following behind her and sounding completely stunned. "I was right!"

"I give up," she muttered, and continued on her way. One thing was clear, the chances that they were going to convert Joe Montcrief to the importance of saving Beaverton were about as good as him learning the names of all her roses.

Chapter 11

She walked into Ernie's to find the aunts there with Ernie and his wife and Napoleon and Madame Dior. The atmosphere was gloomy.

The first meeting of the committee to save Beaverton didn't seem to be going all that well.

She soon found out why. "With the back taxes and penalties, we're looking at several hundred thousand dollars to get the sanitarium property back," Ernie explained.

"Then we'd still have to find a way to keep paying the taxes, or what's the point?" Olive added.

"Where are we going to find that kind of money?" Emmylou asked, letting some of her despair out.

It was as hopeless as it ever was to discuss how they were going to pay the town's back taxes. It had seemed like a boon when Emmet Beaver had willed the town his sanitarium; had he foreseen it would end up as a kitty litter factory, she was sure he'd have done something else with the property.

At the end of an hour, they'd dreamed up a casino, which, given the area's population, didn't seem viable; selling off their combined jewelry; and her personal favorite, robbing a bank.

What they needed, Emmylou realized as the meeting wound down with even less optimism than it had begun, was an advisor. Like Joe, except that Joe was quarterbacking for the other team.

She and the aunts walked back together along with Madame Dior, who'd decided to join them. Emmylou felt so bad that she made them all a cup of tea and then spent a good half hour bitching about big business in general and Joe in particular.

It didn't solve anything, but at least she felt marginally better when she went outside to pick fresh herbs to put on tonight's roast chicken.

Lydia was still watching Emmylou's departing back when Olive said, "I thought we'd never get rid of her. Now, all we have to do is to make Joe and her fall in love. He's smart enough and rich enough to save the town, and she needs a good man."

"What about me? Maybe I'll find someone rich enough to save the town. I could use a good man."

Olive snorted. "What would you do with a good man? You haven't had sex in twenty years."

"Oh, go ahead and laugh. I've had bids on my online auction—and it's got my picture."

"People think it's a joke! You can't sell sex on eBay, it's illegal."

"What do you think I am? Stupid? Of course it doesn't say I'm selling sex. I worded that part very discreetly."

"I bet your bidders are all teenage boys with a sick sense of humor."

"I've got one guy whose handle is Eyes4U. No teenager would remember that song. It used to be my favorite when . . ." Lydia's eyes grew misty and Olive, who knew why, reached over to pat her hand.

"I suspect his handle is slipping and his eyes are long gone. Along with the rest of him."

"We're supposed to be finding out how to enchant Joe and Emmylou so zey fall in love," Madame Dior reminded them.

"Emmylou doesn't believe in love," Olive said, the lines on her face suddenly deepening. "How could she grow up in this place and not believe in love?"

"She's not a romantic, that's all."

"Then Joe will have to throw every romantic trick at her. Because a woman who's never loved is going to fall hard when she finally does fall."

Lydia sighed. Wasn't that the truth. Why had no one ever told her when she was young and so full of herself that one day she'd be old and wrinkled on the outside, but inside she'd still feel like the same girl? That the one great love of her life would be as sharp and poignant at seventy-five as it had been when she was forty. Okay, so she was old and batty. Well, she wasn't as old and batty as Olive. And she didn't steal things or pretend she was French. Damn it, she was a bastion of sanity in this crazy place. And maybe she could give Emmylou what she'd had to give up—the love of a lifetime.

"We don't want her to get hurt," Olive said.

"Love hurts," Lydia said without thinking. She must have sounded sadder than she meant to, for the others stared at her. Olive's eyes got soft.

"Don't worry," Olive said. "We'll make sure they fall in love."

"And how do you plan to do that?"

Olive smiled and her faded blue eyes twinkled. "Dr. Beaver's special tonic."

Lydia nearly swallowed her tongue. "What are you talking about? The last of the tonic was used years ago."

"I found a bottle a few years back. I couldn't believe there was one left."

Lydia felt her eyes bug out so wide she was afraid her eyeballs would pop out and skid down her face. "Why didn't you tell me? I had a right to know."

"What would you have done with the tonic?"

"I'd have used it!"

"Exactly. That's why I didn't tell you."

"Of what are you talking?" asked Madame Dior. When she felt left out of a conversation, she got Frencher than frog's legs.

"There was a sort of medicine that Dr. Emmet used to pre-scribe for patients. It helped focus their libido. When he died, the recipe died with him and there were only a few precious bottles left. The stuff was amazing—sort of a love and lust potion in one. If we slip it to Joe and Emmylou, they'll have great sex, fall in love, Joe will stay, and the town will be saved."

Madame Dior gasped. "Dr. Emmet Beaver passed away more than thirty years ago. You can't feed that stuff to peo-ple now. Why, it could have turned into poison."

"Well, that's true." Olive's face creased in a frown. "Or it could have got stronger with age."

"You'd do better to sell the stuff to make money than waste it on Joe and Emmylou. Why don't you give it to me?" Lydia suggested. "I could sell it on eBay."

"Nonsense. You just want the tonic for yourself."

Damn, that Olive was always too smart for her own good.

"Okay, so we waste the stuff on Emmylou and they get friskier than a pair of teenage rabbits. So what?"

"You're thinking small. They fall in lust, they fall into bed. This stuff doesn't just enhance the libido, it dampens inhibi-tions and spurs creativity. A little of this mixed with any al-cohol, and kaboom. They'll have such a fantastic time, it will hasten the falling in love process." Olive chuckled. "There's no time to lose. We'll feed it to them at dinner. We'll need our earplugs tonight."

"There's only one bottle left," Lydia complained. "Why can't I take it down to the bingo hall on my birthday?"

"Which is more important? An octogenarian orgy or sav-ing this town?"

When Lydia didn't immediately answer, Olive snapped, "Well? Did you fall asleep?"

"I'm thinking."

"We have to save the town."

She was right, but it didn't make Lydia happy to admit it. "Oh, all right. But you'd better come up with a very nice pre-sent on my birthday. No more support hose."

"Support hose are practical."

"So's a casket—maybe I'll get you one of them for your birthday."

As Emmylou walked by Joe, who was arguing with yet another faceless business associate, she wondered if she'd ever find peace again in this garden. It was beginning to sound like the trading floor of the stock exchange.

Unable to resist their lure, she touched the velvet petals of a True Love and on impulse cut a few stems for the dining table. Then she headed for the small brick planter that was her kitchen garden.

The sage was in bloom, its fuzzy purple flowers making her smile. The rosemary was dark, shiny green, and she rubbed a piece between her fingers and inhaled the released aroma. Yes, she decided, rosemary. What else? She snipped some garlic chives and parsley. That would do. Simple was best.

As she walked past Joe once more, she said, "Are you eating here tonight?"

Joe said, "Hang on a minute." To his client, she presumed; he actually looked at her for the first time in hours.

"I'll be working late so I figured on eating here. Do you mind?"

"Of course not." But it would have been nice to have been asked.

"Put it on my bill," he said.

"Yes, sir." Like she was the Plaza Hotel. Sheesh. You wouldn't get garden-raised rosemary and Idaho potatoes grown right here in Idaho in some fancy-schmancy hotel.

Not that he'd notice. She could feed him his own shoes and he'd eat them.

He was a sad, sad case. Her garden was one of the most beautiful, relaxing places on earth, and did he bother to watch the new petals unfurling? Did he stop to smell the goddam roses? No. He stared at the grass. His eyes were pinched with fatigue and his shoulders rode high with the stress she could practically see knotting his neck. Pathetic. But then so was she for caring.

It was, however, nice to cook for someone with a healthy appetite. Olive and Lydia between them ate what she did, minus anything crunchy or chewy in deference to Olive's false teeth. Some days she felt that if she ate another mashed vegetable, she might scream.

When guests stayed in the Shady Lady, she was always happy to serve dinner on request. And usually after a night sitting around Belle's kitchen table, or a night of meatloaf and shooting pool at Ernie's, they did. She didn't push dinner because she didn't believe in taking business away from the tavern and Belle, but she didn't turn customers away if they asked.

Still, it would have been nice to have Joe make the request rather than assume he could snap his fingers, say "Put it on my bill," and everything would be fine.

By the time dinner was almost ready, and the smell of roasting chicken and vegetables filled the kitchen, she decided Joe couldn't keep ignoring his senses forever. Something was bound to slip under his guard, and she wouldn't be a bit surprised if it was her roast chicken.

"Smells great," Lydia said, echoing her thoughts as she came into the kitchen. "Want me to set the table?"

"Yes, thanks."

"I'll use the good stuff. And I'm putting out wineglasses. A sophisticated man like that comes to dinner, you have wine." She pronounced sophisticated with the emphasis on *so*. SOH-phisticated.

"I don't think we need wine."

"Yes, we do. He'll expect it. And we'll charge him double the price we paid, just like in a real hotel. Besides, Dr. Hartnell said a glass of wine is good for my health. Might be good for your health, too."

"There's nothing wrong with my health," Emmylou protested.

"Dr. Beaver would have said you were blocking all your electric circuits. A young thing like you should be having sex every night."

"Dr. Beaver was an old quack who charged people a fortune to come down here and think about nothing but sex. What's so great about that?"

"Plenty, missy. Don't knock it until you've tried it."

For some reason this subject always irritated her, especially when Lydia and Olive ganged up on her. She was just all around peeved enough today, what with Joe treating her like a servant, and not noticing her food or her garden, or—let's face it—her, that she snapped. Stomping into the dining room, she yelled, "What are you suggesting? That I never think about sex?"

"Well? Do you?" Lydia was pulling the good wineglasses from the walnut bowfront cabinet where she stored them. The crystal glittered as the older woman thumped it on the table. "A nice young man like Joe comes along and all you do is cook for him."

"This is a bed and breakfast. It's not a brothel anymore."

"Well, it was a hell of a lot more fun when it was! And I bet that nice young man would love to have sex with you if you gave him half a chance."

Emmylou felt like baying at the moon. Instead of doing that, she threw back her head and screamed, "My sex life is none of your business!"

"You don't have a sex life!" the old woman bellowed right back.

She heard the unmistakable creak of one of the floorboards in the kitchen and knew without turning that Joe was in there. Of course it couldn't be anyone but Joe. She wouldn't feel this excruciatingly mortified if it was anyone else.

There was only one thing to do. She'd act dignified, pretend she didn't know Joe was in the kitchen, and give him time to get the hell out of there. Then, when she saw him again, the whole thing would be forgotten.

She grabbed a linen napkin and began polishing the glasses Lydia had brought out. The kitchen floorboard creaked again. And again, and suddenly Joe was stepping through into the dining room.

Oh, well. He didn't know what he was eating or seeing when he was on that damn cell phone. The chances were he shut his ears to everything but his business, as well.

She risked a glance, but she didn't think the unholy amusement in his eyes was caused by his latest chat with the cat litter king of New York. She narrowed her eyes, telling him silently but pointedly, *Don't you dare!*

He leaned against the door frame, looking so pleased with himself she wanted to kick his shin. "I'm sorry to hear you don't have a sex life, Em. Anything I can do to help?"

She put down the shiny glass and turned, hoping she wasn't blushing. "A gentleman would pretend not to have overheard that."

"I don't suppose gentlemen have much fun."

Lydia chuckled, and scuttled out of the room with more speed than usual. Traitor.

He moved closer, and she moved back only to find her thighs jammed against her dining room table.

She glanced up and his eyes were a kind of smoky blue now, and so very intent. His gaze dropped lazily to her mouth and suddenly heat hit low and then spread. "Now, about getting you that sex life," he said, and lowered his mouth.

Her eyes drifted shut and her lips drifted open.

"What do you want now?" Joe asked in a voice of supreme irritation. She blinked her eyes open and saw him frowning and looking anything but interested in her.

She said, "Hey, I didn't—" but he cut her off with the wave of a hand and she realized his cell phone had come between them. Again.

And instead of being backed against a sturdy mahogany table for a steamy kiss, she was watching his back as he walked out of the room, and *she* was steaming.

Enough already with the cell phone. And so much for improving her sex life. He wasn't a sexually exciting man—Joe Montcrief was a robot and his master was implanted in his ear.

She stomped back to the kitchen and dug out a thick black marker and a pad of foolscap and wrote in block letters: DINNER WILL BE SERVED AT 7 P.M.!

Then, deciding that sounded petulant and snarky, and a businesswoman running an inn should not be either to her only customer, she rewrote the note, leaving out the exclamation point.

"Can you take this in to the office and put it in front of Joe's nose?" Emmylou asked when Lydia came back, holding out a glass of wine like a peace offering.

"Sure, honey. Ah, sorry about earlier."

"So am I."

"I figured you two would be locked in the bedroom by now, the way he was looking at you." The old woman fanned herself. "I thought your blouse was going to start smoking."

"His cell phone is his true love," Emmylou said. "He treats me like a servant."

Lydia thought about that for a minute, deep in thought. "Love slave," she said at last. "Maybe if you dressed up as a love slave. Men have some very peculiar fantasies, dear. Half of your job is tapping in to the right one. I think I still have a costume up in one of the trunks in the attic that—"

"No." The one thing guaranteed to put the capper on her day would be to show up in some moth-eaten *I Dream of Jeannie* costume and have Joe not notice.

"All right. One thing at a time. I'll take your young man a glass of wine. Drink yours. It will do you good."

Normally, Emmylou wasn't much of a drinker, but she was riled enough that she gulped down half the glass. Then licked her lips. "Is this from the case Napoleon sent over for Christmas? It's bitterer than I remember."

"That's the French for you," Lydia said.

Emmylou sipped again. It was good. She was on edge, maybe a drink would help her relax, she thought as she sipped again. The wine might be a shade bitter, but it was growing on her.

Lydia took the metal flask out of the pocket of her house-dress and poured a healthy slug into a second glass of wine. She stirred it in with a silver teaspoon and squinted to make sure there was no clouding or sediment to give her away. Nope.

Carrying the wine carefully, along with the note, she approached the office where Joe was haranguing somebody about something. He was the least restful boy she'd ever known, and she only hoped Olive knew what she was doing making him and Emmylou fall in love. Lydia wasn't at all sure she wanted this one around permanently. Still, she had to help save the town, and if her sacrifice was sharing the Shady Lady with cat-litter boy, she supposed she could do it.

She stuck the note on top of his keyboard, and he nodded. Then she handed him his wine. He pointed to the desktop, but she wasn't born yesterday and if there was one thing she knew about, it was men and one-track minds. Unfortunately, this poor boy's was all on the wrong track. She hoped his little cocktail would cure him. Cock-tail, she muttered. Now there was a good word.

What do you get when you pour a lust potion into a glass of wine? Cock-tail. She chuckled silently at her own joke. She'd have to remember to tell Olive.

Once more, she handed it to him and this time he took it. He kept talking, and for a second she thought he'd forget all about the wine and toss it all over the place before he drank any, but as soon as he stopped talking, he sipped. She let out her breath and backed out of the room.

Unbidden, memories flooded her. She'd been a damn good Intimate Healer, and Dr. Emmet's tonic didn't have much to do with her success. Her tragedy was that most of her clients were there because of problems in their marriages. They were good, decent men and the doctor sent them to her because they couldn't perform or they couldn't bring their wives pleasure. She'd taught them so much, saved many a marriage. She wondered if anyone knew how much it cost her to let those sweet men go once they were cured.

Eddie Parkinson was one such man. Oh, he'd been so tongue-tied and shy when she started working with him. Naturally, since he was a married man, there was never any sexual intercourse between them. What she taught was touch. How to pleasure a woman. How to hold back his own pleasure.

Eddie had blossomed under her and Dr. Emmet's care, and the young husband went on to enjoy a long marriage and several healthy children. He probably had grandchildren now. They'd crossed paths the odd time in the grocery store. Once in a while he and his wife came out for bingo. He always looked at Lydia as though he could see past her exterior to the lonely heart that beat beneath her breasts.

She'd never, ever broken the rules, but if there was one man she wished she'd had sexual intercourse with all those years ago, it was Eddie.

His wife had died almost a year ago, and foolish Lydia had hoped he might call one day. She was still waiting.

When she walked back upstairs to dress for dinner, she heard the slosh of liquid from the flask in her pocket. Even after the healthy doses she'd given Emmylou and Joe, there was plenty left. Probably the stuff didn't keep.

This was the last bottle, too. As far as she knew, the formula had died with Dr. Emmet.

She sighed. If Joe and Emmylou didn't fall in love, get married, have a bunch of babies, and save this town, she was going to be seriously riled.

Chapter 12

To everyone's amazement, Joe didn't miss dinner. He wasn't even very late. He'd washed up and changed his clothes, like a well-mannered boy should, and when he came into the dining room, he brought his glass with him—with the doctored wine she'd served him half drunk.

Lydia blinked when he sat down and a wire swung out from his ear. "Have you got a hearing aid? Young fellow like you?"

"No. It's my cell phone." He glanced over at the swing door as he said it.

"No, Joe," Emmylou said, coming in from the kitchen with a platter of steaming roast chicken. "No cell phones at the table."

"Give me a break, would you? This client's all over me."

She looked like she was going to snap his head off, which meant words might be exchanged and the last bottle of Dr. Emmet's tonic might as well get poured down the toilet. Lydia figured those folks that paid a lot of money to have some fancy stallion mount their thoroughbred mare must feel a little the way she did right now. Like she'd do anything to smooth the path.

"Honey, let Joe have his phone. It's only us, and he is our guest." She didn't, of course, say *paying* guest, but that's what she implied and Emmylou knew it. After a moment of firm lip pinching, Emmylou said, "All right. If you and Olive don't mind."

Well, as a matter of fact, she did mind. It was going to do them no good at all if the damn fool stallion talked to strangers all through dinner instead of flirting with the nicest thoroughbred mare he was ever likely to come across.

What on earth was wrong with youngsters these days? Was his cell phone really more important than enjoying the company of a gorgeous young woman? No wonder America's birth rate was declining and the cell phone population exploding. Lydia shoved the mashed yams on her plate aside to make room for the chicken.

Emmylou sat down and picked up her napkin, then made a choking sound.

"What's the matter?" Joe asked her, half rising and looking ready to do the Heimlich maneuver.

"Nothing." Emmylou waved him back to his seat, while glaring at Lydia, who did her best to look innocent.

She was a big believer in subliminal messages. Except that sometimes subliminal messages were too subtle and a person was better off with more obvious clues.

Emmylou whipped her napkin, still in its napkin ring, off the table and stuck it on her lap. Joe, still watching her, looked puzzled until he turned to his own napkin.

She'd given him the best of the napkin rings. He slipped his starched napkin out and studied the ring for a second, then glanced at Emmylou, who was busy looking at her lap, and then right at Lydia. "These are very interesting napkin rings, Lydia," he said with a gleam in his eye even an old woman could love.

"I chose that one specially for you. You can take it with you for later."

He glanced at Emmyylou again, and said, "Maybe I will."

Olive was so busy watching Emmylou and Joe that when she served herself mashed potatoes, she missed her plate and half the potatoes went splat onto the tablecloth. Any fool could see she'd spent an hour gussying herself up in her black velvet slacks and the cotton sweater Lydia had knit her for Christmas last year. It was black and white and looked even better on Olive than it had on the woman in the pattern.

"You look nice, Olive," Emmylou said.

"Thank you, dear. I'm going visiting after dinner." She looked over at Lydia with a determined expression. "Why don't you come with me?"

That woman was as subtle as a cow pie. Lydia had a plan of her own that would help ensure Joe and Emmylou had the house to themselves, but she didn't intend to announce it to all and sundry. Well, she hadn't; now she had no choice. "Thanks, but I'm doing some visiting of my own. Pass the potatoes."

"That's nice." You could tell the woman was dying to ask Lydia where she was going, but didn't dare in case she'd made it up and was only going to end up watching TV with one of her old friends. French TV if she went to Madame Dior, taped History Channel programs if she went over to Napoleon.

It didn't look like all their careful planning to slip the tonic to the two youngsters and then leave them the house to themselves was going to matter a damn. Emmylou wasn't happy about the black cord hanging out of Joe's ear.

Lydia had almost forgotten what fools men were.

Then he did a most surprising thing. He removed the earpiece and hooked it down on his belt somewhere. "I'm turning my phone off until after dinner," he said, and you could tell that it wasn't easy for him to do that. Emmylou could see it, too. She smiled at him and piled his plate with chicken.

Oh, that was good. Lydia had watched on one of those sex programs on TV where when people fed each other it was like a mating ritual. Emmylou was a little stunted in that area, so maybe for her, piling Joe's plate was her way of telegraphing that she wanted to have sex with him.

No wonder the girl never seemed to get laid. The way she

was loading up the food, Joe was probably thinking she wanted to be his Jewish grandmother. Good thing there was plenty more tonic in the flask. Lydia was going to slip them both another belt of the stuff first chance she got.

They all passed Joe the bowls and dishes and watched him heap his plate so high it was a wonder the table didn't tip with the weight and dump everything in his lap.

"I can't tell you how much I like home cooking. I eat out all the time."

"Can't you cook?" Olive asked. She might be old but she didn't believe in bringing up lazy sons. She and Lydia had always agreed that if they'd ever had any, their boys would have learned to cook, same as the girls.

He said, "I can microwave."

"Oh, that's sad."

He put a bite of food into his mouth and it was like watching someone after their first kiss. He closed his eyes and said, "*Mmmm.*"

In the time it took Olive to cut her chicken pieces tiny enough for her dentures to handle, he'd finished a plateful.

"Would you like some more?" Emmylou asked.

"I shouldn't," he said, putting a hand on his belly, "but it's too good to resist."

Lord alive. They'd have eaten that chicken for a couple more days, the three of them. And after Joe piled his plate again, there wasn't much left but a wishbone.

When Emmylou brought out fresh apple pie and ice cream, he really did groan. "You should have warned me there was dessert."

"It's nice to watch someone enjoying my food," she said. Since Lydia knew what she meant, she didn't get huffy, just hoped that fool Joe would have the sense to eat a big hunk of the dessert Emmylou had obviously made him specially.

He didn't disappoint. He might have eaten the pie slower, but his obvious pleasure radiated across his face, making

Lydia wish she were a few years younger. Oh, what she could show that boy.

Mind you, there was something about him that suggested he had some pretty good moves of his own, and the way he glanced at Emmylou, he was planning to use them on her.

She and Olive shared a conspiratorial wink, and Olive rose and said, "Why don't you two go into the parlor? Lydia and I can do the dishes."

Emmylou's color immediately heightened. "I'm sure Joe wants to get back to his work."

He drained the last of his wine. "It'll keep."

"I set fresh candles out, too. All you need to do is light a match." Oh, that was a good one. Nothing so romantic as candlelight.

"I've got some nice brandy," Emmylou said, finally getting into the spirit of the thing. She glanced at Joe and her lips tilted. "Napoleon brandy."

"Sounds good." Then he rose and said, "Shall we?" He pulled her chair out for her as she stood, just like a head waiter in a fancy restaurant. Lydia was half in love with him herself.

A sharp nudge in the ribs cured her of that and she obligingly followed Olive into the kitchen.

"I get the feeling those two are trying to get us alone together," Joe said, once he'd lit the candles and she'd poured them each a brandy, using the good crystal because, what the hell, it sure didn't get used very often.

"An asteroid landing in the backyard would be more subtle. I'm really sorry."

"Don't be. I've been trying to figure out all day how to get you alone."

"When you weren't wheeling and dealing."

"Right."

"So I'd say getting me alone took about what, a nanosecond of your day?"

"You're forgetting that I'm an artist at multitasking."

"I'm pretty sure I know what kind of an artist you are."

He laughed, and it was the sexiest sound she'd ever heard.

He wasn't only good to look at, but his voice had a wonderfully sexy timbre. Voices were important to her; she liked to imagine how they'd sound in the dark rumbling away beside her on the pillow. His would be a definite turn-on.

She took a sip of her brandy and let it fire-eat its way down to her belly, then put the glass aside. Maybe she'd had more wine than she realized. She felt a little muzzy.

"Are you all right?" he asked.

"Yes. I'm not much of a drinker is all."

"I feel it, too."

"You do?"

"A little dizzy? Slightly off balance?"

She nodded.

"I don't think it's the booze. I think it's this attraction between us that only gets stronger the longer we ignore it."

"Maybe we should stop ignoring it, then," she said.

"I could not agree more," he said, and sinking down beside her on the overstuffed, velvet-covered sofa, he kissed her.

Oh, sure, he'd kissed her before and it had been great, right up there in the pantheon of best kisses of her life, but every time there'd been this internal monologue going on in her head. Sleep with him or not sleep with him? Now the dissenting voice was silent. She was all systems go, mentally and physically, and so instead of wasting time intellectualizing the shoulds and shouldn'ts of the situation, she was putting all her energy into feeling. And she did feel.

Pow-pow. The power of his kiss thrilled through her, so they moved from the initial polite warming-up phase to hot and greedy, open mouths and thrusting tongues, at lightning speed. And lighting feel. And lightning everything.

"I am crazy about you," he muttered huskily when they broke away to draw breath.

Crazy seemed to be the operative word here. It was how

she felt, too. Like all her calm sanity had deserted her and left nothing but blind passion in its place.

And crazy or not, blind passion was feeling pretty good.

Her skin seemed to scorch at his touch. Was it her imagination or was she more sensitive? Her taste sharper? Maybe it had simply been too long since she'd let herself go like this.

After they'd worked themselves up to the hot and bothered stage, she heard cheerful twin good-byes from the aunts and then the thud of the front door.

She glanced at Joe to see his eyes cloudy with passion, his pupils dilated and reflecting the candlelight.

"We're all alone," she said.

"I feel like a teenager and the parents just left." He paused to look at her with a quizzical grin. "Except those two seemed like they really wanted us having hanky-panky in their absence."

"Gee, what was your first clue?"

"I'd have to say it was when I realized Lydia had put cock rings around the napkins. That seemed like a pretty broad hint."

"Knowing Lydia, she'd say it's a shame to see them go to waste if no one's going to use them."

"And the napkins were certainly nice and stiff."

She grinned at him and reached for his hand. They could make love right here, but her aunts didn't keep late hours. The last thing she wanted was to keep listening with half an ear for the sound of them coming home.

"My room," she decided.

"Anywhere," he replied.

They held hands as they sprinted up the staircase, which didn't even squeak in protest. It had been built to withstand great passion.

Built to encourage it, not that the heat burning low in her belly needed any encouragement. She felt that if he touched her there, if he so much as looked too hard, she'd go off like a firecracker.

She led him to her room. It had belonged to her great-great-grandmother, the madam, and she loved the room. It was big and housed a huge, in-your-face bed. The mattress was new, but the bed—like all the antiques in the house—was original. The windows gave a view of leafy trees and overlooked her garden.

"Great room."

"It's the madam's room. It's an honor to be invited in, you know."

"Oh, I know."

He kissed her again, half teasing, mostly serious. "I've never had sex in a brothel before."

She chuckled. "Glad to hear it."

"So," he said, running his lips down her neck so she shivered and his words rumbled against her skin, "what's the protocol here? Do I pay my money first or after I'm satisfied?"

"Oh, honey, you'll be satisfied. And I charge on a sliding scale. Depending on what you bring to the table, as it were, you might get a hefty discount."

"I thought you were here to service me?"

"You thought wrong, bucko." Since he was currently rubbing her breast in a way that brought her all kinds of pleasure, she assumed he was merely teasing. She sure hoped so. She was planning to vent a little of her sexual frustration tonight, not add to it.

He went for her buttons with almost fanatical haste. From the way his cheeks had flushed and his hands shook, she knew he was as anxious as she.

His breathing was loud in the big bedroom, almost drowning out her own, and sweat dampened his brow. Oh, yeah, she was turning him on, all right.

That thought alone heightened her excitement. She felt the tips of her breasts tighten and tingle as he rushed his way through the buttons.

"Unh," he said, or a word to that effect, when he spread

the edges of her blouse and discovered that she wore no bra. He made another strangled sound when he touched his lips to her breasts, as though he'd been robbed of speech.

Normally she liked to take the undressing part slowly, dragging out the anticipation, the same way she unwrapped Christmas and birthday gifts. But not tonight. They'd teased and denied each other long enough. Her blood felt like it was sizzling under her skin—she was beyond horny, her need to be filled almost painful.

He was obviously feeling the same, so they went at each other with frantic speed, dragging off clothes, nipping, licking, biting whatever they uncovered.

He was surprisingly buff for a desk jockey, she discovered. A definite bonus. She hadn't been sure what she'd find under his clothes. If he'd had a full computer setup complete with secretarial service under there, she wouldn't have been surprised.

But no, there was just nice warm male flesh. He had muscles where a woman liked to see muscle, and not a lot of show-offy bulk. His penis was a serviceable type. Not so big as to make a fool of itself, or so small as to make a fool of its owner, but a good length and girth. It was definitely looking up to the job.

"Does he meet with your approval?" Joe asked. He was teasing, but she thought maybe she'd embarrassed him, too. What was wrong with her, staring at a guy's package like that?

"I'm sorry. Frankly, it's been a while. I'm refamiliarizing myself."

He grinned down at her wolfishly and she realized all of him was up for the job. "I'll familiarize you. Don't worry."

And he tipped her back onto the bed. He started to kiss her breasts but she was too needy—she was so desperate to be filled, it was an ache. She reached over and opened her bedside drawer, then handed him a condom. "Please," she said, "I can't wait."

"Thank God," he said. In seconds he was ready, then he rolled over and against her, and then up inside with the power and surge she craved.

"Oh yes," she said. They fit so well together it was like the missing puzzle piece sliding into place. There was none of the awkwardness of a first time, the tilt of hip slightly off, or the fit not quite right. He slid into her body as though it had been made for him.

She closed her eyes and prepared to enjoy herself.

And then didn't enjoy herself at all.

Within moments, the long, drawn-out pleasure she'd hoped for was no more. He grabbed her breast with about as much finesse as a vise shows a two-by-four. A couple of flailing thrusts inside her body, a sound between a grunt and a groan, and he collapsed on top of her, panting against her neck like the little engine that couldn't quite make it to the top of the hill.

She lay there underneath the dead weight of him, stunned.

That was it? All the passionate kissing and fondling downstairs had led her to believe he was a promising lover, and he turned out to be the biggest dud of her life.

She squirmed her hips a bit, hoping for something, anything to put her out of her burning misery. But there was no response.

He didn't even have the courtesy to move off of her, just lay there, panting.

And suddenly all her pent-up excitement sublimated into bitchiness. "Female orgasm is a concept you might want to explore sometime."

Maybe there were women who could get off on two strokes and a clawing at the breast. She didn't seem to be one of them.

She should have realized this whole thing was hopeless when he chose his cell phone over kissing her. A man who didn't have enough sensuality to distinguish a tuna sandwich from beef, and who could spend all day in her garden and not remember a single flower—well, what had she been thinking? On the sensuality scale, this one rated "do not resuscitate."

He whispered something in her ear; she assumed it was an apology, but it was so faint she couldn't make out the words.

"What?"

"Can't breathe," he panted.

He should try it from her perspective, lying flat with his whole weight pressing on her. Her lungs must look like a pair of Pringles.

What did he mean exactly, "Can't breathe"? His breath was loud enough in her ear, like an old man about to snore.

He groaned as though he were in pain and a drop of sweat plopped onto her shoulder.

"Are you okay?" she asked, finally calming down enough to wonder if he had more wrong with him than his sexual technique.

"Sick," he managed.

Oh, no.

"What do you mean, sick?"

"Chest. Hurts," he managed.

Shit. There wasn't much she could do from underneath him, and of course there was no help to be had in the house since both the aunts had gone out. She heaved and shoved at the dead weight of him until she got him rolled off her and onto his side, then she pushed him onto his back.

She reached out and flicked on a light, and realized with a shock that he looked as pale as though the bride of Dracula had just given him a very long good-night kiss. His forehead was damp and his breathing definitely off.

"Show me where it hurts," she said as calmly as she could.

"Chest," he gasped. And his arm flopped onto his chest like a dead fish. Left side of his chest.

Oh my God, she thought, *he's too young to have a heart attack,* but then she thought about his lifestyle of constant stress and wondered. "Any pain in your arm?" she asked, crossing her fingers that the answer would be no.

He nodded as though speaking were too much of an effort, then with a gasp said, "Left arm."

Shit. Shit. Shit. Rapidly she reviewed her options. If she called 911 she was looking at twenty minutes for the ambulance to get here. She could drive him to the hospital herself in that time. But what if he died en route? He really didn't look all that hot.

"I'll be right back. Hang on. If you die in my bed, I'm going to kill you," she warned him.

Beaverton boasted a fairly new hospital that served the region. Gord Hartnett wasn't only her former lover, he was also her friend. She called him while she threw on her clothes, briefly described the situation.

"The ambulance is out on a call. It'll be faster if you drive him in yourself. I'll meet you there."

"Thanks," she said, knowing if anyone could save Joe it was Gordon.

She ran down the stairs, pulled her car around to the front door and left it running, then she sprinted back up the stairs. *Please don't die,* she silently pleaded as she pushed Joe's legs into his slacks, not wasting time on underwear or socks, and forced his arms into the sleeves of his shirt. She managed to get two buttons fastened with shaking fingers and decided that was plenty. Together they staggered down the stairs.

"I'm all right," he insisted. "I feel better."

"When you can stand up straight and say that without wincing with pain, I might actually believe you," she said, bundling him into the car.

"I don't want to go to the hospital."

"They can give you something to make you feel better," she said. She tried to sound confident, like his condition was the equivalent of a scrape needing a Band-Aid when she secretly suspected he might need the paddles and the cardiac jumper cables that scared the pants off her when she saw them on TV.

She got him belted into the passenger seat of her car, and he slumped against the seat. His breathing wasn't as loud now. Was that a good sign?

Please don't die.

She drove faster than she'd ever driven in her life, thankful that she'd grown up here and knew every bend in every road. There wasn't enough population to worry about traffic.

She drove with her hands gripping the wheel, her entire being focused on getting medical help. *Please don't die.*

"Are we going to a real hospital?" Joe's voice startled her.

"Of course," she said cheerfully. Whatever she did, she had to make him feel confident that he was going to be okay.

Joe made a sound like a faint snort. "It's probably some guy named Freddie who got a plastic doctor bag when he was a kid and now he thinks he's an MD. He'll stick a plastic thermometer up my ass and give me forty-year-old candy pills to make me all better."

If he could get all that out without taking a breath, he must be feeling a little easier. Her hands loosened their grip on the steering wheel and she let her foot ease off the gas pedal. It wouldn't do either of them any good if she smacked up the car. "I called the best doctor in the area. He's a friend of mine. He's meeting us at the hospital."

"Turn the car around."

"Are you going delirious on me?"

"No. But I swear if Napoleon or Edith Piaf tries to touch me, they'll be slapped with a malpractice suit faster than you can say Kevorkian."

"Trust me. Dr. Hartnett's an excellent doctor." He'd been a good lover, too, but she was surprised how little she missed him.

"You're the only one around here I do trust," he said softly.

She turned her head and smiled at him. "How's the left arm?"

"Tingling."

"Chest pain?"

"It feels like somebody's squeezing it in a vice. Hurts like a sonofabitch."

"Hang on and try to relax."

Like that was possible. In the dark car, she felt the tension in his body.

"You're going to be fine," she promised him softly, hoping she was right.

"Em . . ."

"Yes?"

"If I die, call my assistant at the number you'll find on my business card. Her name is Anna. She knows where my will is. She'll take care of everything."

He patted his pockets, probably looking for his damn business card. Even on the way to the hospital he was trying to do business. No wonder he was having a heart attack in his thirties.

"Put your wallet back. If I need the business card I'll dig it out. But I'm not going to need it."

Thankfully, the small hospital drew into view and she drove straight up to the emergency door.

She was glad she'd phoned ahead when a stretcher came wheeling through the emergency door manned by a couple of paramedics. Dr. Hartnett ran alongside.

They loaded Joe on the stretcher while the doctor peppered him with questions. He was in good hands. She'd gotten him here alive. For that she was grateful. Realizing she still held the wallet Joe had thrust at her, she called, "I'll park the car and check Joe in."

The doctor waved to let her know he'd heard and understood, but it was obvious he was more interested in Joe's health than the status of his Blue Cross.

She bet Joe wouldn't get this kind of treatment in New York.

She got back in the car to move it and realized her hands were shaking and she was dizzy. Only then did she realize how scared she'd been.

If ever a man had had a wake-up call, that man was Joe Montcrief.

If he lived through this, she was going to make it her personal mission to teach him how to relax. And if he hated it, too bad. After what he'd put her through, she was going to show him there was a better way to live. She liked him too much to watch him kill himself with work and stress.

Chapter 13

Lydia hadn't felt this nervous since . . . well, it had been years. She ran her hands down her hips. As though she could suddenly make them smaller, or her varicose veins disappear, or the lines on her face erase.

She'd come on a fool's errand, she realized, and feeling like a silly old woman trying to reach back to her youth, she turned slowly away. But her carry bag bumped her knee as she did, and the half full wine bottle she'd snitched off the dinner table clanked against the flask with Dr. Emmet's cordial.

Oh, the hell with it. If she wasn't foolish now, when did she think she was going to act crazy? In the great beyond?

Pulling herself to her full height of five feet four inches and pasting a smile on her face, she knocked.

A long time passed and she thought maybe no one was home. She was just debating whether to knock again when the door opened and a man stood there.

For an age he stared at her, then he said, "Lydia."

"Hello, Eddie." Now what? She'd gotten to his doorstep on sheer guts and bravado. Now she didn't know what to do or say.

He blinked at her a couple of times from behind his glasses and she wondered if he was waiting for her to ask for a donation or something.

"I came for a visit. If that's okay."

"Lydia," he said again, and she realized he was falling back in time, just as she did when she looked at him. Oh, he'd aged; who hadn't? But his kindly, wrinkled face was as dear to her as when it had been unlined and anxious. His eyes were faded and hidden behind glasses now, but they were still his eyes.

"Welcome," he said finally, and opened the door all the way.

He led her to a stuffy living room that smelled stale. She could hear the sounds of a game show from somewhere down the hall. She perched on a chair and wished she'd gone with Olive instead. Who was she kidding? The past was gone. Over. Best left to memory.

"How have you been, Lydia?"

"Fine. I've been fine."

Somebody must have won something on the game show for she heard cheering and clapping. A glance at the mahogany coffee table told her Eddie didn't dust much. Even the half dozen Scotch mints in the crystal candy dish sported a layer of dust.

His wife must have decorated this room, she thought, and he probably hadn't changed a thing. He probably never came in here. "I was sorry to hear about your wife."

"Thank you. It takes a while to get used to."

She nodded and squeezed her ankles and knees together.

"Would you like something to drink?"

"I—" She'd brought the wine and the cordial, but now it didn't seem right. "Maybe later. I only came by to say . . . well, it would be nice if we could be friends."

"Friends."

He looked slowly up at her and she felt a layer of dust peel away from her own life. "I've thought about you so many times," he said.

"Have you?"

He nodded.

"You could have come to call."

"I didn't want to presume," he said softly. Of course he didn't. She should have realized. He'd always been shy, maybe that's what had first endeared him to her. A lovely man who saw himself as so much less than he was.

If they sat in this dying room much longer, what little courage she had left would wither. "What's on TV?" she asked.

He brightened. "I think it's changed over now. Want to come see?"

"Sure."

The den gave her hope. It was obviously Eddie's favorite room, with a leather couch, big-screen TV, a well-thumbed *TV Guide*, and the faintest scent of microwave popcorn.

She sank onto the couch. "You got any more of that popcorn?"

He chuckled. "I buy it in bulk."

She didn't worry about matching up her knees and her ankles, but curled her legs beneath her. By the time they'd split a bowl of popcorn and talked through two game shows, she knew he was the same Eddie she remembered. Only better. Age had faded him in some ways, but it had strengthened him in others. He was funny. A little more sure of himself. And when he drew closer on the couch, she saw the gleam of interest in his eyes.

"I'm glad you came, Lydia."

"Well, I got tired of waiting for you to come to me." She'd meant it to sound light—good old Lydia, giving the guy on the couch a hard time—but it didn't come out that way. She heard her own voice sound wistful and sad.

Eddie touched her knee. "Oh, don't you worry, lady. I had my eye on you, all right. I was bidding for you."

Her old, bruised heart sped almost painfully. "What are you . . . who . . . ?"

"I thought you would have figured it out. Don't you remember how you used to play that old record I liked? 'I Only Have Eyes for You'?"

Her eyes misted. "Of course, Eyes4U."

"That's me."

"Well." She wanted to throw herself on his chest and weep for the sheer joy of the moment, but she was Lydia and she'd spent a lifetime being the tough cookie. "Well. You've got competition, you know. And I'm not going cheap."

"I know," he said, and kissed her. She realized in that moment that one of the reasons he'd crawled into her heart all those years ago, when she hadn't suspected a thing, was that he saw the woman she really was inside. He did know.

Maybe you couldn't turn the clock back, but sometimes, if you were very lucky, you could time-travel through memory. She rediscovered the feel of him, and the taste and smell of him, different and yet the same. The young man and the old. When her emotions nearly claimed her again, she grabbed for her bag.

"I almost forgot," she said. "I brought some wine we had left over from dinner."

By the time the news came on, they were going at it like teenagers. Oh, she thought, she'd taught him well.

He had her panties off and was about to enter her body, which she'd been wishing for off and on for forty years, when he suddenly stopped. "What am I thinking? I'm sorry, Lydia. I shouldn't rush this. Maybe we should get to know each other better first."

"Eddie," she said, laying her hand against his cheek, "I've known you most of my life. Now shut up and get on with it."

He chuckled and kissed her, then entered her as slowly and carefully as a man with a new bride. Foolish tears filled her eyes, and then spilled over.

He kissed them away.

"No more crying," he said. "No more being alone."

Joe stared at the dull green ceiling, painted to match the dull green walls. He felt like shit, but he figured that was good news since it meant he was still alive.

The county hospital smelled like hospitals everywhere. The food tasted like hospital food everywhere. "Do you suppose there's some great hospital food factory somewhere? Hidden from prying eyes and guarded like a toxic waste dump?" Joe asked Emmylou as his gaze moved from the ceiling to the Jell-o on his lunch tray—also green.

It looked exactly like something out of a toxic dump.

At least he was out of ICU and in a private room now.

Emmylou was fussing with a big bouquet of flowers from her own garden, arranged in a cut glass vase. He liked them a lot better than the formal arrangement his office had sent. Although just seeing the floral tribute from his colleagues and staff reminded him that he had a bone to pick with Ms. Busybody Innkeeper. "I told you to contact Anna if I died. I didn't say anything about telling them I was in hospital."

"Anna phoned," Emmylou said. She poked a finger into the bottom of the office arrangement, then added water from the plastic water glass on his bedside table. She couldn't seem to help herself around growing things.

"What do you mean she phoned? Did you answer my cell?" He sounded sharp but he didn't really care. He'd begged, wheedled, and bullied her, but she refused to bring his cell to the hospital. Patients in the Back of Beyond ER weren't allowed to make long-distance calls. So he was stuck, isolated, wondering what deals were falling like dominoes because he wasn't there to complete them.

"Of course I didn't answer your cell phone. She called the Shady Lady. I told her what happened." She plucked a tissue from the dispenser by his bed and wiped a bit of damp moss from her finger. "I assumed, since the woman knows all your affairs including where your will is kept and your final wishes, that you'd want her to know you were in the hospital. I apologize if I've done wrong." She didn't sound sorry, though; she sounded like someone who'd been told not to get the weak heart in 3B all worked up.

Naturally, the very idea of being treated with kid gloves

riled him considerably. But just because he might have a weak heart didn't mean his intellect had to follow suit.

"No. You did the right thing. Of course they have to know." He gazed at the corporate bouquet moodily. How many times had he told Anna to send one of these very arrangements out to clients having babies, inking new deals, opening apartment buildings, factories, airline hangars, and the like. He never imagined receiving one himself.

"I feel fine and I need to get back to work. I want to get out of here."

"Of course you do," she said in her soothing tone. "And as soon as the doctor has all your test results and knows how to treat you, then you will get out of here."

She was looking prettier than anything in that vase, and just gazing at her made him feel better. But she treated him the way he imagined she'd treat any guest who nearly kicked the bucket while staying in her B&B. She was calm, pleasant, friendly, helpful.

He might never have been anywhere near her naked body. It was like there was an invisible force field of friendliness that she could hide behind so he couldn't even apologize for not only almost dying in her bed, but for making a complete fool of himself while doing it.

He ought to be worrying about his heart, but in truth he felt like his pride was the more damaged. Soon they'd have all the bazillion test results back, then he could get the hell out of here.

It didn't matter that he'd nearly died; all he could think about was that he'd choked in bed.

When Emmylou had finished fussing, she kissed him on the forehead on her way out. And didn't that just tell the whole story?

When she reached his door, he was tempted to call her back and drag her into his hospital bed. If he was going to have a heart attack while making love, at least he should complete one or the other. They'd both have a satisfactory climax or he'd die. Anything seemed preferable to the kiss-on-the-forehead treatment.

But she no sooner reached the door than the great Dr. Hartnett himself entered the small room.

She didn't treat the doc like a retard, he noted. She treated him like a man whose body wouldn't let him down at crucial moments. As she left, he got the feeling the doctor would have opened the door and held it for her, except that Joe's door was permanently open so anyone in the world could walk by and gape at him. One more joy of hospital life.

"How are you feeling today, Joe?" the doctor asked him.

"Like shit."

"Sorry to hear that. I've got good news."

Since he'd been expecting everything from a month to live to a triple bypass, his ears perked up.

"You were lucky."

Hah! If his attack had come an hour later—even a quarter of an hour later—he would have died happy. There was nothing lucky about humiliating himself while inside Emmy-lou. Nothing.

"Your heart is fine."

"I had a heart attack and my heart's fine?" Why, oh, why couldn't this have happened in a normal city?

"That's the good news. You didn't have a heart attack. You had a gastric attack."

A long pause ensued. Somebody was paged, a food trolley rattled by his ever-open door, and still he couldn't find words.

"It was your stomach, Joe. Not your heart."

"Indigestion?" Joe couldn't believe what he was hearing. He'd come to trust Gord Hartnett, but obviously he was as qualified to be a doctor as Beaverton's ersatz Napoleon was to rule France, or Katie the Kleptomaniac to be in charge of security for Tiffany's. "I had all the symptoms of a heart attack."

"Yes, I know. We checked everything and the good news is your heart's strong and healthy. Your cholesterol's good.

Blood pressure's a little high but that's probably stress and lifestyle related. What you have is a hiatal hernia. Basically, it means you're going to have to change your diet, eat small and often, and avoid stress. Also avoid large heavy meals and alcohol right before bed."

Dr. Hartnett sat down on the chair beside Joe's bed in true television-doctor-bonding-with-patient pose. "Joe, what happened is a wake-up call. From what you and Emmylou have told me, I'd say you're a heart attack waiting to happen."

"Well, you're wrong. You can't have it both ways, doc. If there's nothing wrong with my heart, then I'm not an attack waiting to happen. If I am, then this can't be indigestion."

"I didn't say it was indigestion. I said it was a gastric attack. Of course you should be glad there's nothing wrong with your heart, but your body is still sending you a strong message. Take it easy. Enjoy life. Stop and smell the roses."

"You sound like Emmylou."

"Emmylou is a very intelligent and sensitive woman. You should listen to her." Something about Hartnett's tone made the hair on the back of Joe's neck prickle. But then Hartnett was speaking again and he forgot the odd momentary impression.

"I want you to rest and take it easy for a week, then come and see me in my office."

Joe shook his head. "I can't hang around for a week. I've got a business, clients, a life."

"Remember when you thought you were having a heart attack?"

Joe nodded, remembering all too well, not only the acute pain but the fear that his life would suddenly be over before he'd had a chance to live it.

"You'll have a lot more of a life if you treat your body with respect."

"Yeah, yeah. But why can't I fly home and see my own doctor? I can rest in New York."

"Can you? Emmylou will follow my advice and feed you

what I tell her to. You can relax and let your esophagus heal. It's been burned, you know. It needs a rest. Do you have someone in New York who can nurse you?"

Joe eyed him with disfavor. "Are we talking boiled chicken and milk?"

"The diet's not so bad. Don't worry. You'll be in good hands."

It suddenly struck Joe as a little pathetic that he had to rely on the proprietor of a bed and breakfast to look after him, but the truth was the Shady Lady was a hell of a lot more homelike than his apartment, and if he went home, who'd look after him there?

"Emmylou is a very restful woman," the doctor was saying, as though he knew her well. Joe cocked an eyebrow.

"She was good to me when I first moved here, and she and my wife have become close friends."

Joe liked the sound of the wife. Not that he had any claim on Emmylou, but still, he liked the sound of that wife.

Something the doctor said played back in his head, and since this was Back of Beyond, Idaho, the doc seemed to have all the time in the world to chatter. So he kicked the old conversational ball in the air. "You said she was good to you when you first moved here."

"Yes. She was." Was it Joe's imagination or did he seem guarded? Maybe Emmylou had done more for the good doctor than bake him welcome-to-the-neighborhood brownies? Not that it mattered, of course. The part that had him curious was that the man said he'd moved here. He could understand someone like Emmylou being born here and coming back when she inherited the old brothel—at least, if he tried really hard, he got it. But who'd move here?

"Why would you choose to live here?"

The doctor looked at Joe as though he might be running a very high, delirium-causing fever. "Beaverton's a great place to live."

"It's the back end of nowhere and it's full of lunatics."

Gord Hartnett smiled. "Some of the residents around here are a little eccentric, it's true, but they're good people. Crime's nil—"

"Hah, don't forget Klepto Katie."

"Miss Trevellen. Yes. An unfortunate habit, but she always returns what she's, um . . . borrowed. It's also gorgeous countryside, and the weather's good. We're close to the mountains, if you like skiing and hiking."

He encountered a blank stare from Joe, whose idea of mountain climbing was taking the stairs when his elevator was out of order. He exercised with maximum efficiency and liked to be into the gym, exercised, showered, and out within sixty minutes. No steam rooms, no rubdown, just get in, sweat, breathe hard, get out. No likelihood of encountering bears or cougars.

"I'll tell you something interesting," continued Dr. Hartnett, obviously realizing a list of outdoor recreation opportunities wasn't going to convert Joe into a Beaverton cheerleader, "the people in this area are healthier." He crossed his arms and leaned back in a classic doctor-ruminating-over-fascinating-research-data pose. "They are statistically healthier than their counterparts elsewhere in the country."

"Statistics can be misleading."

"They live longer, too. About five to seven years longer, on average. Now why do you suppose that is?"

"They're all too crazy to know how old they are or if they're sick?" Joe wondered aloud.

"You are a very intolerant man. Pretty typical of serious type A's. And I suspect you're harboring a great deal of unexpressed anger."

"Oh, give me a break. You want to live in this town, fine. But spare me the real estate pitch and the bonus head-shrinking. All right?"

"I'll say good-bye then," Dr. Hartnett said, rising and holding out a hand. "You'll be released tomorrow. If you decide to stay a week, call my office and set up an appointment. If you go home, get your doctor to get in touch and I'll send over the file."

Knowing he'd been surly to a guy who was doing his best, Joe smiled and shook hands. "Thanks. You took good care of me."

"Now start taking care of yourself."

And with that parting zinger he was gone, his mountaineering, outdoors-guy stride taking him rapidly out into the corridor.

Joe was back to contemplating life from inside a pale blue gown that left his ass hanging out.

But the good news was he was getting out of here tomorrow. When he judged she'd had time to get home, he called Emmylou—luckily not a long-distance number—and she picked up herself on the second ring. "How are you feeling?" she asked when he'd identified himself.

"Great. I'm breaking out of the joint tomorrow."

She laughed dutifully. "That's wonderful. I'll drive the getaway car."

"I was hoping you'd say that," he admitted. "Do you mind coming to get me?"

"Not at all."

"I never asked you to keep my room for me, by the way. I hope you did."

There was a tiny pause. "I'm not exactly overrun with guests at the moment, Joe. The room's yours as long as you need it."

"Well, tomorrow night anyway. I'm going back to New York the next day."

"But Dr. Hartnett said—" She cut herself off. Why was he not surprised that the doc was discussing him with his hostess? Hell, she'd probably seen the pictures of the inside of his stomach.

"The doctor advised me to stay, but it's a bad case of heartburn. They have doctors in New York." He didn't mean to sound sarcastic, but telling him to avoid New York was like telling a chocoholic to stay away from Lucerne.

"All right. But I think you should at least stay the weekend. For the play. It's the highlight of our summer here in Beaverton. Lydia and Olive and the others will be so disappointed if you miss their show."

"What about you? Will you be disappointed if I leave?"

A pause. Then a soft, "Yes," as though she wished she didn't have to admit the truth.

What was he going to do on the weekend anyway? Suddenly, a few days of Emmylou's care seemed like a great idea. But only a couple. "Okay. Get hold of Anna. Tell her to find me some way out Monday. Got it?"

"Yes, sir."

He blew out a breath. "Sorry. I know you're not my secretary, but could you please phone Anna and tell her to plan me a route home?"

"Get some rest. I'll see you tomorrow."

"Thanks." It looked like he was going to have to do some flower buying, after all Emmylou had done for him.

Chapter 14

Emmylou put down the phone. Then picked it up again. She called Gregory. "Joe's planning to leave Monday. We're back with the original plan."

"Right."

Then she called Madame Dior. An organized woman, Emmylou had set up a phone tree to relay information relevant to the current crisis. She called three women, and they each phoned three people, and before you knew it, the whole town was informed. She kept her messages simple, of course. This one said, "Joe's out of the hospital tomorrow. Meeting tonight at the bingo hall, seven o'clock."

How dare he go back to New York, she fumed. She'd assumed the townspeople had at least a week or ten days for him to recuperate quietly while they figured out how to raise the money for the back taxes. Or at least worked out how to prevent him and his employers from destroying Beaverton.

A gastric attack so bad he thought he might die was not going to endear Beaverton to Joe, and so far no one had found either an alternative buyer for the property or a few hundred thou in spare change to pay the back taxes.

Joe's cell phone picked that moment to go off, jangling in time with her irritation. He was so stupid. How could he walk away knowing he was going to destroy such a wonderful community? How could he walk away from her?

While she fumed, she stalked into the library cum office and snatched the phone up. "Yes?"

A female voice said, "Is this Joe's phone?"

"Yes, it is." Emmylou said, thinking she had no right to answer his phone. What on earth was she doing? She could barely hear the woman, so she marched outside into the middle of the lawn as she'd seen Joe do.

"This is Anna, his assistant. I'm wondering how he's doing."

"He's been very ill, Anna," Emmylou said, thinking Anna sounded much too young and attractive. "His doctor has advised him to have complete quiet and rest for the next seven to ten days."

"But what about—"

"It's a matter of life and death." Okay, not Joe's life, but the life of Beaverton and every one of its residents, and if a little prevarication would save them all, she'd indulge. This once.

"Oh my God. I had no idea."

The woman sounded truly distressed, so Emmylou relented. One day Joe was going to find out about this conversation and then he'd kill her. "With complete rest, the doctors have every confidence in a full recovery. Of course, he can't be disturbed with calls or e-mails or reminders of work."

"Wow. I wish he wasn't so near to closing a deal." The assistant blew out a noisy breath, but Emmylou got the feeling she was more concerned about everything she'd have to do than about Joe's health, so she didn't worry too much about her little white lie. Okay, big, fat, black lie. And also, she had no intention of asking Anna to organize Joe's transport out of here as he'd requested. But then she hadn't said she would, so that wasn't exactly a lie.

"I'm sorry. But it could have been a massive heart attack and he could be dead. That would be worse for business, I'm sure."

"I don't know. I think the client would get it that he's dead. Anything else is going to be a tough sell."

Emmylou had a sudden picture of Anna. She probably had long dark hair, wore a power suit with killer heels, carried a thin briefcase, and had a cell phone earpiece hanging out of her ear that matched Joe's. She was probably multitasking while she talked to Emmylou. Writing the company's annual report, updating her resume in case Joe didn't make it, and filing her nails.

"Joe's only resting comfortably because he knows he can count on you."

"Yeah. Yes, of course. Tell him to take care, okay?"

"I will. And you promise not to let anyone bother him?"

"I'll do my best. Um, would it be okay if I called you for updates on his condition?"

Emmylou thought about that. It seemed only fair. "Sure. You've got the phone number here at the bed and breakfast."

"Can't I call his cell?"

"No. The doctor insisted he not be disturbed. He won't be answering his cell."

"Wow. That doesn't sound like Joe. He must be sick."

"Seriously."

"Oh, okay. Thanks a lot. Tell Joe to call me as soon as he's feeling better. I don't think he's ever missed a day of work before for sickness. Huh."

Why was she not surprised?

"Thank you for calling, and Joe asked me to pass on his thanks for all you're doing."

"Yeah. Tell him to remember that at salary review time. This is not going to be easy."

Emmylou pressed *End* and then looked at the little package of trouble in her hand. Not only were her town and her friends in trouble, but so was Joe if he ever stopped for a second to think about his life.

What she was about to do was for everyone's good.

Returning to the house, she went into the library and unplugged the cell phone's cradle, then took it and the phone into the parlor and locked them in the safe behind her great-grandmother's portrait.

If anyone would approve of Emmylou's actions, she knew it would be her great-grandmother, and she couldn't think of a more fitting guard to watch over the safe and its contents.

That done, she went back to the office. Joe's laptop still sat on the desk where he'd left it. She tapped her fingers against the desk surface, thinking. Once more she picked up her phone. This time she called Harry Farnsworth from the computer shop, who'd set up the Internet for her.

"Harry," she said when she got him, "I need your help with the Internet connection."

"Is it acting up?" he asked.

"No. But I need it to. I need to mysteriously lose online access for the next week."

"Not a request I get every day. Is Olive spending too much time on porn sites?"

"No! At least I don't think so."

He laughed. "She knows her way around the Internet. You'd better tell her you want the connection to stay down or she's likely to fix it for you."

"Okay. Got it. I don't want Joe having access to his business, that's all. He needs to rest." She was cutting the poor guy off from his world. In trying to save him, she might kill him. She felt like a cross between Florence Nightingale and Dolores Claiborne.

"Harry, have you heard about the meeting tonight?"

"Yeah. Just got the call."

"Good." The phone tree was working, then. "Can you come back to the Shady Lady after the meeting and disable the Internet connection?"

"No problem."

Now she'd taken care of preventing Joe from leaving, she had to make him fall in love with the town. Plan A was to get the money together to save Beaverton, but Plan B was to stop

Joe and his clients from wanting to locate their factory here in the first place.

She didn't know which plan was more fraught with failure, but she'd give them both her best shot.

Her great-grandmother had made a booming success against worse odds.

Chapter 15

Joe was not in the best of moods. He'd lost a fight with a nurse about a wheelchair and felt like a toddler in a stroller as the big-armed, big-voiced nurse wheeled him toward Emmylou, who waited at the patient discharge exit.

Em looked like the first ray of sunshine to a guy emerging from prison. His heart jumped at the sight of her, which only pissed him off more. If he'd ever made a bigger fool of himself in front of a woman he was trying to impress, it was buried so deep no therapy on earth could dig up the memory.

Having a coronary while doing the nasty was a humiliating cliché, but he hadn't even managed a real heart attack. He should be glad, of course, that he was essentially healthy, and naturally he was, but at least if he'd choked in bed because of a heart attack, no one would hold it against him.

Mighty Joe Montcrief had been felled in the act by indigestion. A faint burn began to work its way up his esophagus and he breathed deep and slow to try and get it under control.

Emmylou smiled and waved when she saw him and walked quickly forward. She obviously couldn't decide how to greet him with Nurse Maude chugging along behind, so she settled on a cheery "Hi," and then walked awkwardly alongside the wheels of his rolling throne. He hated having to look up at her.

"Hi." He sounded surly and he knew it.

"Somebody's a grumpy bear today," his nurse informed Emmylou and everyone else within a twelve-block radius.

"Somebody's a fat-assed dominatrix wanna-be," he muttered almost but not quite under his breath.

Emmylou choked on a laugh, then spoke over his head. "Has he been a troublesome patient?"

"The young men are always the worst. Don't want to take their medicine, don't like following hospital rules, like the one where we always leave in a wheelchair." She spoke the last bit down to him in the voice a nursery school teacher would use to a kid who'd peed on the floor.

If he'd known his departure from the hospital would be as ignominious as his arrival, he'd have called a cab, or he'd have taken a bus. Hell, he'd have walked all the way to the Shady Lady.

"Thank you, Maude," he said, as the exit approached. "Little Joey can walk on his own two legs now."

"Well, your nice young lady's here in case you fall down. Hold her arm, now. There's no shame in being weak."

Now he was standing, he felt a little more in control. "Thanks for taking good care of me, Maude," he said, giving her a smile and extending his hand.

"Oh, you are one sweet boy," she said, ignoring his hand and pulling him into her massive bosom for a hug so suffocating that he almost landed back in the ER.

" 'Bye," he managed when he could breathe again. The nurse beamed at him as though his recovery from indigestion was a miracle.

"Are you okay to walk on your own?" Emmylou asked, looking at him anxiously.

He hadn't touched her yet today and she sure hadn't treated him like a man who'd been inside her body, albeit he'd only been there for about seven seconds before pain so severe had struck that his cock had about shriveled and died on the spot.

"No," he lied, and threw an arm around her shoulders. This left her with little choice but to put her arm around his waist.

Behind him he heard a large lungful of sentimental sigh follow him out the door.

"Nurse Maude thinks we make a cute couple," he said, turning his head and leaning down to murmur in the general direction of Emmylou's ear. The sun caught her hair and it sparkled gold and platinum.

"If she'd heard those things you were saying, she'd have thought something worse."

"Worse than that I was a grumpy bear?"

She laughed. She felt good against his body. Tucked under his arm, she fit nicely. They walked with an easy rhythm, as though they'd been going steady for years. The sunshine felt good against his skin. When he breathed he caught the smell of her hair, like flowers and spice. "You know what I wish?"

"That I'd stocked up on green Jell-O?"

"Close. I wish my gastric attack had held off another hour."

The perfect harmony of their stride was marred when she stumbled over her feet.

"Oh, well. I, um . . ." He didn't need to look at her face to know she was blushing.

"I hope you're trying to say you'll give me another chance." Maybe it wasn't exactly suave to be hitting on her the second he got out of the hospital, but he'd thought of little else but picking up where they'd so disastrously left off the other night in her bed.

"Look, Joe." She turned to him, but he didn't give her a chance to blow him off in the hospital parking lot. He cupped the back of her head and kissed her. She made a startled sound, which was good because her lips needed to part for any sound to get out. And then he had her. He poured everything he had into that kiss, not only because he felt he had to make up for the other night but because the minute their lips met he felt the rush of heat between them. He pulled her gently against him until there wasn't a hint of space between them.

He'd meant the kiss as a teasing reminder that they weren't nearly finished with each other yet, but he was blindsided by the power that slammed into him. Her lips trembled beneath his and he couldn't resist taking the kiss deeper, possessing her mouth the way he wanted to possess her body.

He felt her hands on his back, all over the place, as though frantic to feel him. She tugged him closer, but there wasn't any closer—not with their clothes on. What her body was trying to tell them both was that it wanted him inside her. And he rubbed against her, letting her feel the hard-on he had for her, letting her body know the feeling was mutual.

They might have stayed there all day, except for the intrusion of a car that pulled into the lot. With a shaken laugh she pulled away, giving him a glimpse of passion-drenched blue eyes, wet, swollen lips, and a stunned expression.

As he threw his arm back across her shoulders, he felt he'd gone a long way to restoring the tone of their relationship.

"How do you feel?" Emmylou asked him once they were in her car and pulling out of the hospital parking lot.

"Up for anything you've got in mind," he said, and he did mean up. As though to compensate for the way it had let him down during his gastric attack, his cock was standing at attention now. He'd had a taste of paradise and he couldn't wait for more.

With a prescription for super antacid in his pocket and his last hospital meal already nothing but a tasteless memory, he felt better than any man just released from hospital ought to feel.

"Could you handle a little tour of the area?" she asked him. "I've got some things to drop off at Potter's Farm. It's out this way."

"Sure." And if he could drag Emmylou behind a handy haystack, so much the better.

They drove out of the hospital grounds, and within minutes were heading into rural territory. Joe had been inside bilious green walls—exactly the color a guy wanted to stare at when he was bilious himself—too long. As he looked out the window of the car he noticed how big the views were here. He liked his usual views. High-rises, the East River. Falafel and pretzel vendors on every corner. Here there was vastness, a lot of stuff that looked like wheat waving around and not a Starbucks in sight.

The sky seemed bigger, higher somehow, and a whole lot bluer. He had a sudden urge to walk outside and smell the air.

Ah, what was he thinking? It would smell like dirt and cow dung.

They didn't talk much. He drifted along with the rhythm of the road, letting his thoughts trail.

The Gellman brothers were going to be beyond ballistic by now. They wanted the land and factory tied up ASAP, but right now Joe was having trouble getting too worked up. Anna would be holding them at bay. He'd call the second he got back and pick up where he'd left off. So they lost a few days. America's cats weren't going to run out of litter anytime soon.

The merger would or would not merge. They'd figure it out.

The car bumped down a rutted road and he saw a farmhouse ahead. A white farmhouse with boxes of red geraniums out front and a yellow lab on the front porch. It looked like a setting from a movie featuring a farmhouse more than a real one.

"Well, how about that?" he said, amazed.

"Pretty, isn't it?" Emmylou said.

"Yeah." She got out and so did he. The car doors thunked behind them.

He stretched and breathed in. Okay, so he didn't smell dirt and cow pies. It was more like dry grass and a hint of horse. The dog barely bothered to bark, managing only one half-hearted woof. It was an old one with an arthritic hind leg, he saw, when it hoisted itself to its feet and took the stairs slowly before ambling toward them, its tail waving slowly as though anything more vigorous would hurt.

Emmylou gave it a pat on the head and kept walking, but Joe squatted and gave the poor old mutt a good rub. The dog wriggled in ecstasy and rolled to its back for more.

"Can you teach Emmylou to do that for me?" Joe asked, rubbing the dog's belly. When he hit a certain spot, the dog's back leg—not the arthritic one—twitched. Joe laughed. "You're a sorry sonofabitch, aren't you? Somebody should have put you down long ago."

The dog thanked him for his opinion by licking his hand.

When he got to his feet, Emmylou emerged on the porch with another woman. She was one of the youngest he'd seen in town. Early forties at a guess. She looked like the kind of woman who kept a loom in her living room and wove her own curtains. She wore a flowing skirt and a man's work shirt, round glasses, and long blond hair in pigtails.

"I hear you're a visitor in town," she said with a wide smile, coming down the front steps to shake his hand.

"That's right. Joe Montcrief."

"Welcome. I'm Amy Potter."

"Pretty place," he said, feeling something was required.

"Would you like a tour?"

No. He'd like to get back to the Shady Lady, call the office, get his deal back on track, and then take Emmylou to bed, where he was going to wipe from her mind their last unfortunate intimate encounter and replace it with something a whole lot better. But this woman looked so eager, and he doubted she got a lot of company. "Well, maybe a quick one."

He cursed himself as she said, "Come on, Buster. Let's take Joe for a tour," and they all had to slow their pace to that of the old dog.

They walked behind the barn and he saw a collection of

the saddest, most pathetic horses he'd ever seen. They made Buster here look like a Westminster Dog Show champ.

Emmylou walked to the fence and leaned on it. As though somebody'd rung the dinner gong, the horses started to plod, limp, and shuffle their way forward. "I'll get some apples," Amy said, and disappeared into an open barn.

"I hate to be the one to break it to you, but those horses belong in a glue factory."

"And that's exactly where they'd be if Amy didn't rescue them. There's nothing wrong with those horses. They're healthy, just old. Some of them aren't even old. They were raised and kept pregnant to provide urine for hormone replacement therapy."

He glanced a question at her.

"For women going through menopause? Pregnant mare pee has a ton of estrogen in it. But when hormone replacement therapy was linked to cancer, the market kind of dropped out of the pregnant mare business. All those mares weren't needed any more, nor were most of the foals." Emmylou shrugged.

"She's running a haven for wayward mares?" There was something ludicrous in the notion.

"Don't they deserve some dignity?"

"How does she feed them all?" he asked, figuring there had to be a hefty hay bill out there.

"She runs a riding stable so the horses get exercise and the locals get a chance to ride. That helps pay for their feed. She and her husband also grow organic herbs and vegetables. They get by."

By the skin of their teeth, he bet. His esophagus tickled when he looked out at all those horses. One came right up to him and put its massive head on his shoulder.

"Hey!" he said with a laugh.

Amy Potter laughed from right behind him.

"She thinks you've got a treat. My husband likes to tease them sometimes. He puts carrots behind his ears."

That hubby. What a trickster.

Amy handed him a small and wormy-looking apple that had to be left over from last year since it was in about as good shape as the horses, but the Apaloosa who'd been nuzzling his neck seemed happy to see it, worms and all, and took it delicately from his palm.

They stayed and fed horses until everybody who wanted one got an apple. There was a nice-looking brown quarter horse that might be up to his weight, he thought, then mentally shook his head. What was he thinking? If he wanted to ride there was a stable in New Jersey where he rode the odd weekend. The horses were top-of-the-line thoroughbreds. These sorry creatures looked like he'd have to carry them.

"Do the Potters own those fields?" he asked after they'd said good-bye and made their way back to the car.

"No. They own a little land around the house. But they rent the fields from Gus Carver. He's a potato farmer. When he rests his fields, that's where the horses go. It works out for everyone."

Joe wasn't sure the arrangement was still going to work out when the mineral rights were claimed by the Gellmans. Their business interests would take precedence over the needs of a bunch of worn-out and generally useless horses. Didn't seem fair they should end up as glue or dog food, though.

"You're quiet," Emmylou said after they drove away. "Are you tired?"

"No. I was thinking, hot flashes gave those horses life and cancer almost ended it. Funny how that works."

"Amy is one of the nicest people I know. If there's a stray or a wounded animal, it gets taken to her."

"There's no vet in town?"

"No. Amy's a pretty good alternative pet healer, but if it's very serious, Gordon Hartnett will take a look."

Joe jerked his head her way so hard he almost twisted it right off his neck. He stared at her. "You're telling me I put my life in the hands of a guy who also practices on animals?"

He could tell she was biting back a smile. "He hardly ever loses a patient," she said at last.

He snorted. Oh, great. Now he was sounding like a horse. No doubt the good doctor had something to do with that. Probably gave him horse pills by accident.

The sooner he got out of this crazy town the better.

"Animals love you," she said after a minute, sounding surprised.

"So do women. It's my natural charm."

"No. They really do. Mae West frankly loves men, so I discounted that even though Aunt Olive swears the cat's abandoned her to sleep on your bed at night."

He didn't say a word, but kept looking out the window. He'd thought at least a cat could keep a secret. But not if she was female, apparently.

"Then the old dog today and the horses. And you know what I find really interesting?"

"Look." He pointed through the window at the sky. "Isn't that a UFO? Probably one of your neighbors coming home."

"You love animals."

What had she thought? That he tortured bunnies for fun?

When he didn't answer, she said. "It's not a crime, you know."

"Of course not. I just can't believe you're making such a big deal of it."

"It shows a soft side, that's all."

"Hunh. Hitler loved animals." He had no idea if that were true, but it sounded good.

"Do you have pets?"

"I live in a Manhattan high-rise and I'm never home. What do you think?" Though he did feed Mutt and Jeff, a pair of pigeons that had taken to hanging around his roof patio.

"What about when you were a kid? Did you have a favorite pet?"

"I was the favorite pet," he said, and then was appalled at how bitter he'd sounded. What was the matter with him? He never whined about all that boo-hoo, unhappy childhood crap. He tried to backtrack fast. "My parents were society types. My dad was a big-time banker and my mom ran their social set. They had me late in life. We traveled too much to have a dog or cat, they said." Even though they'd employed full-time servants.

"Oh, how sad. Do you have brothers or sisters?"

He shook his head.

"I never did, either. I would have loved a sister."

And he'd have loved a brother. Somebody he could talk to and who could share the blame if there was a mess around the house, or a window got broken or a potted plant over-turned.

"I spent most of my time in boarding and prep schools. That was like having a couple of hundred siblings."

"Was that as much fun as it sounds?"

He thought about it. Nodded. "Yes. A lot of the time it was great. I'm still friends with some of those guys."

"But you never had a real home."

He didn't answer, but was impressed at her acuity.

"I didn't have a traditional home, either. Funny how im-portant it seemed at the time."

"Now you create a home for other people. You do a fan-tastic job." He could see her with a houseful of kids some-time in the future. She'd be terrific at it, he knew. The pang that crossed his heart came and went so fast he hardly no-ticed it.

Chapter 16

When they reached home, Joe realized his R&R at the Beaverton General, followed by a revivifying visit to the stable of the walking dead, was over. A glance at his watch told him he could get a couple of hours in before business closed down in New York.

"Thanks for the lift," he said when they pulled into the parking area. He glanced over to where his rental had been parked. He wasn't very surprised to see it still wasn't back from the garage. Beaverton hadn't been good for the health of either him or the rental car. The sooner they were back where they belonged, the better.

"You're welcome. You should probably go straight up to bed and rest."

He was already out of the car by the time she finished her sentence. "Have to check in with the office," he said, and strode to the door of the Shady Lady.

Nothing seemed to have changed in the time he'd been away. The place still smelled like old wood and lemon polish, and whatever flowers Emmylou had put around the place. She loved those flowers.

"Afternoon, ladies," he said when he saw Olive and Lydia gossiping in the hall.

"Well, aren't you a sight for sore eyes."

"Are you feeling better, dear?" They peered at him with

equal worried expressions, almost as though they'd put him in the hospital.

"You bet I do. You'll have to try harder next time to kill me," he joked.

"We never—" Lydia, the plumper one, said.

The older, skinnier one, wavered before his eyes and had to put a hand to the wall to steady herself.

"Whoa, there," he said, stepping quickly forward. "Are you all right?"

"Yes. Of course. Time for my nap, that's all," she said weakly. She really didn't look all that hot.

"Do you need some help up the stairs?"

"No. I'll be fine." And she tottered off, Lydia in her wake. They started whispering the minute they turned the corner. They obviously thought they were out of earshot, but he heard the odd word, including "cordial." Good, he thought. A stiff drink was just what Olive looked as though she needed.

Mae West had obviously heard his voice. She came lounging up to him and curled her body around his ankles, whining at him the whole time.

"Look, it wasn't my idea to end up in the hospital," he told the thing, picking it up and laying it over his shoulder where it started to purr. "But don't get used to me. I'll be leaving soon."

He went straight to the library where he'd left his cell phone. It was gone. Fair enough. Emmylou had probably moved it to his room. Hiking up the stairs with the cat almost deafening him with her purring, he went to his room. And for the first time since he'd left the Shady Lady in agony, he felt himself relax. No one was going to take his blood or stick a microscopic camera into his guts. No one was going to wake him at five or insist he eat food fit for a toddler with no taste buds.

This room, like this house, was relaxing. Emmylou was in the right profession, he realized. She was a relaxing woman who knew how to create a serene atmosphere. He yawned and eyed the big bed with longing. After he'd talked to Anna and then soothed his clients, he'd take a nap.

He glanced around for his cell phone, but it didn't seem to be in the room. His laptop sat on the rolltop desk, the power cord neatly coiled, but his cell phone wasn't visible.

He pulled open drawers and even checked the closet.

After placing the cat on the bed where she sent him a "come join me" glance that made him grin—she was well-named, that one—he headed back downstairs in search of Emmylou.

Naturally she was outside tending her flowers. She'd probably been away from them all of four hours.

"Hey," he said. "Have you seen my cell?"

She didn't look at him, but kept snipping off dead blooms. "Did you look in the office?"

"Yes. And in my room. It's not there."

"How odd."

"Very odd. If this were New York I'd figure it was stolen, but out here in never-never land . . ." A bad feeling swamped him. Oh, they had their fair share of thefts out here. He'd witnessed one with his own eyes. "Has that klepto been over for tea lately?"

"I wish you wouldn't call her that," Emmylou said, not bothering to turn her head and look at him. She seemed to be awfully busy deadheading roses.

"I'll call her something a damn sight worse if she's messed with my phone. It's my lifeline. I'll go crazy without it."

She mumbled something that sounded like, "Oh, and you're so sane now," but he decided to assume he'd heard wrong.

"I'm going over there to get my phone back."

"You can't go and yell at her. Anyway, how do you know it's her? You have no proof."

Hmmph. "Who else would take it? I'll go have a look around her place, that's all. And when I see it I'll go gaga about how I've always wanted one. Especially today. I've seen the routine. I know how it works."

"Well, you can't go now." Emmylou finally turned her head to look at him, shading her eyes against the sun. "The play's tonight. You'll have to get your phone tomorrow."

"The play. Right. I remember. We have a date."

"You're sure you're okay?"

"Yes. I have to check in with my secretary. Can I use your phone?"

She stared at him a moment as though she were going to argue, then nodded. What was with everyone today?

Emmylou had never felt guiltier in her life. In trying to save Joe from a heart attack she had an awful suspicion she was giving him one. He emerged from the house not two minutes after he entered it, his face a dangerous shade of dark red. "Your long-distance line seems to be down. Did you forget to pay your phone bill?"

She hadn't thought to ask Harry to mess with her phone; he must have done that on his own initiative. She wondered if they could take incoming calls. She didn't want to miss business if there was any to be had.

"Of course I've paid the bill. There's no need to insult me. Our system isn't as efficient as yours."

"I'm sorry, Emmylou. That was totally out of line. I'm just frustrated. There's a deal cooking right now. A couple of them." He blew out a breath, then ran his fingers through his hair so it stuck up in spikes. "I shouldn't have taken it out on you. You've been wonderful to me."

Oh, why not stick a knife in her arm? She couldn't feel more guilty, and now he was being nice.

When he found out she was to blame for the loss of his cell phone, he was going to be pissed. When he found out she was trying to sabotage his business deal, he'd probably blow a gasket. And when he found out that the blown gasket on his rental car was her idea, as well . . . She didn't even want to think that far ahead.

"You could try relaxing," she said.

"I guess." He was tempted to ask her to come up to bed with him, but he did feel more tired than he cared to admit and he wanted to be in tip-top shape the next time he made a move on her. Reluctantly, he told his libido to put a sock in it and, taking her advice, headed upstairs for a nap.

Of course, Mae West was hogging as much of the bed as she could, including most of his pillow. He moved her out of the way, but as soon as he was under the covers she curled herself against the small of his back.

The warmth was comforting. To his surprise he found even the sound of her purring was soothing. He'd sleep now. Not because he was tired, exactly, but to recruit his strength for later. He hoped Emmylou was taking the opportunity for a nap also.

She was going to need it.

He had a grin on his face when he fell asleep.

Emmylou wished Joe was gone, even as she plotted to make him stay. Of course she had to do what she could to save Beaverton, even if that meant conniving to keep a man here against his will.

But every part of her that wasn't concerned with saving the town wanted him gone. He was too driven, too complicated, and most of all too damned attractive. She didn't want to be drawn to him; she didn't want to feel so . . . twitchy and hyperaware when he was around.

She sighed, wondering where all this was going to end. She had a bad feeling that when Joe figured out what was going on behind his back—which he inevitably would—there was going to be a lot of yelling. Of which she'd be the main recipient.

She wondered if they'd ever get to have sex—and if she wanted to any longer.

While she was staring at her rosebushes, lost in thought, Aunt Olive came out of the house in a loose cotton house-dress straight out of the fifties. She'd been to Terrea for Old Lady One and now her fairy godmother white hair sat in perfect roller shapes on her head. "What are you doing out here without a sun hat, darling girl?" she said when she saw Emmylou. "You'll get skin cancer."

"Oh, let her be," Lydia said, emerging in her wake. "She could use some color. Besides, I read that people stay out of the sun too much these days."

"Maybe if you read the news instead of the feature pages and the TV listings you'd have an intelligent thought in your head."

"Hah. You know what I read on the front page? Scientists are working on a kind of chocolate that, when you eat it, gives you an orgasm."

"That would sure save a lot of trouble," Olive said. "Where do you get that stuff?"

"They haven't finished inventing it yet."

"Too bad," Emmylou said, though she had a sneaking suspicion she'd rather have a Joe orgasm than a chocolate one. Probably.

"Anyhow, we have something we have to tell you," Aunt Olive said, looking surprisingly unsure of herself.

It was so unlike her that Emmylou felt panic clutch her chest. "You're not sick?" she asked glancing from one to the other.

"Now see what you did? You made her worry. I told you we should keep our mouths shut, but when did you ever listen?" Lydia said.

"Tell me what?" Emmylou demanded.

"We think we might have put Joe in the hospital," Olive said, with a quiver in her voice.

"No, we don't think that. *You* think it. I'm telling you Dr. Emmet's cordial had nothing to do with it."

"Dr. Emmet's cordial? Joe? What are you two talking about?"

"I guess I'd better explain," said Olive, pulling at an aging rose bloom until the petals fell into her hand.

"I guess you'd better 'cause I sure as hell won't," Lydia assured her.

"Dr. Emmet had this cordial he sometimes used to treat a . . . um . . . reluctant member."

"Reluctant member," Emmylou repeated, getting a bad feeling about where this was going.

"Oh, don't talk that twitter-pated nonsense, woman. It was an elixir, specially formulated for a man who couldn't get it up. Trouble in the old erection shop. No lead in the pencil, a salt-petered peter, a—"

"I get it. Thanks."

"Don't mention it."

"And what does this cordial have to do with Joe?"

Olive fiddled with the petals in her palm and even Lydia kept quiet. A bee flew by as loud as a fighter jet in the heavy silence.

"Well?"

"We discovered, when we were working with Dr. Emmet, that the cordial had quite an astonishing effect on people who drank it, even if they didn't have any problems with the initial excitement phase."

"Oh, would you stop being so mealy-mouthed," Lydia said. "The stuff makes you so horny you'd think somebody'd poured itching powder in your pants. Works on everybody, too. Not just men."

"You're not suggesting . . ." She couldn't even finish the sentence, she was so horrified.

"There was only one bottle left. I would have saved it for my birthday." Lydia glared at Olive. "But Olive and me wanted to make Joe fall in love with you and stay right here in Beaverton. Well, he's a good man and he makes a pretty decent living, best we can figure."

"How dare you—"

"Oh, don't be so coy, girl. Any fool can see from the way you two look at each other that it's springtime in the Rockies."

Emmylou took a breath, tried to remember that Lydia had never taken well to the idea of retiring as a sex healer, and that she truly had been just trying to help. "Let's get back to the cordial for a moment."

"There was one bottle left that Olive found. Olive figured we could do the whole town and you and Joe a big favor if we could get the two of you together, since you were doing such a pathetic job on your own."

"You didn't . . ." But she knew from their faces they had.

"It never caused any problems for anyone before. It was Dr. Emmet's secret recipe, but it was only some herbs and things. So we opened the last bottle and slipped some to you and Joe. You have to take it with alcohol before it works, see."

"That night," she said, seeing all too clearly. "The wine."

"Yes." Olive took up the tale again. "It's never made anybody sick before, but we're wondering if maybe it got a little stale."

"Stale?" Emmylou sounded like a harpy, but she didn't care. She was livid. "Emmet Beaver's been dead for thirty years. My God. You don't even know what's in that stuff, or what might have gone wrong. You could have killed us both. That elixir is obviously rotten." She slapped a hand to her chest. "Joe could sue if he finds out. Oh, this is awful."

"Don't get your panties in a twist. You didn't get sick. I gave you an extra big dose."

"You did what?"

"Sure. You've been hanging around old ladies too long. You ask me, you're starting to act like one."

Olive snorted. "Not like you."

"Well, maybe she should act like me. You both should, you'd have a great time. And just so's you both know, I took a dose of cordial that night and gave some to a . . . friend of mine. It worked fine. Exactly the way it's supposed to. Joe got sick because he works all the time and ate like a pig that night. You ask me, he'd have been better with a dose of bicarbonate of soda than a trip to the hospital."

Lydia stuck her nose in the air and walked back toward the house, leaving Olive and Emmylou staring at her retreating figure. Just as she was about to go inside, Olive yelled, "Who are you having sex with?"

They got back a sly grin tossed over her shoulder. "Wouldn't you like to know?"

Emmylou wasn't sure about that. But at least now she knew why Lydia had been so darned happy the past few days. Come to think of it, she didn't seem to be around as much as usual. Emmylou had been too busy worrying about Joe and visiting the hospital to give much thought to the aunts, but she hadn't seen much of Lydia.

"I thought you two went out visiting together that night."

"No. We left together but she said she was visiting another friend. I didn't think anything of it."

The sun, which moments ago had felt warm and pleasant, now pounded down on her head. On top of everything else, she had to worry about her septuagenarian, oversexed aunt having an affair. "Any idea who she's seeing?"

"I know they're all nuts in this town, but I didn't think anyone was so far gone as to take up with that old loon." Olive thought for a moment. "It does make you think that the cordial must have still been good. I mean at our age, honey, sex is like pulling a car up hill with a rope."

In spite of her angst that Joe might sue the B&B, she'd drunk heaven knew what concoction of thirty-year-old love potion, and her aunt had tumbled right off the rocker this time, Emmylou had to smile.

Olive grinned back at her. "Or sticking a marshmallow in a piggy bank."

Emmylou choked and then the pair of them started to laugh. "Oh dear, whatever are we going to do?"

"I for one am going to see if I can find the recipe for that stuff."

"You don't think maybe Lydia made up that story so I'd stop being so mad?"

Olive shook her head. "Lydia would never lie about sex. If she says she's getting it, she's getting it."

"You sound almost wistful."

"Wistful? Girl, I'm jealous as hell." She glanced quickly up, her blue eyes speculative. "So, did you feel anything?"

Emmylou felt her skin warming in a way she couldn't blame on the sun. It was ridiculous to feel shy in front of a former Intimate Healer, but she felt foolish admitting the utter disaster that had been her and Joe's big night.

"Sure, I felt something. He's very attractive and we're . . . attracted to each other and, um . . . I felt . . . excited."

"More so than usual?"

It had been kind of a while. Hard to tell if she'd been more or less excited than usual, especially since that night would forever be colored in her memory with the fact that it had culminated not in mutual ecstasy but in a trip to the ER.

She had felt excited, though. She'd barely been able to get through dinner, and once they reached the parlor and Joe had kissed her, she'd felt her body flame all over. Even after everything was over and she'd been driving home from the hospital, she'd noticed that her hormones hadn't died down to normal.

"Yes," she said. "Definitely more than usual."

Olive sighed. "It was working, then."

"But what about Joe? It was awful what happened to him." She lowered her voice instinctively. She couldn't imagine how awful it would be if he overheard them.

"I tend to agree with Lydia. Four of you had some and only one got sick. Seems like it might be a fluke."

"I don't like the odds. Anyhow, we're getting rid of the rest of that stuff."

"Oh, honey, no. You can't spoil Lydia's fun."

"What if her lover dies? He's got to be a senior citizen. What if he already has a weak heart and this sends him over the edge? Lydia would be a murderer."

Olive paled. "I hadn't thought of that."

"Let me have it."

"What will you do with it?"

"Pour it down the toilet."

"Hmmph. There'll be some happy sewer rats tonight." Olive shook her white head. "And I can guarantee you their population is going to spike."

"Come on. Let's get this over with."

As they made their way upstairs to Olive's room, they passed Lydia coming down. "Where are you off to?"

Lydia wore lipstick and one of her clingy silk dresses. She looked like someone's very sexy grandmother.

"Have you got that stuff? That potion?" Emmylou demanded.

"There was still half a bottle in my room," Olive said.

"It's still there," Lydia said. Then frowned. "What are you planning to do with it?"

"Flush it."

"What?" Lydia gasped. "But that is the last of the famous Dr. Emmet Beaver's cordial. It should be donated to science. In fact," she said, warming to her theme, "there should be test subjects who'd swallow the potion and report on how it worked. It could be studied by modern science. We could be famous. Maybe we could make enough money to save this town, have you ever thought of that, missy?" She struck a dramatic pose, forgetting she was on the stairs. She wobbled alarmingly for a moment, then grabbed the banister and intoned, "The Town That Sex Saved."

She cackled, delighted with herself. "We could have our own reality show. Maybe that Simon Cowell would come. He's cute."

"Yeah, and you'd be voted off the show first."

"Oh no, I wouldn't. I," she said haughtily, "am a character."

Emmylou felt like there was too much going on for her to ever catch up. She concentrated on one thing. "Where are you going?"

"On a date."

Lydia obviously didn't want to give any more details and Emmylou decided not to press. Not much could happen to a person in Beaverton. Besides, since everyone knew everybody else's business, she'd soon have the name of the boyfriend. Emmylou only had one qualm. "He's not married, is he?"

"I have never been a home-wrecker, young lady. And I never will be." She turned to glide regally down the stairs, then fell off her dignity long enough to turn and say, "Not that I didn't have plenty of opportunities."

Emmylou and Olive continued upstairs. When they got to Olive's room, she fished out the bottle from the back of her clothes closet. Emmylou had expected a dusty old beaker of some sort, but in fact the bottle looked like a regular liquor bottle made of clear glass. There was a cork stopper.

It was slightly less than half full of a murky yellow liquid, and there was some sediment on the bottom.

"Was it sealed in any way?"

"Of course. The bottles were always sealed with wax."

Gingerly, Emmylou eased out the cork and sniffed at the concoction. It smelled surprisingly pleasant, sort of like chamomile tea. She ought to toss it, but what if she was wrong? Who was she to destroy the last of Emmet Beaver's cordials? Especially when she had empirical evidence that it was effective. Though possibly dangerous to the health.

Lydia's words suddenly came back to her. "You know, Lydia was right," she said to Aunt Olive.

"Impossible."

"About the cordial. This should be studied. Dr. Hartnett has been doing research on how people in Beaverton live longer and don't get sick as often. He's had a passing interest in Emmet Beaver's work since he first learned of the old sanitarium. Maybe he'd like to study this. He may also be able to tell us once and for all if this stuff is what made Joe sick." She nodded briskly. "I'm going to take it to him."

"You sure you don't want to keep a little for yourself and Joe?"

"Positive. I don't think the associations of the other night are pleasant enough that either of us wants to take another chance."

"Too bad."

"And just so nobody gets any ideas, I'm putting this in the safe."

After she'd locked the cordial away, she called Gord Hartnett and told him she wanted to see him.

"Are you sick?" he asked, sounding surprised. "You're never sick."

"No. I've . . . found something relating to Emmet Beaver's research that I think might interest you."

"Great. Tomorrow's a pretty easy day. Why don't you come by the office in the morning."

"Will do. And thanks for all you did for Joe."

"Joe needs what I found in this town. Only he doesn't know yet how much he needs it."

"He sure could relax a little."

"Have you heard of the slow movement?"

"You mean those gourmet types from Italy and France who celebrate a slowly prepared and leisurely eaten meal?"

"Yes. It started with that, but there's a whole movement now into living life in the slow lane. That's what Beaverton is. America's slow lane."

"Some days it feels like the rest stop."

He laughed. "I'll see you tomorrow."

Right. That done, she could turn her attention to tonight's cuisine. It wasn't part of her regular service to cook dinner for her clients, and it certainly wasn't her responsibility to cook them a special diet supplied by the hospital dietician. On the other hand, she felt some responsibility for almost killing the man while under her roof. And all in the name of love.

The trick, she suspected, was going to be cooking something healthy and suitable for Joe to eat while not letting on to him that he was getting a special diet. She glanced at the sheet of suggestions and figured she was going to have to get very creative with fresh herbs.

And, unfortunately, in order to disguise the fact that Joe was on a special diet, she and the aunts were going to have to join him. Okay, so the aunts' taste buds weren't as sharp as they'd once been, and they liked simple food, but she wasn't sure that fish baked in milk was going to go over big.

She could bake a chicken, but the last time she'd tried that it hadn't ended up so successfully. For all she knew, Joe had developed an aversion to baked chicken for life.

She was still trying to decide what to cook her guest when the man himself came downstairs. He was a little heavy-eyed from recent sleep but otherwise looked as good as ever, with an expression in his eyes that made her warm all over.

"Hi," she said, feeling very much alone with him and suddenly remembering the steamy parking lot kiss. Maybe there was still a little of Dr. E.'s cordial remaining in her system, for she responded to the warm expression in Joe's eyes by going from zero to a hundred on the sexual desire scale in under two seconds.

"Hi," he said back, giving her a crooked smile.

"How are you feeling?"

"Well enough to take my date to the play."

Olive walked in at that moment, her hair so full of curlers it looked like a mechanical device. "Oh, good. You're coming to the play. I guarantee you won't be disappointed. Nobody can act, sing, or dance but we all have a hell of a good time doing it."

"Joe should be resting."

"From a tummy ache?"

Joe laughed. "Really, I want to go. There's not much I can do until I get my cell phone back." He glanced at Emmylou. "Tomorrow morning."

Chapter 17

The rustling of Xeroxed programs diminished, the shift and mutter of bodies on the wooden bleachers of the high school gymnasium/theater settled, and the orchestra—which was mostly the high school band brought together for their one summer gig—exploded into the overture of *West Side Story*.

Within several bars Joe caught the familiar refrain of "Maria." After that he wasn't so sure what they were playing, but he'd never had much of an ear for music. Though he suspected most of the members of the Beaverton High School Band didn't have much of an ear for music either.

Then, with a sound like popcorn near the end of the popping cycle, the drummer gamely wrapped up the overture and the faded blue curtain creaked open to enormous applause.

Joe clapped as loudly as anyone, since he realized he knew almost everyone performing. How odd.

Emmylou had promised him these were the best seats in the house when she sat them close to the front but off to one side. Seemed like an odd choice to him, but in his acquaintance with her, he'd realized that Emmylou mostly knew what she was doing.

Joe had seen one of the revivals on Broadway, and—not

that he wanted to be a snob or anything—he had to admit
the rival gang members had been a little more convincing.
Still, these guys were doing their best.

" 'When you're a Jet, you're a Jet,' " sang Edgar Kew, the
town barber, in a voice that made up in volume what it
lacked in tone. His gang followed him around the stage,
singing and dancing, one Jet a few steps behind on account of
his walker.

Most of these Jets were a little closer to their dying breath
than their first cigarette, but nobody in the audience seemed
to care. Including Joe. He was as into it as anyone when his
date gasped.

"Oh my God," Emmylou said beside him, and he followed
her startled gaze to where Ernie, the proprietor of Ernie's bar,
whose curly black wig might once have belonged to Burt
Reynolds, snapped open a switchblade.

"Must be a method actor," Joe whispered back. No rubber
or plastic for old Ernie. He had a real knife with a wicked-
looking blade, and the way that dance number was going,
somebody was going to lose a limb. Fascinated, and rapidly
reviewing what he knew of emergency first aid, he watched
the rest of the number, but the other Jets weren't stupid. They
kept a good distance from Switchblade Ernie.

When they were done, the gymnasium walls shook from
the sound of loud applause. Joe doubted the original cast ever
got a better reception on Broadway.

When the last Jet had swaggered through the number, mostly
without bumping into any other Jets, he heard a voice order,
and none too softly, "Okay, get off now, get off."

Startled, he stared into the wings, of which he had a good
view, from where Emmylou had seated them. A middle-aged
woman he didn't think he'd seen before had a clipboard in
hand and a pair of reading glasses on the end of her nose.
The glasses were on a chain she hung around her neck.

"Is she part of the act?" he whispered to Emmylou.

"Stage manager. She's deaf as a post and thinks everybody else is, too."

From that moment, Joe settled back to enjoy himself. No wonder everybody in town got so excited about their summer production.

Maybe these weren't the greatest actors in the world, but that didn't stop them for a second.

And "Tony" had a surprisingly good voice. Joe recognized him. His name was Eddie something and he was a polite older man. Emmylou had told him the guy was recently widowed, but she hadn't needed to. The man walked on the right edge of the sidewalk as though there were someone walking by his side.

When he came out for his "Maria" song, Eddie got a good clap. He acknowledged this with a bow. "Mar-eee-er," he said in a good, strong baritone, sounding a lot like Ted Kennedy. Usually, he dressed as though he were going to the office, in a shirt and tie and blazer of some kind, but obviously that wouldn't do to play the part of a Polish West Side gang member, so he was in costume.

And Joe loved his costume almost as much as he loved Ernie's wig. Tony's khakis were neatly pressed, his black wing tips shone, and his short-sleeved checked shirt still bore the creases where it had been folded in the package.

Then he started to sing. The man had a great voice, and was putting every bit of emotion he could into it. When he got to the chorus, where he repeated his love's name over and over, he paused for a gracious moment for the audience's applause to die down, then took a deep breath and added even more gusto to his final, "Mar-eee-er!"

There was something bothering Joe about the show, and suddenly he realized what it was. He leaned over to Emmylou. "Didn't Olive and Lydia say they were playing—"

"Nuns," the woman with the clipboard snapped, and just

as the poor Tony took another breath, a gaggle of nuns tumbled out on stage.

" 'How do you solve a problem like Maria?' " they chorused, clearly under the impression that this year's production was *The Sound of Music*.

For a moment the nuns stared at Tony and he stared back.

After a long moment of agonizing silence, Tony rallied. " 'I've just met a girl named Mar-ee-er,' " he sang, sounding less sure of himself.

The nuns looked at each other. And at the audience. And at Tony. Joe noted that one particular nun had shortened her habit to midthigh, showing off a nice pair of legs in black stockings. She'd also let enough red curls peek out of the white nun-thing on her head that he recognized Lydia.

" 'How do you catch a cloud and pin it down?' " the nuns questioned.

" 'And suddenly that name will never be the same . . .' "

Oh, you said it, brother.

Back and forth they went, Tony and the nuns, singing about their two Marias. It wasn't the best-timed duet Joe had ever heard, and the band wasn't sure what to do with it, so they mostly seemed to play whatever the hell notes they felt like. They did their best, but at the end of it, you had to wonder about who this Maria was. A flibbertigibbet Austrian training to be a nun or a soulful Puerto Rican shop girl?

He might have suspected the nuns interrupting Tony was deliberate if Emmylou hadn't started shaking beside him in silent giggles.

Now he remembered that the two factions refused to rehearse together, and he supposed that somewhere along the way there'd been a slight misunderstanding about which play they were putting on; perfectly normal for what he'd seen of Beaverton.

Well, after that, holding a wave upon the sand would have been a cinch compared to holding Beaverton's production of

West Side Story together. Frank Elbart, the man with no short-term memory, was supposed to play Bernardo, Maria's brother who is accidentally killed by her new love Tony. It was a part he'd played many times as a young man, Emmylou had explained, so the part was firmly imbedded in his long-term memory. The poor guy couldn't remember what he'd eaten for breakfast but he remembered soliloquies from thirty years ago. However, he became understandably confused when he stepped on stage as Bernardo to find a bunch of nuns who displayed some odd habits.

In the melee, Ernie had walked on to see what was going on, and he still held his switchblade.

Watching Mr. Elbart, Joe was amazed at how the man transformed the instant he clapped eyes on that knife. He wasn't a geriatric gang member anymore. Suddenly imbued with fierce dignity and a commanding air, he stalked forward toward Ernie, whose wig had slipped over one ear. Everybody stared at Frank Elbart. You couldn't help it. He was mesmerizing.

He wrested the switchblade from Ernie, turned to the audience, and held the knife high so the overhead gym lights flashed off the razor-sharp blade. Joe wondered whether anyone could possibly get here in time if he called 911.

" 'Is this a dagger which I see before me? The handle toward my hand?' " Frank Elbart intoned gravely.

"Oh my God," Joe whispered to Emmylou. "He thinks he's Macbeth."

"We did that one last year. He's a brilliant Macbeth."

Elbart continued, speaking to the knife as though he doubted it were real.

> " *'Come, let me clutch thee.*
> *I have thee not, and yet I see thee still.*
> *Art thou not, fatal vision, sensible*
> *To feeling as to sight? Or art thou but*
> *A dagger of the mind, a false creation,*
> *Proceeding from the heat-oppressed brain?' "*

Talk about a heat-oppressed brain! In his passion, Frank waved the knife over his head with flair. He was a tall man to begin with, and the reach of his arm was commanding, certainly long enough to slice through the fly rope suspended above his head. There was a funny noise, like a large balloon popping.

"Oh, shit," said the stage manager, dropping her clipboard with a thump.

In seconds, flimsy paper hearts and tiny silver stars floated down on the heads of everyone on stage like a twirling silver and pink snowstorm.

Every single person on stage turned to the stage manager as though she'd know what to do. Joe had to give her credit. She might have been hard of hearing, but she didn't lack aplomb.

"Kiss her," the stage manager yelled to Tony. "Kiss Maria."

"She's not on stage!" he called back. And Joe had a feeling she was the only cast member who wasn't.

"Well, kiss anybody."

Then Tony glanced at the assembled company. With a shrug, he walked smack up to Lydia, easy to spot in her minidress nun's habit, and kissed her full on the lips.

The stage manager stepped forward and started clapping, so they all joined in. Emmylou wiped the tears of laughter from her face while the actors began bowing.

The poor band, meanwhile, was in a fix. Those who'd ever figured out their place in the music had long since lost it. A lone clarinet piped out a few notes and gave up.

It seemed as though the musical would end with a whimper when a lanky kid with a tuba, who Joe guessed would one day be mayor, suddenly stood and yelled to his band mates, " 'In the Mood.' " He snapped his fingers and counted them in, "And a one, two, three!"

Well, the Beaverton High School band might not know Bernstein's score to *West Side Story* as intimately as possible, but they knew "In the Mood." All the band members rose and went at it with gusto, enthusiasm, and volume. Eddie/Tony, who'd been kissing Lydia a pretty long time considering the woman was supposed to be a nun, grabbed her hand and began to boogie. Not to be outdone, Macbeth took the stage manager's hand and started to swing, kicking up puffs of pink and silver paper.

The audience clapped and laughed and catcalled, and then they all started dancing: cast, crew, and audience.

Joe turned to Emmylou and said, "May I have this dance?"

She blinked and looked dubious, as though she thought he'd mash her toes.

So naturally, being a competitive sort, he led her down the bleacher steps to the gym floor, then spun her into a complicated jive sequence that ended with her locked right up against his body.

"I didn't know you could dance," she said a little breathlessly.

"I can not only jive, but I can fox-trot, samba, waltz—both fast and slow—and do pretty much any dance called for at weddings, dinner dances, or on cruise ships."

"A man of many talents, then," she said with a laugh.

"And you keep up just fine," he told her, pleased at how easily they'd fit together even in an impromptu sock hop.

It lasted until the band ran out of music. When "In the Mood" came around for the second time, Joe said, "Let's go," and walked his girl out into the starry evening.

"I have a couple of questions about tonight's performance," he said after a few minutes of blessed silence.

"I'll bet you do." Her voice sounded a little strained, which he suspected was from laughing so hard while trying not to make any sound.

"What were the hearts and stars floating from above all about?"

"They weren't supposed to be released until the grand finale at the end, when Maria and Tony kiss."

They walked a few more steps. "The last time I saw *West Side Story* it was a tragedy. I could have sworn Tony got knifed to death."

"Well, the Beaverton Little Theatre Company thinks that there are enough sad stories in life, so they pretty much give every play we do a happy ending. In this version, Tony gives Bernardo a bloody nose, and Tony gets a cut requiring no more than a Band-Aid. After the blissful final kiss, I believe he and Maria move to Queens and open a dry cleaners."

"Ah."

"Do you want to know how they fixed *Macbeth* last year?"

He thought about it. Then said, "No." Some things were better left unknown.

They walked hand in hand just like a couple of high school sweethearts and Joe began to wonder if Emmylou really needed rescuing from this place—or if he should worry that he was starting to appreciate its distinctive attributes.

"Are you up for the cast party? It's at Ernie's."

"Oh, I am." So they altered course and soon found themselves in a packed, raucous bar where cast and crew showed up—some still in costume. As far as Joe could tell, there were no hard feelings about the tiny misunderstandings. He got the feeling that sort of thing happened all the time.

He chatted to those he knew, met some new people, grabbed a couple of beers, and passed one to Emmylou. He mingled, and she mingled, but he was always aware of her position in the crowded place. A couple of times they made brief eye contact, and he knew she was as aware of him as he was of her.

When the aunts arrived, the party really started, and continued for several hours, including an impromptu sing-along as well as passages from *Hamlet* and *Death of a Salesman*, courtesy of the versatile Mr. Elbart.

When Joe and Emmylou returned to the B&B much later,

Joe realized he was crazy about this women, crazy in a way he'd never felt before. They paused outside the front door and, maybe because the high school sweetheart image was still with him, he leaned in and kissed her softly. "Thanks for a truly unique evening."

Chapter 18

"Morning, ladies," Joe said as he walked into the dining room the next morning, looking awfully good for a guy just out of hospital.

"What are you going to do today, Joe?" Olive asked him.

"I'm going to visit Miss Trevellen, and Emmylou's coming with me. Right, Em?"

"That's right. But we shouldn't go too early. She's probably tired from last night."

"Nonsense. She's always up with the larks. What are you going over there for?"

"Joe wants to see her collection of toy soldiers," Emmylou said before he could let the aunts in on his true purpose.

"She's quite a collector. And a walk will do you both good. Very relaxing, walking."

Not for Emmylou, knowing that Miss Trevellen didn't have Joe's cell phone.

In short order, Joe realized she didn't have it either. They arrived at her door and she seemed delighted to see them, if puzzled. Crafty old thing. Emmylou had always half suspected her pilfering was connected to loneliness. She often had fresh baking on hand when Emmylou arrived to retrieve one of her things.

Joe, to give him credit, acted genuinely happy to see the

older woman and gave as his excuse his desire to see her snuff box collection again.

"Of course, my dear young man. I'll make some coffee." While she was gone, Joe quickly scanned the room but, of course, there were no cell phones.

"Where is it?" he asked in an undertone.

"If she'd borrowed it, it would be in this room."

Once more he walked around, shifting objects to look behind them, opening a cigar box to see if the phone was inside.

Emmylou wasn't enough of a hypocrite to help him when she knew perfectly well the phone wasn't there. Instead she went out to the kitchen to help their hostess with the coffee. In a few minutes Joe joined them, using the opportunity to scan the kitchen. There was one old wall phone. Miss Trevellen wasn't even in the age of the portable, never mind the cell.

He pointed to it with a smile. "That's a pretty old-fashioned phone, Miss Trevellen."

"Oh. Well. I don't much care for the telephone. I don't spend much time on it and if I had one of those carry-around ones, I'd only lose it."

"Don't tell me you don't have a cell phone."

"Goodness, no. I wouldn't know what to do with one."

"Well, I would," he muttered.

They drank their coffee and chatted about the weather and Joe's recent illness, and even about antique snuff boxes and toy soldiers. Emmylou was impressed that he actually did know something about antiques.

He didn't mention the phone again and she didn't bring up the subject. Instead, on the way back to the Shady Lady he said, "Can I book my room for the next week?"

"Of course."

He laughed. "You're not a very astute businesswoman, you know. You should at least tell me you have to check your bookings."

She sent him a rueful glance. "You strike me as an intelligent man. You must have figured out by now that business at the Shady Lady isn't exactly booming."

"Business in Beaverton isn't booming."

"Oh, well. We all get by. And you can't put a price on happiness." She sent him a pointed glance. "Or health."

"Is there any chance of adding dinners into the equation?"

"Tonight's is already in the oven."

He let out a breath. "Thanks."

They entered the Shady Lady and he followed her into the kitchen. When she'd taken a seminar in Boise on running a B&B, there was an entire workshop session on how to keep the proper distance from guests while still making them feel at home. Somehow she'd botched things up completely with Joe. He had her cooking dinners for him as well as breakfast, he'd technically had sex with her, and he followed her into the kitchen without so much as asking permission.

He picked up her kitchen phone as though he had every right, and she only stopped herself from snatching it away from him when she realized that his New York office would be closed on Saturday. He could phone, but he wouldn't reach anyone.

He punched in numbers and she was startled when he said, "Here, would you take this?" and handed her the receiver.

"What—?"

"I called my cell phone. It's ringing. I must have lost it here in the house somewhere."

"Oh, but . . ." There was little point in continuing to speak when he'd left the kitchen. She could hang up, of course, but she'd practiced enough passive deception today.

She sank onto a stool at the breakfast bar and waited.

She didn't have to wait long.

"Emmylou," Joe said, when he came back into the kitchen. He thrust his hands in his pants pockets and leaned back against her countertop. The position might have looked casual, but it was clear he was anything but. "Your great-grandmother appears to have swallowed my cell phone."

"Ah." Okay, "ah" wasn't going to cut it, but she wasn't sure how to handle this situation—yet another one that had never cropped up during her weekend seminar on running a B&B. Honestly, she was beginning to think she should ask for her money back from that useless seminar. After her brilliant "ah," silence reigned for a few moments.

"Of course, it occurs to me that a painting couldn't swallow a phone."

"No. I suppose not."

"I'm guessing there's a safe behind the picture."

"Good guess."

"Let me go one further. I'm guessing that you locked my phone in your safe."

"Right again."

"For safekeeping?"

"Oh, you can just shove your snotty sarcasm. You want an explanation for why I locked your phone in my safe? I'll give you one. I'm trying to save your life here, Joe."

"By ruining my business?" he yelled.

"Joe, you've had a warning from your body. If you don't slow down, the next pain in your chest will be a heart attack."

He closed his eyes briefly. She distinctly hoped he was counting slowly to ten so he wouldn't yell at her again. It was a weak hope at best, and clearly unfounded. "What did you tell Anna?"

"The truth. Mostly. I told her your doctor recommended rest and quiet and she shouldn't contact you until next week."

A menacing pause ensued. "And did you happen to pass on to Anna my instructions to get me out of here?"

She breathed in slowly. "No."

"What is she going to tell the client who's been breathing down my neck about getting this deal sewn up?"

"I think she's going to tell them to chill."

He stalked forward until his body was completely in her

personal space. With the counter at her back, there was nowhere to go. She was literally backed into a corner.

He seemed suddenly very fierce and strong. Not a bit like a man who'd just been released from hospital. She had to admit to herself that she was in trouble here.

His eyes bored into hers, fierce and molten lead, the planes of his face sharp and unyielding. "Are you going to give me my phone back?"

She swallowed hard, glanced up into his implacable countenance, and shook her head. Why was she doing this? She should give him the damn thing and let him kill himself with work if he wanted to so badly. Except that she cared about him. More than she wanted to admit.

They'd had the briefest affair in the history of sex, but he had been inside her body, and she didn't let anyone in that she didn't care about. She had confiscated his phone out of the highest regard for his health and well-being, and he'd better be smart enough to realize it.

"You're not going to give me back my own property if I ask for it?"

"No. I'm not."

"Then you leave me no alternative." He was acting all huffy, but she sensed he wasn't as angry as she'd assumed. In fact, he moved in on her until they were touching.

She felt the heat coming off him. "What are you going to do?" she asked.

"Punish you," he said in a low voice that made her skin warm. He lowered his head until their lips almost touched.

"I thought punishing kisses were only doled out in old romance novels."

He dropped a kiss on her lips that was anything but a punishment—more of a teasing promise. "My methods are much more subtle and cruel."

"Really? We're not talking leather whips and chain mail here, are we?"

He kissed her a few more times, light teasing kisses that

landed and then took off before she had a chance to fully engage. "You don't give me any credit at all, do you?" His fingers trailed up the front of her top to toy with the undersides of her breasts. "I was thinking of making you so hot you'd beg me to send you over the edge."

She felt the warmth of his body, smelled the scent of his skin, and was caught in the sexual promise glittering in his eyes. Already she was humming with anticipation and a wanting so strong it bordered on need.

After the amazing almost-sex in her office the night Greg was disabling his car, then the pseudo-heart-attack sex of the other night, she figured she was ready for something that would put an end to her ever-mounting frustration. She did not, however, have to make things easy for him.

"I will make you a bet," she said, letting her own fingers sneak under his shirt to find taut, warm belly.

He dropped his head until their foreheads met. "This is supposed to be a punishment, not a wager."

"That is a very severe punishment," she agreed, giving his lower lip a tiny nip just to let him know she could hold her own if punishing was on the agenda. "But I'm thinking that getting me to the point of no return is going to put quite a strain on your own self-control."

"You let me worry about that," he said.

"But that's the whole point. Let's both worry about it. You're so sure I'll be a slave to your will. I think you'll be begging a lot sooner than I will."

"What's at stake? I want my phone back. What do you want?" When he spoke to her in just that tone, with his fingers toying with her breasts what she wanted was to stop talking and make love. But she also wanted to save Joe from himself, for reasons she didn't entirely understand.

"If I win, then your laptop joins your cell phone in the safe."

His head jerked up and the teasing left his voice. "Are you out of your mind?"

"No! Second to the cell phone, that laptop is your biggest problem. You're addicted to technology like a junkie on heroin. Cold turkey, baby. It's your only hope."

"Fine," he snapped. "I'm not worried."

"Good. Neither am I."

"Okay. Let's do it then."

She felt a sudden qualm. Sex with her had already hospitalized him once. "Physically, are you sure you're up for it?"

"Em, I am more up for it than you can imagine."

"But you've been in the hospital . . ."

"I haven't forgotten where we were when my stomach interrupted us. Have you?"

"No." And she never would.

"It's been four days of coitus interruptus for me. After I stopped feeling like hell, all I did was lay in bed all day and think about making love to you."

She felt absurdly flattered. "You did?"

"Well, it's not like I had anything else to do apart from eating lime Jell-O. No phone. No laptop . . ."

"And I hope you got used to it."

"Getting a little ahead of yourself, aren't you?"

She kissed his nose. "I am going to win this bet."

In lieu of a reply, he kissed her until her toes curled.

"I have to go lock the door," she said when she came up for air.

"I'll meet you in your room. I have to shave first." When his eyes did that yummy crinkly thing at the corners, her heart sped up. "I don't want any stubble getting in the way of your pleasure."

She laughed—hah, hah, hah—like a bit of smooth skin was going to have her swooning with desire. But secretly, just the idea of him shaving, and thinking about all the places on her body he might be planning not to leave whisker burn, had her erogenous zones on high alert.

"See you in five," he said, and leaned forward and kissed her once more, slowly and sweetly.

Sure enough, when he pulled her in tight and deepened the kiss, she could feel a hint of stubble. His chin brushed hers and she felt a slight scrape, but she curled into him anyway, putting everything she had into that kiss. He pulled away, sucked in a deep breath, and stared at her for a moment. Not feeling quite so sure of himself now, was he? He'd obviously forgotten her lineage.

Knowing that the aunts were having a post-production coffee party at Betsy Carmichael's place, and would likely be there for several hours, she locked the door and put the rarely used "Please Call Again Later" sign up to deter any chance visitors.

As she climbed the stairs she felt excitement bubbling deep inside. Maybe they'd had a couple of false starts, but this time they'd get it right.

She heard the creaking of the old water pipes that told her her guest was taking a shower.

She smiled. When he emerged, she'd have a surprise for him.

Chapter 19

As warm water cascaded down his body, Joe wondered if he'd ever wanted anything as much as he wanted to make love to Em. As the anticipation built, he let it, knowing from experience that it sharpened desire.

His razor probably didn't need a new blade, but he took the time to replace it. Then he shaved carefully, scraping the blade twice over any area that might touch a part of Emmylou. He pushed his tongue against the dent between his lips and his chin and took the blade down in a straight line.

Maybe it was the way he'd been stuck in bed for days thinking about her, but he was so eager he could barely take the time to prepare himself for her. He brushed his teeth, flossed, gargled with mouthwash, and all the while his body hummed with anticipation. He imagined her waiting for him in her bed, and that thought had him grabbing his robe and stuffing the pocket with as many condoms as it would hold.

He was nothing if not an optimist.

Oh, how he was going to love the moment when she first went starry-eyed and helpless in his arms. When her passion overcame her competitive instinct and she climaxed gloriously.

He wasn't even aware he was smiling until he strolled out of the bathroom toward the bedside table where he'd left the

history of Romania and stopped dead in his tracks, all no-
tions of Romania forgotten.

Emmylou was stretched out on his bed and the only thing
she was wearing was a welcoming smile. She lay on her side
facing him, her chin propped in her hand.

If he could have formed a word, he'd have told her how
beautiful she looked stretched out, her languorous smile in
perfect harmony with her lush body.

Since he couldn't speak, he let his eyes worship her as he
moved closer. He'd seen her undressed before, but it had
been a blur of rush and need and then intense pain, so the
whole thing was more an impression than a memory. But
looking at her now, he knew he was forming a memory that
would last forever.

Hair that blond and tumbled was designed to be spread
out on a man's pillow, as hers was this moment. Her neck
was long and slender, her shoulders graceful. Her breasts
were plump and full with cappuccino-colored nipples. His
palms itched to touch them but he made himself wait. He
could see from the way those beautiful breasts rose and fell
that she was becoming aroused under his gaze.

She was enjoying being on display, stoked by his evident
pleasure in her body. Dragging his gaze lower, he saw that
she had a very nice belly, with a hint of muscle and a curvy
waist and hips. He couldn't hold his gaze there. Back up it
went. When he'd had her on his lap in her office, her bra had
stretched across the top slope of her breasts. Now they were
gorgeously open to him and he had to have another look. He
was a breast man, and his reaction to hers was sharp and vis-
ceral. He wanted to taste them, lick them, touch them. Fuck
them.

Her nipples tightened beneath his gaze, the aureoles puck-
ering to thrust the tips at him.

He swallowed. Back to the belly. Oh, nice belly. Hips,
round like a woman's should be. The triangle of hair glossy

and deep gold. A tiny sound came from his throat. Like a plea from his body to quit looking and start touching.

No. No touching. Not yet. He didn't care about his laptop, but he wanted to make sure of her pleasure.

"I want you so badly," he said. Her skin was beginning to pinken in interesting places. He bet that flush darkened and spread when she came. *No. Don't think about coming. Not yet.*

She stretched her toes and arched her back just enough to tilt her breasts toward him; it was like she already knew his weakness. Daylight streamed in from the window behind her so she was backlit, and for a moment he was mesmerized by the graceful curve of her throat, her shoulder, and the fluid line of her arm resting at her side. After only letting himself look, the impulse to touch was irresistible, and so he followed that gorgeous curve, gilded by the light.

He touched her throat, ran his fingertips down to her shoulder and then slowly down her arm. Her skin was soft and warm as a sigh. He leaned closer to her while she remained motionless for him, like a painting or a statue. He kissed her shoulder, and her shudder of reaction proved her neither painting nor statue but wonderfully warm and alive beside him.

He traced his lips upward, to the meeting place of shoulder and neck, feeling the warmth of her skin beneath his lips, smelling the scent of her skin, which reminded him of the roses in her garden. Maybe she'd tended them so often that she'd somehow absorbed their scent. He ran his hand down her arm again, feeling the soft down on her forearm and the smooth skin of her upper arm, resilient with muscle.

When he could stand it no longer, he pushed her to her back and curled his fingers around her breasts. He leaned into them, burying his face, kissing and licking, plumping them with his hands.

Not only were they spectacular, he discovered, but they

were extraordinarily sensitive. She thrashed helplessly as he pulled a nipple into his mouth and tongued it.

How could he do this? How could he excite and arouse this wonderful, responsive, giving woman and not stoke his own arousal to the danger point? It couldn't be done.

He should leave her breasts alone to give him some breathing room, but at this moment nothing in the universe mattered more to him than feeling her nipple tight and hard under his tongue.

She reached for him. "I want to see you," she said, "I need to touch you." Right. He'd almost forgotten he still wore the robe. He rose as she reached out to pull the tie free, and he shrugged out of the thing and let it fall.

He was standing there naked looking down and she was looking up, so his eagerly jutting cock seemed to be the point at which their gazes met. A slow smile curved her lips and then she hoisted herself onto her elbow for a closer look. The seat of his pride swelled a little more, if that was possible, at her obvious approval. This wasn't their first time in bed but, damn, it sure felt like it.

She reached out to touch him, and as he felt her fingers close around his shaft he figured he could kiss his business good-bye. Odd how unimportant toppling mergers, spa locations, and cat litter factories seemed at this moment.

"Are you going for an unfair advantage here?" he managed.

She bit her lip and then, with obvious reluctance, pulled her hand away. She rolled to her back and regarded him. "Perhaps we need some rules."

"Rules?"

"Yes. You get five minutes to do whatever you like to me. I get five minutes to do whatever I like to you. We change over every time the buzzer goes. Should I get the kitchen timer?"

He looked down at her, so absolutely perfect, from her lithe body to her kind heart to her warped sense of fair play.

He picked up one of the condoms from the bedside table and sheathed himself. "I have a better idea," he said, joining her on the bed and nuzzling the sweet spot where her shoulder met her neck. "Forget the timer. Forget the rules. This is a free-for-all." Then he scooped both wrists into one hand and held them above her head, which made her chest arch, and her breasts practically popped up toward where his mouth hovered.

He closed his lips around one nipple, knowing he couldn't stay away.

He took his time, pulling with slow suction against the nipple until there was a tiny pop and his lips were free. "Oh, that feels so good," she murmured.

The next thing he knew, she'd squirmed around until her hips were directly beneath his, then she arched against him, teasing him with her slick cleft. Oh, he wanted to plunge, hard and fast, so badly he felt sweat build on his forehead as he refused his body the pleasure it had craved since the first time he'd met Emmylou.

Instead he tongued her nipples in a way that made her pant harder, and he tried to ignore the torment as she teased him with her hips and lured him into her body.

He was panting as hard as Emmylou, and as much as he loved kissing her breasts, he wanted her mouth, so he moved up to kiss her, and as his tongue slipped into her mouth, his cock took over and plunged inside her body.

The move startled both of them.

Emmylou made a strangled sound in her throat and rose up to meet him as he plunged again and again. He let go of her wrists and instead they linked fingers, holding hard as they mated with mouths, and bodies struggling and thrusting, no longer opponents, and no longer playing games.

There was nothing in the world he could do to stop the tide that built from deep within him. The only loser in this contest, he realized, would be a man who rated his laptop over making love to the most special woman he'd ever known.

He'd wanted to pleasure her first, for his own pride's sake more than anything, but he wasn't going to make it, not when she was gripping him, kneading him, all clinging, wet heat and he was all but drowning in the feel of her, the sound of her, the scent of her.

Suddenly, she arched against him and that slight change in angle did it. He felt the explosion, felt it roll out of him in agonizing bursts of pleasure. While he was half lost to reason, he became aware that his weren't the only cries in the room, nor his the only intense climax. Emmylou's fingers gripped his feverishly, her body milking him as she rode out her own orgasm.

His heart thundered, his breathing was ragged, and he'd never felt so good in his life.

He wanted to tell her, say something, let her know what she meant to him, but he couldn't find the right words, so he kissed her slowly, tasting her, swallowing the last of her sighs of pleasure while she traced the shape of his shoulders with fingers that weren't quite steady.

He raised himself up on his elbows and looked down into her face, which was passion pink, her eyes still barely focused, her lips swollen and wet. "Emmylou, that was . . ." He couldn't finish. What was it he was trying to say? It felt like something amazing had happened, something way beyond the sexual.

Words were floating through his head. Scary words. The kind a man like him didn't say to a woman. He felt more emotion swirling in the room than was good for either of them. She wasn't blabbing, though, or kissing him to stop herself from blabbing. Of the two of them, he'd say she was the more shocked.

He traced the shape of her ear with his fingertip, thinking he could spend a year getting to know every unique part of her, then he pulled her in for a big, goofy hug and held on, feeling all the emotions he was too wary to name.

"I told you I'd win," Emmylou said when her heart finally slowed and she felt as though she could speak without making a fool of herself. She was wrapped snuggly in Joe's arms.

The hair on his forearm brushed her chin when he tightened his grip and pulled her against his chest. She loved the feel of him, the warm fuzzy brush of his chest hair against her back, the way his forearm crossed her breast.

"I think we both won," he said, dropping a kiss on her head.

"I meant the bet."

"Oh, that," he said with a pretty good imitation of casualness, considering the technology slave was about to lose his master. "We came together, it's a draw."

He was right, of course, but she wasn't giving up that easily. "Your orgasm triggered mine, therefore, technically, I won."

"I let you win."

"Oh, you liar. You did not."

He chuckled and she felt the rumble of his chest behind her. "Yes, I did. I probably could have held out for a few more seconds."

"And why did you let me win?"

She felt the mattress shift slightly as he moved. "One, because you might be right. Maybe I should try living without my phone and computer for a few days."

"You said one. Is there a two?"

"Yeah. This client's a pain in the ass. It won't hurt them to discover I don't always jump when they yank my strings."

"Cool. Does that mean you're also going to tell me what they've got you working on down here?"

He pulled her down beside him. "Tomorrow. I'm doing my best to take a day off here, don't remind me I'm a workaholic."

She could have kicked herself. "Right. Sorry."

Just because they'd achieved such an incredible physical intimacy didn't mean he was going to share his devious purpose in coming to town. Yeah, great postcoital chitchat. *That was fantastic, honey. The earth moved. And speaking of moving earth . . . we'll be moving most of yours around here to mine cat litter.*

Okay, she wasn't going to spoil her own wonderful bliss by even thinking about his true purpose in coming to Beaverton. Tomorrow she'd challenge him and then maybe she could start talking some decency into the man. He had the sense to let her lock up his high-tech toolbelt, maybe he was on the road to enlightenment.

Amazingly, he did take the day off, most of which they spent in bed. She crawled out in the late afternoon to ensure the ceremonial locking up of the laptop took place, then Joe helped her make dinner. She loved the intimacy and the way his eyes warmed whenever they glanced her way. Which was often.

Luckily, the aunts didn't come home until dinnertime, so she was spared any teasing, knowing looks, or even worse, how-to suggestions.

She took Joe for a long walk after dinner and then he announced he was heading off to bed early, sending her a significant glance that had her body blooming once again with desire.

She snuck into his room a little later, feeling young and foolish and determined to be so quiet that two nosy old ladies would be kept in ignorance of what was going down in the Blue Room. Joe held a history book in his hands, but it was clear from the terrain of the bedsheet that he'd been waiting for her. She stripped in seconds and climbed in, putting a finger to his lips as she straddled him, riding him slowly until they were both sweat-damp and spent.

Feeling deliciously postcoital and heavy-eyed, she snuggled

against his warmth and enjoyed the sense of drowsy euphoria that echoed great sex.

"I've never slept in this room before," she told him. "It's nice. I love the way the ceiling slopes."

"Yes. It's a great room. Nice firm mattress, too." He sounded wide awake, and she opened her eyes fully, then turned to see that Joe was not in a similar drowsy zone. His eyes were wide and he was staring at the ceiling.

Oh, jeez. She'd forgotten his problem, and here she was about to fall asleep in his bed.

Trying to act cool about it, she leaned over and kissed him good night.

"Stay," he said, when she rolled out and fumbled into her clothes.

She smiled. "I don't want to give the aunts the satisfaction of seeing me roll out of your room in the morning."

She got to the door and glanced back, and she thought she'd never seen anyone look so lonely. "I wish it didn't have to be like this," he said.

Her smile wasn't large, but she managed one. "Me, too." And then she slipped out and padded to her own room. The sheets on her bed seemed chilled and it took her a long while to fall asleep.

Chapter 20

Joe hauled himself out of bed, realizing he'd have to hurry if he didn't want to miss the advertised breakfast hours. He didn't want Emmylou to think he was taking advantage just because they were having sex. And they'd better be having a lot of it to take his mind off the loss of his cell, his laptop, and—at the last minute—the sneaky way she'd grabbed his Palm pilot and shoved that in the safe.

After showering and shaving, he pulled on the most casual clothes he'd brought, jeans and a Knicks shirt, then ran lightly down the stairs.

Well, it seemed he hadn't missed breakfast, he realized when he got to the dining room and saw the two older gals sitting over their coffee and the morning paper.

Some toast crusts sat on a white plate in front of Olive, and Lydia was spooning up the last of a bowl of oatmeal.

"Morning, ladies," he said, hoping Emmylou had something a little more substantial on the menu for him. He'd been looking forward to another of her breakfasts and he had worked up quite an appetite in the night.

"Well, aren't you a sight for sore eyes," Lydia said, giving her brassy hair a pat.

"You took the words right out of my mouth," he said, feeling in charity with the whole world this morning.

She cackled at him. Then yelled, "Emmylou? Joe's ready for his breakfast."

"Be right there," came her voice from the kitchen. He wanted to walk right in there and kiss her good morning properly, but with the two aunts looking on he felt that maybe he should restrain himself.

"You want some coffee?" Olive asked as he sat down at a place set between them.

He opened his mouth when Emmylou came swinging through the door in one of her endless aprons over a jean skirt and—he wasn't sure what. From where he sat all he could see was apron front—for all he knew she didn't have anything on underneath it.

Now that was an idea. Emmylou in nothing but an apron . . .

Sexual fantasy was promptly forgotten when she said, "Herbal tea for Joe."

"Herbal tea? Don't you know by now that I like coffee?"

"Doctor's orders; until your esophagus has healed, he doesn't want you drinking coffee. Didn't he tell you that?"

Now he felt like a kid who didn't want to take his medicine. "He might have," he admitted. She put the tea in front of him and he caught her gaze. She looked exactly the same as always. Where was the blush? The exchange of intimate glances? He'd planned to be circumspect in front of the old ladies, but Emmylou was taking things a little far. It was like their night hadn't affected her at all.

She poured something pink into his cup and his mood soured further. "What is that?" he asked.

"Raspberry tea. It's good for the stomach."

He sipped, decided it was as putrid as it looked, and added up the things she'd taken away from him. One: cell phone. Two: laptop. Three: Palm pilot. Four: coffee. Five: this morning's good mood.

"Did you sleep well, Joe?"

"Never better, Olive," he lied, watching Emmylou as she turned and headed back for the kitchen, seemingly completely uninterested. "And you?"

"I always sleep poorly," she said. "It's age."

Lydia made a rude noise. "When I was as young as you, I didn't waste all my nights sleeping. I don't know what's wrong with you and Emmylou. So hot for each other you scorch the air when you look in each other's eyes, and acting like a pair of scared virgins."

Right. That was it.

Rising, and placing his linen napkin on the table beside the pink tea, he strode around the table, catching Emmylou just before she reached the swing door leading back into the kitchen. He grasped her shoulder and turned her around bodily. Surprise was written all over her face.

"I forgot to say good morning to you properly, Emmylou," he said pleasantly, then kissed her.

Not a kiss on the cheek, or a peck on the lips, either. Oh, no. He grabbed the back of her head, kissed her the way a man ought to kiss the woman he'd made love to most of the night, bending her back so they probably looked like a pair of passionate tango dancers to the interested onlookers at the breakfast table.

He felt the moment she gave in and kissed him back, putting her arm around his neck and pressing against him. He felt her heart thump against his chest and he was pretty sure that was her nipples he felt rubbing against him.

When he straightened them both, she blinked at him, dazed, her color a little heightened.

He walked back to the dining table, sat down, and put his napkin back in his lap.

Even the pink tea didn't taste so bad this time he sipped it.

There was total silence in the room and he knew all three of the women were staring at him.

He felt he'd made his point.

Not even the plain poached eggs Emmylou served him

with butterless toast could dim his sudden verve. There were no further references to the lack of initiative in young people today.

The two old ladies conversed with him over breakfast with great good humor, sharing such nuggets from the morning paper as the fact that more hummingbirds had been counted in the area this year than last.

"Oh, look. You made page three," Olive informed him as though he ought to be pleased.

He put down the forkful of egg and toast he'd been about to eat. "What do you mean?"

She folded over the paper and handed it to him. Sure enough, there was the headline: NEW YORK BUSINESSMAN FELLED BY BEAVERTON.

He shook his head and shoved the paper back at her. Usually, he was mentioned in the business pages. But not even the fact that his ignominious gastric attack had made the news section of the paper could dampen his mood.

Emmylou came through the swing door several more times, but it was fair to say that she no longer appeared as though this morning was just like any other. When she saw him she blushed like a schoolgirl after her first kiss.

That was more like it.

Emmylou felt like she was presenting the largest urine sample in history when she placed the half-full liquor bottle of yellow cordial on Gord Hartnett's desk.

He looked at the bottle, cocked an eyebrow, and turned his attention to Emmylou, who settled into one of the chairs in his office. It wasn't a very comfortable chair—she suspected doctors chose chairs the same way fast food restaurants did, to get people out of them again as soon as possible.

"What's up?" he asked, settling into his own executive chair behind the desk, which looked a hell of a lot more comfy than the vinyl and chrome job on which she perched.

Gord wasn't big into chitchat or wasted time. That was

one of the things that had made their affair work so well, she realized now; neither of them had ever pretended to more than they felt. They'd both had obligations and lives to live, and while they'd felt affection for each other, she knew they both viewed their relationship as a convenient, efficient way to meet their sexual needs. The incredible thing to her was how different he'd been the second he met his wife-to-be. He'd ended things with Emmylou almost before Terri's tonsils bit the dust.

She opened her mouth and completely different words emerged than the ones she'd planned. "When you broke things off with me, had you even asked Terri for a date?"

Gord blinked, obviously as taken aback by what she'd said as she was. He leaned back a little, as though seeking the right position in his chair in which to have this unexpected conversation.

"No," he said, when he had his back flat against the chair back and his arms on the armrests. He looked like a man about to face a firing squad but open to his fate.

"But what if she'd said no, she didn't want to go out with you? What then?"

"Emmylou, I'm sorry. I always thought you were okay with the way things ended between us. Forgive me, but I thought we both felt that our relationship was—"

"Temporary." She completed the sentence for him cheerfully. "Yes, absolutely. We were convenient for each other. But I just now wondered what made you so certain things would work out with you and Terri that you ended things with me when you did. It's funny, I never thought of that before."

He turned his head so he was looking past her, and Emmylou suddenly knew without having to follow his gaze that there was a picture of his wife behind her. "I think I fell in love with Terri the first time I saw her."

"With a hundred and three temperature and her throat swollen?"

He gave a short laugh. "I know. She can't believe it either, but it's true. At first she was just another patient, of course, but every time I looked into her eyes it was like seeing someone I'd known a long time ago and had missed really badly. Then I touched her and . . . I don't know. It sounds corny and completely unlike me, but I knew." He glanced back at Emmylou. "But I never, ever meant to hurt you in any way. You know I think—"

"No, it's fine. I think the world of you, too, and I have no regrets. We were always destined to end up friends, not lovers."

He nodded and she felt the relief coming off him in waves.

But she still felt puzzled, as though there was something just out of her grasp. "The thing is that I always thought we were alike. We're practical about sex."

"But I turned out to be a romantic in love." He turned a little pink as though embarrassed even to be talking like this. "I never saw it coming. Never."

"Wow. So even if she'd—once she could talk normally again—even if she'd said thanks but no thanks, and left the state, you'd have—"

"I'd have kept trying to change her mind. I wouldn't have felt right making love to one woman when I'd fallen in love with another."

She couldn't help her smile. "So you are an old-fashioned romantic at heart."

"Let me ask you something. If she'd left and I'd tried to rekindle things with you, would you have gone for it?"

She'd never thought about that before. So she did now. That was one thing she'd always liked about her relationship with Gord, and obviously the reason their friendship continued after the affair was all but forgotten. They could talk about anything.

Her head was shaking before she realized she knew the answer. "No," she said. "I guess once you'd fallen for Terri, whatever happened, the sex was over for us."

He nodded. They smiled at each other and there was the

affection of friends. She admitted, "I missed the sex for a while, though."

"I don't mean to pry, but I have a feeling one of my recent patients would be more than happy . . ."

"You mean Joe." She didn't feel like talking much about her and Joe. It was too new. Last night had been too blindingly fantastic for her peace of mind. However, what had happened between her and Joe was partly why she was in this office.

"Well, that gives me a great segue into what I'm doing here. First, I need your word that what I am about to tell you will remain confidential." She'd heard about doctor/patient privilege on TV crime shows, but she wasn't putting her aunts at risk based on a *Law and Order* rerun. "I can't have anything bad happen to . . . anyone else in the story who might have accidentally caused someone harm."

His brow creased in a frown. "I'm not sure I can—"

"Oh, no one died and there's been no permanent harm."

He looked at her for another searching minute, then at the bottle on his desk. He nodded. "You have my word."

She didn't know whether he gave his word as doctor or friend, but it didn't matter. If he said he'd keep his mouth shut, he would.

Briefly, she described what had happened the night Joe had his attack, including the previously unknown fact that both he and she had been secretly dosed with the cordial.

By the time she finished, Gord was sitting on the edge of his chair, dividing his attention between her face as she spoke and the bottle of cordial on his desk.

"And they slipped this stuff to both of you. In wine."

"Yes. According to the aunts, it needs to be mixed with alcohol to become effective."

He pulled a legal sized notepad toward him and started scribbling. "And how long after ingesting the liquid did Joe have his attack?"

She eyed his notepad with disfavor and kept quiet until he

glanced up and caught the direction of her gaze. "This is just for my own research. I gave you my word, Emmylou. This conversation stays between us."

She nodded. "Okay. I think it was about an hour to an hour and a half later."

"Did you feel any effects of the tonic?"

She hesitated. "I had no stomach trouble."

"How about other symptoms? It's supposed to be some kind of sex enhancer, the way you described it. Did you notice anything in that regard?"

"Yes."

"Come on, I'm a doctor. This is fascinating."

"I felt extremely aroused. Before he even touched me."

"How long did those feelings last?"

"Several hours."

"And you said your aunt Lydia also took some of the stuff?"

"Yes. According to her, she also shared it with a man."

He glanced up, his eyebrows raised in query. Like her, he must have been wondering who Lydia's new beau was. "I have no idea who it was, but she says they were both fine afterward."

"And did she say whether it had an . . . arousing effect on her and her partner?"

"Yes, she did. According to her they had fantastic sex. She's very angry with me for taking away the rest of the bottle."

He smiled briefly. "I'll bet."

"So what do you think? Could the cordial or whatever it is have caused Joe's attack? I just feel sick that someone in my house could have caused him harm."

"Do you have any idea what's in this stuff?" he asked.

"No. Olive and Lydia say it's mostly herbs, but they believe the recipe died with Dr. Beaver."

Gord removed the cork and sniffed, then recorked it. "I'll have a complete chemical analysis done." He sat back and tapped his pen on the pad of scribbles. "My best guess is that this stuff may have contributed to Joe's attack, but there were a lot of other factors involved. And no one else got sick, so I wouldn't worry too much."

"But you'll let me know what you find out?"

"Absolutely." He stared at the liquid in the bottle intently. "You know, the more I learn about Emmet Beaver, the more I believe he was a genius."

She rose to leave, oddly flattered to have her grandfather termed a genius. "Thanks for taking a look at that stuff for me."

"Thank you for bringing it. I'm truly interested in Dr. Beaver's work and a sample of one of his medications is quite a find." He sounded pretty pumped. So long as there was nothing in that bottle that could have made Joe sick, she was willing to let him have his fun.

As she rose, Gord also stood. "Emmylou, I hope the same kind of fall-flat-on-your-face love happens for you, too."

She smiled at him, and on impulse leaned over to kiss his cheek. "Thanks, Gord."

What she didn't tell him was that she had an awful feeling it already had happened. And with the man who was planning to destroy her town.

Meanwhile, now that she'd unburdened her conscience, she had to go get something for the town-wrecker's dinner.

Something bland but interesting, not spicy but tasty. Or maybe she'd give him fish baked in milk and then play footsie with him under the table to distract him from what he was eating.

Joe wandered up Main Street, gazing into windows and doing something he never did. Strolling. Stopping to chat to the people who knew him, and knew all about his business and his recent medical troubles—and that was pretty much everybody.

He wanted to buy Emmylou a present. It was difficult to think of the right kind of gift, though, for there were several things he wanted his gift to convey.

First, there was thanks for driving him to the hospital, visiting him, bringing him home—all that "going beyond the call of duty as an innkeeper" activity for which he was profoundly grateful.

He also wanted to buy a gift for Emmylou the woman, who'd given him so much joy last night. If he were at home, he'd send a couple of dozen long-stemmed roses. An uncomfortable image flashed across his mind of the arrangement his office had sent him in the hospital. That same standard arrangement they sent everyone; was he as predictable with the long-stemmed roses?

Well, he wasn't going to buy roses for Em. There didn't seem to be a florist in Beaverton, and besides, Emmylou had a garden full of flowers. She spent half her life out there tending roses, which obviously gave her pleasure. The last thing he wanted to do was send her the cut variety.

He wandered up Main Street. The trouble with wandering when there was no phone attached to his ear was that it gave him too much time to think. Too much time to remember the look on Emmylou's face when she'd left his room last night.

Why hadn't he pretended to fall asleep? At least then he'd have had the pleasure of holding her while she slept. He'd have given up his own rest. It wouldn't have made much difference. After she left he had a crap sleep anyway.

If the shopping told a great deal about a town—and Joe had never thought about this one way or another, not being much of a shopper—then Beaverton was one very odd place.

Not that he needed a lot of extra evidence.

The art gallery specialized in a number of painters he was unfamiliar with whose work featured nudes. Nudes recumbent, nudes standing, nudes playing croquet, pairs of nudes going at it. As interesting as the art no doubt was, he kept walking.

He left there and wandered next door to the gift shop. Massage oil, scent o' sex candles, lingerie that made him swallow hard when he pictured it on Emmylou, and hand-blown glass sculptures in sensuous flowing lines that made him think of naked women. The only thing unique to Beaverton was the plastic replicas of the town's gigantic mascot, most dandruffed with dust.

He kept going.

The barbers in the barbershop he'd been warned never to set foot in waved gaily as he passed, the woman never stopping her snipping.

He wasn't a stroller. A wanderer. A browser. And yet, with no cell phone, no laptop, nothing to do, he didn't know what else to do with himself. Emmylou had gone out so he'd decided to do the same, but all he wanted was to get her alone again. Desire for her thrummed beneath his skin in a steady beat, like his pulse.

He passed a bakery. Oh, how they all waved, but he wasn't that naïve. Emmylou was a terrific cook. What could he buy her at a bakery that she couldn't bake better herself?

He waved back at the friendly strangers and kept walking. He knew he'd find something, if he just kept looking.

There was a dog lying with its head on his paws outside the bakery. When Joe looked down at him, his tail wagged feebly.

"Hi, Buster," he said, squatting to pat the poor old beast. Buster licked his hand and wriggled his arthritic body—which for Buster was like turning cartwheels. "Oh, you're a good old boy, aren't you?"

Buster agreed, and wagged his tail some more.

"He sure did take to you," said the kindly plain woman who owned not only Buster, but the Ranch of the Damned.

Joe rose. "Hi, Amy. Nice day." And then was inspired to ask this woman, who was obviously one of Emmylou's friends, if she had an idea for a gift for his landlady.

"Emmylou's a classy woman," she said with a slight frown. "Most of what this town sells, she wouldn't want."

"I was afraid of that. I thought of roses, but there's no florist. And anyway, she grows them."

"I've got some new hybrid bushes in."

"You have? You mean real rosebushes?"

"Sure."

He beamed at the woman, beamed at Buster. Of course giving a rosebush to a woman who loved to grow roses had to be better than the cut kind. "Perfect."

Chapter 21

Emmylou had spent most of the time since she'd returned from Gord's office dodging the aunts. Okay, so she had slept with Joe. So what? It was her business. His business. Not Olive and Lydia's business. But did they know that? Oh, no.

And after all but fully consummating their relationship again over the breakfast table, what had he done? He'd gone, that's what. He'd left the Shady Lady while she was on her errand to see Gord, and when she returned no one knew where he'd gone. It wasn't that she cared exactly, but where the hell was he? A workaholic with no toys? She'd expected that he'd be haunting her every second, bored out of his mind, not that he'd disappear.

As always when she felt churned up, she picked up her caddy of garden tools and went outside, where the scent of roses soothed, the glossy leaves welcomed her, and the bees buzzed like old friends.

She had no idea how long she'd been out there when she heard Joe's voice. "Hi." That's all he said and she felt her heart jump.

She turned toward him in what she hoped was a casual way, and saw he had his hands behind his back and an air of suppressed excitement.

"Hi," she replied.

"I had a good time last night," he said.

The smile that bloomed came from somewhere deep inside. "Me, too," she said.

"I wanted to get you flowers. So I did."

He brought his hands out front and her jaw dropped. "That is so perfect," she cried.

As she walked toward him, he held out a potted rosebush. "I tried to find a color I didn't think you had."

Mr. I-don't-know-what's-in-my-sandwich had taken the trouble to learn the colors of her roses? All the parts of her that should have been strong and held out against his charm suddenly softened. She loved roses. He'd seen that and found her one she didn't have growing in her garden.

"Thank you, Joe," she said. She felt a little foolish. No, not foolish exactly, more flustered. How odd. She never acted like this. She couldn't even raise her gaze from the tight bud of the apricot-colored hybrid tea rose. She reached out and touched the peachy pink edge that flirted from behind the tight green bud. "I can't think of anything that would have meant more."

"I'm glad," he said simply.

There was a pause. Finally she glanced up and found him staring at her so seriously, she wished she'd kept her gaze on the rose.

"Well," she said after a moment. "Where should I plant it?"

They both looked around the garden, so overflowing with green stalks and leaves and colorful blooms that Joe wondered where she'd even find room for another rose. She didn't seem to see any problem, however. "I want it to go somewhere prominent, so that I remember you every time I look at it"

Something to remember him by? He felt just a little huffy to be so quickly dismissed from her near future, until he realized that of course he was intending to go and had never pretended otherwise.

She was a practical woman, that Emmylou, not one to let a little romance cloud her thinking.

Romance. He considered the woman standing in front of him admiring her rosebush, clearly obsessed with finding it the ideal location. No doubt she was thinking about soil variables and hours of sunlight and not about the man who'd given her the plant. Romance? He'd never seen a woman less given to romance than Emmylou.

He thought about earlier, in the kitchen. The fact that she was facing him at breakfast after they'd slept together hadn't fazed her at all, but his kiss in front of her aunts had rattled her shutters, all right. They weren't the sort of aunts to mind a little kissing over the breakfast table—in fact, he guessed they'd be a damn sight happier to see Emmylou bent backward over a man's arm than they were to see their daily bran flakes.

Suddenly, he got it, the thing that had bothered him this morning. Emmylou had enjoyed sex with him, but she didn't seem to have any romantic feelings toward him. Of course, that ought to make her his ideal woman, so why did he want her to try to talk to him about his feelings? Why did he want her to suggest a picnic or the movies or any one of a thousand foolish activities he wouldn't have time for if he had his computer and phone?

He didn't question his motives too closely, only followed the irresistible impulse to see if he was right.

"You see sex and romance as two different things, don't you?"

"They are two different things," she said, looking at him as though he weren't too bright.

"Not to most women."

"I am not most women."

"Thank you, I can see that."

"What is bothering you, Joe?"

"I don't know. It's strange to meet someone who only wants me for sex, I guess."

She laughed. "You're leaving in a few days. I had a great time last night. I loved our time together and I'm hoping we'll do it again tonight, but I'm not going to swoon all over you and start planning the wedding. Do you have a problem with that?"

"No! I only want to feel like you'll still remember my name a week from now."

She patted his cheek. He could not believe it. She patted his cheek. "I'll always remember you with fondness, Joe. And I'll have your beautiful roses to remind me of you."

"So you equate romance with permanent commitment, is that it?"

"Are you writing a thesis on this topic?"

"No. I'm making conversation." Though he wondered why he bothered. It was clear the woman was more inter- ested in yanking up weeds and slopping fertilizer around than she was in talking to the man who'd spent some of the nicest moments of his life inside her body.

All right. Fine, then. He'd talk about something she might find interesting.

"I haven't told you why I'm here."

She glanced up at him, her expression unreadable. "No. You haven't."

"I think you're going to like what I have to tell you."

This time her expression was perfectly legible. She looked astonished. "You do?"

What did she think he was doing here, destroying the place? She really had some opinion of him. He was anxious to let her know the truth. "I'm here to save Beaverton."

"Really." She was on her knees squinting up at him, so he must have misread her expression. She looked disgusted, but how could she be? Maybe she thought he was planning to take all the credit personally for saving her town.

"Well, not me personally, of course, but I'm here repre- senting a company that wants to inject a great deal of capital into the area. They're going to open a factory that will employ a number of people. If all goes well, the workforce will increase, businesses will prosper. The Shady Lady will be packed every night; Emmylou, we'll put this place on the map."

She looked at him the way she might have looked at one of the insects crawling among her roses, one she couldn't immediately identify. "What kind of factory?"

"It's not the type of factory that's important, so much as the benefits it will bring to the area."

"Still, I'm curious."

"Well, to tell you the truth, it's kind of a funny one." Which ought to fit fine around here. "The company makes . . . uh, cat litter."

"Cat litter."

"That's right. I was pretty skeptical myself at first, so believe me, I looked into the company's history and profitability. There's money to be made in cat litter."

"I'm sure there is." She rose and turned to him. "What's the process exactly? And why Beaverton?"

"Two excellent questions."

"I hope you have two excellent answers."

"Emmylou, would you cut the attitude? I'm telling you, I can help save this town. Okay, so cat litter's not the sexiest commodity going, but we're talking cash infusion, an expanded workforce, progress, Em, progress."

"And the answers to my questions?"

"Right." She could drop the hostility. That would help. "The process, and why we chose Beaverton."

She nodded.

"Well, the process isn't something I completely understand, frankly. It has a lot to do with absorption properties and odor control. A lot of chemical mumbo jumbo which leads to the reason Beaverton is such a good site. It's got two things going for it. There's a great deal of phosphate under the soil, which is easily mined, and the old sanitarium property has been closed for years. The company I represent will take it over and turn it into a factory."

She gave him a steely-eyed, Gary Cooper in *High Noon*, unblinking stare. "How do you get the phosphate out of the ground, Joe?"

"It's a surface mining technique."

"But the 'surfaces' around here are all in use."

"Look, I realize there's going to be some ruffled feathers and inconvenience, but progress always causes some opposition. It's human nature to resist change. I thought you would be more forward thinking."

"Forward thinking? Joe, these are people's lives, their livelihoods."

He snorted.

"Okay, so they're not Fortune 500 companies, but what about Amy Potter's horses? Where are they going to go while the land is stripped from under them? What about her organic vegetables? Or Max's potato farm? You can't simply yank the phosphate out from under them and think it won't completely mess up their lives."

"Actually, Em, we can. Mineral rights can be claimed by anyone."

"Oh, that is so unfair."

"They'll be compensated."

"Hah. What kind of compensation is there for those poor horses? Can you compensate my roses if they're yanked out of the ground? Can you compensate me for the memories that are in this garden and the love and attention I've devoted to it?"

"Nobody's going to mine your back garden, Emmylou. Get a grip."

"But don't you see? Everyone feels the way I do about their little corner of paradise." As they'd been talking, she'd planted the rose, added another hint of paradise to the garden. "That's what this place is to us. Nobody here is looking to get rich. Beaverton is a community where people get along and look after each other, where nobody cares if you're eccentric or different. How many places like that exist in this country, Joe? Or in the world? Can you put a value on that?"

"You're looking at this emotionally," he said, wishing she hadn't mentioned those horses. He'd have to see what would happen in a case like that. "Try to be practical."

"I can't be practical about this. My great-grandfather built the sanitarium and he left it to the town of Beaverton. He never intended that it would end up a factory."

"Then maybe the town should have paid the taxes," he said pleasantly, but through gritted teeth. He'd thought Emmylou would be jumping for joy at his news, not looking at him like he'd shot her puppy.

"Come on," she said, brushing the dirt from her hands. "I'm going to show you something."

"If it's anything to do with cat outhouses, I'm not interested."

"Oh, I think you'll be interested in this. It's the sanitarium."

"You have keys to get inside?"

"Yes."

Figured. "I've already seen it."

"Not the way I can show it to you. I'm going to wash up and change my jeans. I'll meet you at my car in five minutes."

Right. Her car. He wondered if he was ever going to have his rental car running again. He'd arrived here with so much more than he now seemed to possess.

Except time, he realized, as he picked up Em's discarded clippers and resumed deadheading the roses. She had so many roses, there were always things that needed doing. He found the repetitive task soothing, and as he fell into a rhythm, he noticed that his stomach was feeling better. Not just better than since his attack, but better than it had in months. Probably the gastric thing had been coming on for ages and he hadn't noticed.

"Fire, fire!" yelled a familiar voice. Since Em was upstairs and probably out of earshot of the frantic middle-aged fireman with his plastic hat, Joe pointed out the freshly planted rose. He figured it could use a good soaking.

Now that he wasn't busy either getting his panicked heartbeat back in control or pondering the lunacy of this town, he took a moment to admire the way the fireman focused on his task, watering the roses so he got their roots and not their leaves. After he was done, he coiled the hose neatly, saluted smartly, and was on his way.

"You're looking kind of stunned," Emmylou said when she emerged in a clean pair of jeans and a tank top that was the same color as the rose she'd planted. "What's up?"

How to explain that he was starting to get what she meant about this town? How would the new influx of factory workers and small business owners take to an old guy in a red plastic fireman's helmet? Or a sweet old lady kleptomaniac? Would all those people who lived in Beaverton because it was the kind of place where they would never be laughed out of town, suddenly be laughed out of town?

It was nothing to do with him, of course, but still. He wondered.

"That top is the same color as the rose you just planted," he said, since it was easier to talk about her clothes than about his feelings about the townspeople.

She'd started the engine, and the car was rolling forward, but at his words, she slammed on the brakes, leaned across the emergency brake, and kissed his mouth.

"What was that for?"

"You noticed. You actually noticed the color of one of the flowers in my garden."

He noticed more than that. He noticed the contour of her breasts in that top, and unless he was very much mistaken, there was no bra between her skin and the bright cotton top.

He slid a hand across and wrapped it around her thigh, enjoying the play of muscle and flesh as she drove.

He knew something about Emmylou that he hadn't known earlier. She was totally open and uninhibited about sex, which was to be expected given her upbringing, he supposed. But the woman was starved for romance.

Joe didn't consider himself a big romantic, but he suddenly wanted to give that to Emmylou. He wanted to serenade her by singing ballads under her window at night. He wanted to bring her silly gifts so he could see her flustered pleasure. But if he did that, then she might do something he suspected she'd never done before. She might fall in love with him.

Ooh, bad idea. Unless he was willing to do something he'd never done before. And what would be the point? They had no future together. He should be smart like Em. Enjoy the sex and part with a smile.

They were mostly silent as they drove through town and then bumped down the rutted lane that led to the former sanitarium.

She undid the padlock, and he unwound the rusty chain and opened the gate for her to drive through. Unlike the last time he'd been here, they didn't bother relocking the gates behind then.

They mounted the wide marble steps, cracking slightly with age but still in pretty good shape, and she fitted a big old key into the lock that opened one of the enormous double oak doors. There was an inscription in faded gold lettering above the door.

Mens sana in corpore, he read. "Healthy in mind and body."

"You know Latin?"

"They still teach it in my prep school."

She smiled but didn't say anything, merely opened the door and ushered him in ahead of her.

His footsteps echoed in the dim marble entranceway. It was massive. Dim because of course the electricity wasn't hooked up, but the twelve-foot windows let in streamers of sunlight. No one had bothered to board up the windows, and not one was broken.

Ahead of him was the double curving staircase, and the twelve-foot phallic columns gave the place a Greco-Roman orgy look. In the center of the foyer was the dry shell fountain with its pearl inside.

He glanced at the whole setup, and looked over at Emmylou, who was watching him in some amusement.

When he'd seen this stuff in the company of the realtor, he'd been bemused. Now he was enjoying seeing it in Em's company. "Your great-grandpa didn't believe in subtlety, did he?"

She laughed. "Nope. You should see it when the water's flowing."

"I'd love to. Is this place anything but a big wet dream?" His voice echoed oddly in the cavernous space. It was like being in a huge cave surrounded by sexually suggestive stalagmites. He looked around and felt a sudden urge to take Emmylou against one of those gigantic marble penises and get her fountain running, pearl and all. He doubted he was the first man to have that reaction.

"Emmet was ahead of his time, I think. But his beliefs were sincere. He thought sexual repression was the root of a lot of illnesses, both mental and physical. In those days he was probably right."

"In these days, too."

"Do you think so? But everything is so much more open now, and there's therapy and help available for most sexual troubles, without any stigma attached."

"People are still fucked up about sex, though. Look at us."

Oh, that got her attention. She swung around. "Us? What's wrong with us?"

"Oh, gee. Let's see. I can't fall asleep in the same room as a woman and you treat sex like a fast food meal."

"What?" The word echoed around them.

"You need sex, like you need food, but you're not interested in romance."

"That's the stupidest thing I've ever heard. This from a man I've slept with exactly twice."

"I've had a lot of time to think without my usual toys, and it's amazing how perceptive I've turned out to be."

"Delusional, you mean."

"I thought you were afraid of romance."

"That's ridiculous. No one's afraid of romance."

"Exactly. I'm pretty new at this perceptive stuff, so I got off on the wrong track."

She rolled her eyes.

"You're not afraid of romance. You're afraid of love."

Her mouth opened and closed a few times and her chest rose and fell. "How dare you say something like that, about a woman you barely know?"

"I haven't known you a long time, but it's been pretty intense. I'm no Freud, I'm not even a Dr. Beaver, but I'm sticking by my diagnosis."

"I do love people. I love Lydia and Olive. I loved my grandmother so much it hurts me every time I think about her."

She was looking open and vulnerable, her eyes wide and her cheeks pink. Maybe he should shut the hell up and back off. This wasn't his business, and she was right, he certainly didn't have much background or right to give her a drive-through psych exam. And yet something pushed him on. Something in her that he now saw he'd recognized because it mirrored something inside him.

"Em, you're trying to bullshit the master, here. You don't have to. I get it."

"What do you get? You lay awake beside me in bed and instead of realizing how fucked up your own head is, you decided to analyze mine?"

Her voice rose and he felt oddly protective of her. Okay,

she didn't want to poke at her own psychic sore places. But maybe it was time she did. Maybe it was time they both did.

"Your mother abandoned you. She'd rather shoot badminton birdies out her quiff than hang around and be there for you. You don't even know who your father is."

"Thank you. I'm aware of those facts."

She drew in a deep breath so shaky he wanted to pull her into his arms and make her forget her pain. "You haven't seen a lot of happy marriages in your family, have you? It's all about fixing problems and sex circuits, but I don't think you believe love is for you. You're scared of the very thing you want most." He stepped forward and she stepped around him.

"Just like you, Joe."

He felt dizzy for a moment, like the ghost of old Emmet himself had just clocked him one.

"This was a stupid idea," she said. "Forget it. You want to try and destroy this town? Fine. But we're going to fight back."

She started to charge past him but he grabbed her. "Hey, please don't run away. I'm sorry. I was out of line. You're right. I don't know anything about you." He let her go but she didn't move, just stood there staring at him with her too-big eyes. Obviously, no one had ever challenged her before. It wasn't his place, and maybe it wasn't the time.

Her breath was deep and slow, like someone counting to ten before blasting off in anger. She seemed undecided about what she was going to do, then suddenly stiffened her spine. "I do want to show you this place."

"Great. Based on the foyer, I'm dying to see it."

She laughed. He hugged her to him with one arm, and by tacit agreement they let their earlier tension go.

But he was determined that before they were much older, it was going to rear its ugly head again.

Because he saw, as he couldn't have seen before coming to Beaverton, that if he could help Emmylou, he could help himself.

Chapter 22

Who the hell did Joe think he was? Emmylou fumed as she played nicey-nice on the outside. The man had about as many qualifications to shrink her head as he did to fix his own car.

And yet, she had to admit, her anger was out of all proportion to the offense. So he'd busted in to her private affairs, why should that stress her out so much? If they were talking mergers and acquisitions, she'd listen, for in that arena he'd earned the right to be heard. But if ever a man had less qualifications to judge another's heart, it was Joe.

Looking into her was like looking into a mirror?

In what funhouse?

"We can start on this level with the treatment rooms," she said. "They're gorgeous. You couldn't replace the luxury today. The cost would be stupid."

She tried to see the place through his eyes. There was enough marble to rival the Vatican, some of it was carved in what she could only term a medical-erotic style. There were marble massage tables, and the carved masseuses and masseurs were naked, as were their patients.

Joe gazed around, realizing he hadn't come this far with the realtor. He hadn't bothered, assuming they'd pull down the old facility. There was a steam room with gold-plated faucets. And then there were the bathing rooms. They had large mirrors with cavorting cherubs on the gilt frames. Faded gold script stenciled around the walls challenged his Latin.

Mostly he worked out vague meanings about health and electricity, well-being and freedom.

"Some of these baths are private, and some built for two."

"Which two?"

She tapped him on the nose with her index finger. "It wasn't rare for rich couples who were having trouble conceiving a child, or who simply had troubles in the conjugal bed, to come here together. The regimen, as I understand it from Emmet's notes, was to treat them separately and also together. I suspect a lot of their together time was simply a chance to practice the new skills, or take the time to enjoy each other."

"So time was a problem even then."

"I guess so."

The room they were currently in was gorgeous. There was no other term for it. Marble, gold, cherubs doing things that no cherub should even know about, and a deep marble basin with something he hadn't noticed before. Several holes in the marble that looked like water intake valves.

"What are those things?" he asked Em.

"This is one of the earliest examples in America of the double Jacuzzi."

"You're putting me on."

"No. This area has natural hot springs. Emmet thought they were as good or better than the ones in Baden-Baden in Germany or Bath in England. That's why he chose this site for his sanitarium."

"A double Jacuzzi. I don't believe it."

She sent him a mischievous look. "I know how to turn it on. Want to try?"

"You mean it still works?"

"Sure. We can't pay the taxes on this place, but we do keep it up."

"But you can't be on city water."

"No, of course not. The hot springs are piped in directly, mixed with cold water from the well on the property. Give me five minutes."

She disappeared and he went in for a closer look. It was amazing.

He was even more amazed when Emmylou reappeared a couple of minutes later and turned a gold tap in the floor. Water gushed into the tub. But it flowed out again almost as quickly. "I think you've got a leak," he said.

"Don't worry, it's supposed to do that." She put her hands on the bottom of her tank top and yanked it over her head. He didn't much care if the entire place flooded. He was looking once more at a pair of the nicest breasts he'd ever seen. As he'd suspected, there'd been no bra under there. When she stepped out of her jeans, there was nothing left but a bright pink thong.

He wanted to remove it himself, and before he'd formed words, she was sliding the pink slip of fabric down her legs and off.

She glanced at him standing there. "Well? It's for two."

"Right," he managed. "Right."

He was as naked as she in seconds. The tub was still bubbling and gurgling, and the water was rising, but at a very sedate pace thanks to the drain in the bottom.

"You still don't get it, do you?" she said looking at his face.

"Get what?"

"I like to call this one Lady's Choice." She stepped in and settled herself on a marble seat; as the water gushed around her, she let her legs slip apart. There was nothing random about the way the water flowed, and once more he was reminded of the fountain in the foyer.

With more haste than elegance, he scrambled into the copilot's seat behind her.

Warm water gurgled and sloshed around them, emitting

the aroma of rotten eggs. "Couldn't the genius doctor have done something about the smell?"

"It's the sulfur. All good springs smell. You'll get used to it."

"I could definitely get used to this," he said, slipping his hands around her and cupping her breasts.

"Mmmm." She was already closing her eyes and leaning back against him. He kissed her neck, where steam-dampened tendrils were already clinging. The water was perfect, hot but not too hot, so you could stay in here a while if you had a mind to. Or, based on the sounds already coming from Emmylou, be out pretty damned quick if you so desired.

Her breasts were wet and slick. He'd have liked some soap or gel, but of course there wasn't any, so he made do with the water, splashing it up onto her chest and following the track of the water with his fingertips. Her nipples beaded and her head fell back against him.

He reached down under the bubbling water to the center of her body, where water streamed in a steady flow. He intercepted it, pressing a hand against her. She bucked against him, part protest, and part longing for more. He could feel the beat of the water against his hand, feel its diluted impact on her flesh, which was already swelling with desire.

He sported a smaller version of the marble pillars downstairs, and wanted nothing more than to enact one of the many ideas about sex and health that were no less provocative for being spelled out in Latin.

He hoisted her up and slid into her.

"Oh," she cried as she settled on his lap. With her legs wide, the water stream hit both of them—it was a strange feeling to have his balls caught in the stream of water, but nice.

For Em it was obviously more than nice. She started to squirm on his lap, milking him as her excitement rose. He found by using his hand to intercept the flow he could slow her down and then slip his fingers away to put her back in the jet's stream.

She turned her head and kissed him wetly while he felt her excitement build, felt his own keep pace, until there was no stopping the explosion that rocked them.

Afterward, she turned her body all the way around so they were pressed chest to chest in the warm bubbling water, and kissing as though they'd soon be torn apart forever.

They didn't talk much as they used their shirts to dry themselves off and then dragged on their clothes over still damp skin. Once she'd drained the tub and turned the water off again, they headed out, by tacit agreement not bothering with the rest of the tour. Joe had seen what she needed him to see.

This was a place founded on the principals of love and connection. To change its focus to cat poo just wouldn't be right.

When they got back to the foyer, Joe kissed her, sweet and tender, and she realized she was in trouble when she clung to him, not wanting to break the kiss, not ever.

"Will you do something for me, Emmylou?"

She almost replied, *Anything*, but stopped herself in time. "What?"

"Will you let me address the community and at least tell them about the positive aspects of this proposed development?"

Oh, lord. She'd been thinking he might ask her to have dinner with him tonight, go back with him to New York, marry him, even, and he wanted to address a town meeting. No wonder she kept her ideas about sex and love separate. She was good at one and clueless about the other.

Okay, she readjusted her thoughts with an effort. His request was fair and logical. The people of Beaverton deserved a chance to hear his proposal from an unbiased source. However, Joe was a business type and he'd expect some negotiation, so she couldn't just say yes, even though she knew it was a great idea, not least because she knew what Joe didn't, that no one in this town wanted a factory. They weren't interested in money and big profits and union wage jobs; they were interested in their eccentric livelihoods and this tiny paradise where anyone could do whatever they liked with their time so long as they didn't hurt anyone.

If Joe addressed them on the benefits of his mining and factory plan, the people of this town were going to address him right back, and he might learn that there were probably other communities where his program would be a lot more welcome than this one.

She made him wait, as though she were contemplating his request, while she locked up. When they were outside on the grounds, she put her head to one side and screwed up her face as though she really, really hated this idea. Then she said, after a suitable pause for reflection, "I'll tell you what. If I agree to set up this meeting for you, then you have to promise to stay in town for the rest of the week and go and see Gordon Hartnett at the end of it."

Joe looked at her and raised his eyebrows, but a smile lurked in his pewter blue eyes. "Still trying to save my life?"

"More than ever."

"So, if I stay for another week, you'll let me speak to some kind of town meeting."

"I'll even organize the meeting."

He nodded and held out his hand. "Agreed."

She put out hers to shake, and he pulled her so she tumbled off balance and into his arms, where he kissed her with all the passion she craved. In truth, she was much more pleased than she should have been to confirm that he'd be around for the better part of another week.

"Maybe now the mechanic will find time to fix my car."

"What are—"

"And I'd like to book a flight to check out the local terrain, but maybe you can let the pilot know he doesn't have to crash the plane or lose his way or something else to ensure I don't leave town."

Her mouth felt suddenly dry and her tongue as rubbery as a three-day-old tuna. "Exactly what . . . ?"

"Honey, I am on to you. It was too much of a coincidence that my car didn't work the same morning that you, who only cook prunes and toast most mornings, had French toast on the go."

Darn. She never should have tried to appease him with the French toast. What a fool.

"Then, suddenly, there are all these reasons why I should stay."

"Well!" She manufactured as much indignation as she could under the circumstances. "I hope you don't think I put you in the hospital!" And Lord, did she ever hope no one else in her household had, either.

"No. I think you were right about me. My body was getting ready to rebel. I'm glad my stomach blew out before my heart."

"Really?" This was the best news she'd had in ages. "You recognize that I was right about you?"

"Yes. In a lot of ways I think you may have saved my life."

Her smile bloomed bigger than the American Beauty that had opened to full flower this morning.

He held up his index finger. "But like I said, I'm on to you. I'll stay until this thing is resolved, so no more pranks. And do you think I could get my car fixed?"

She bit her lip. "I'm not admitting anything."

"I'm not asking you to."

"But I'll talk to the mechanic and see if he can get that car part in a bit sooner."

"I would really appreciate that."

He slung an arm around her and they walked back out into the sunshine.

"Hey, Joe?"

"Mmm-hmmm?"

"You're smarter than you look."

"So if I'm going to be here another week, can we negotiate the return of my cell phone and laptop?"

"Of course we can."

"Great."

"You're not getting them back. There, we negotiated."

"Palm pilot?"

She shook her head.

She expected outrage or wheedling, or maybe a few tears and tantrums, but Joe was silent. She glanced over at him. "Did you die from shock?"

"No. But I know when I'm beaten. I don't have the combination to your safe."

"Well, that's a little wimpy. Aren't you going to try and torture the information out of me or something?"

" 'Or something' sounds good, but I'm probably just going to let it go."

"Really?"

"Emmylou, it kills me to tell you this, but you were right. I feel like an addict going cold turkey. I feel twitchy when I wake up and can't check voice and e-mail. If there's a second in my day I'm not busy, I'm reaching for the laptop."

She nodded. No surprise there, except the surprising fact that he'd noticed his own addiction. "So the Shady Lady is like the Betty Ford for techno junkies?" She hooked her arm through his. "I like that. What are you finding in those moments when you reach for your fix and it's not there?"

"Silence." They walked on for a minute. "In my life there's no silence. It's all noise and action, deals and more deals and . . . well, you saw that before I did."

"And what do you hear in that silence?"

"I don't know yet." He blew out a breath. "My life's all out of balance, I see that. I've got enough money to last at least a lifetime, but I'm too young to retire. I need to do something with my life. Maybe I just want to run one of the companies I buy and sell for people. Maybe I want to be in a business that offers a real service or provides a useful product." He shrugged, and she felt his discomfort. She doubted he was used to sharing intimate thoughts. "I just want to feel that at the end of it all, when they put me in my casket, I'll leave something useful behind me."

She put her head against his shoulder.

"You think I'm crazy?"

"No. I think a few days without your electronic world has been very good for you. You're starting to sound sane."

He kicked a pebble and it skittered across the scrubby lawn. "Yeah. A month of this and I'll be Buddha."

She chuckled. "Don't knock it. I think you're going to end up a much happier and more interesting man than you would have if you'd stayed on the same course."

"I opened my eyes, Em. And I listened when someone very smart told me the truth." He turned and looked deep into her eyes, so she felt everything waver and start to melt. "You should try it sometime."

"But not today," she managed.

He held her a moment longer, still looking at her, seeing deeper than she imagined anyone ever had. He nodded slowly. "But not today."

She wasn't a fool, though. She'd seen Joe's fierce focus on whatever project he undertook. She had an awful feeling that she was his newest project. If she was smart, she'd give him back his toys so he'd leave her alone.

"Hey," he said, "come up in the plane with me tomorrow."

"I already promised you there won't be any mysterious accidents. You'll be perfectly safe."

"I know. I want your company. You took all my toys away, the least you can do is come play with me."

"I have things to do, you know. A life to live."

"Come on. It will be fun. You can be my tour guide and

offer the bird's-eye view on why mining in this area is a bad idea."

"I can't believe you're joking about this."

"Look. I take what I do seriously. I think what we're proposing will be a boon to Beaverton. I'm open to an opposing viewpoint. That's serious, but we don't have to wear black suits and pontificate to each other."

"All right, then. But you should know I'm not an agree-to-disagree type, not when something I care about deeply is at stake."

"Fair enough. So will you come with me tomorrow?"

"I am perfectly aware that you are manipulating me into saying yes," she said loftily.

"So will you?"

"Yes."

"Great. You know, since I'm being so good about letting you keep my stuff locked up, you should act as my tour guide for the area."

"That is a fantastic idea." Things were working out better than she'd hoped. If she showed him all over Beaverton and the surrounding countryside, he was going to fall in love with this place for sure. Then he couldn't possibly let a cat litter company come in and ruin it.

Could he?

Chapter 23

Joe heard banging. This was such a quiet area of the world, he was instantly awake. Oh, the banging was on his door.

"Come in," he said in a less than cheery tone. There'd been enough banging in the night that someone besides him should have been dead tired today. The trouble was that Emmylou had fallen asleep by his side and he'd watched her rather than wake her.

He'd watched a lot of women sleep, for one reason and another, but he'd never seen anyone who made it look as good as Emmylou did. Her hair was a silky gold pillow, her cheeks looked as soft as a child's, and her lashes were those long, curly, amazing ones that made spiky crescent shadows against her skin. She never snored, only breathed soft and deep between lips that were sexy even in sleep.

She held on to him while she slept. He knew it was done unconsciously, because it wasn't until after she was asleep that he felt her hand curl around his arm, or her body tuck itself into the contours of his.

He read more about the fascinating history of Romania, he thought about what he was going to do when this job was finished and he had no reason to stay on in Beaverton. And he watched the hours tick by. Finally, around three, Mae West had come in from hunting or whatever she did outside all night and leapt right onto Em before he could catch her.

That was one jealous cat.

Em woke with a start, and glanced at Mae West and then at him, consternation flooding her face. "Oh, Joe. You should have woken me. I'm sorry."

"Don't be," he assured her. "I like having you here."

She cupped his cheek with her palm. "But you need your sleep." And with a sleepy yawn, she'd crawled naked out of bed, found her clothes, and stuffed them under her arm.

He cursed himself and whatever demons he harbored that made it impossible for him to sleep with Em. Really, really sleep with her.

"Night," she said, glancing back at him sadly from the doorway.

"Night," he said, hoping he wasn't telegraphing to her how howlingly lonely he felt watching her leave his bedroom.

Even after that he hadn't slept for a long time.

Now that he'd finally managed to get to REM, he didn't appreciate the wake-up call. He squinted at the clock as Emmylou came in bearing a cup of revolting raspberry tea.

"It's eight in the morning," he groused. "Why do I have to get up?"

She walked up to him and kissed him right on his scowling mouth. "Because it's a beautiful day and I'm taking us for a picnic."

"Nobody has a picnic at eight in the morning."

"We have to ride a fair way."

"Ride?" He sipped the tea, wondering when his doctor and the vigilante innkeeper would let him have coffee.

"On a horse."

Reluctant excitement ignited in the part of him where his inner child apparently still lived. But naturally he didn't let on.

"I hope you aren't referring to those broken-down soon-to-be glue sticks when you say horse."

"Oh, please. Those are lovely horses, gentle and safe."

He snorted. "I'm not worrying one will bolt. It will take them all day to get us across the field."

She kissed him again, and since she was already leaning over him, it was easy work to topple her on top of him where the kissing quickly turned hot and heavy. Their week was already half over and it was as though they both realized if they didn't make use of every minute together, they'd always regret the missed ones. He might never be able to get enough of this woman.

"Why don't we have a picnic right here in bed?" he suggested.

"Because I have something else to show you."

He groaned. Emmylou was a one-woman Chamber of Commerce, tourism center, and welcome wagon. She'd flown with him—in a perfectly nice little Cessna—and he had agreed that the scenery was amazing. Well, that hadn't been difficult; it was amazing. In an hour's flying time, he'd seen green, fertile fields of crops, herds of grazing animals, wooded areas, then mountains, lakes, and streams. But he'd also seen a less than affluent-looking trailer park, and a couple of small communities that were more down at heel than Beaverton. Commerce, he pointed out to Em, wasn't all bad.

She'd naturally rebutted with more of her "save the land" spiel, and since then she'd been at him constantly. He'd met pretty much everybody in town now, toured every single business, and heard from more nosy neighbors than he cared to count that they did not want a mine in their backyard, no sir.

To everyone, he'd been polite and attentive and hadn't bothered to argue, except to ask them to keep an open mind until the town meeting took place in three days.

Somehow, he was going to have to figure out how to bring them all around to the merits of the cat litter factory, but he hadn't figured out his strategy yet. He wasn't worried; he always performed well under pressure. And he'd recognized a couple of souls who gave lip service to Emmylou and her "save the town" campaign, but whose eyes lit up when he mentioned economic prosperity.

Luckily for him and his company, everyone wasn't above the lure of profit.

Right now the lure of sex was heavily on his mind, and he was still trying to wrestle her into submission—and definitely winning—when the phone rang out in the hall. She disentangled herself and went to answer it, and he decided to be a good sport and go with her on the picnic. If he knew Em, there'd be a secluded spot where more than the contents of the picnic basket would get eaten.

He stirred at the thought. If there was one thing he had to say about Em, she was not a bashful woman. In all his life, he'd never met a woman who approached sex with such open-minded gusto.

"Hi, Gordon," she said far too chirpily. She'd left the door of his bedroom wide open in her race to get to the phone, so it was easy to hear her conversation. He put together her open-minded gusto about sex with Dr. Gordon Harnett and he didn't like the conclusion he drew.

There was something intimate in her tone when she talked to the good doctor. And he, at somewhere around Joe's own age, was an outsider with no more inherent nuttiness than an insane desire to live in this crazy town. Otherwise, he seemed like a pretty good-looking guy, and he was obviously athletic. He looked like the kind of doctor you'd find on TV in a white coat, a concerned expression on his face as he held a young, frantic woman's hand.

Okay, so Joe didn't live here and Emmylou had a right to her private life, but still, did she have to be so damned chirpy with the guy? Right outside his door?

He didn't even bother to lie to himself about his reasons for eavesdropping on a private conversation. He just sat very still and strained his ears, not that a lot of strain was required. His new lover didn't bother lowering her voice when she spoke to another man.

There was sex between those two. He could feel it.

Then her voice suddenly changed and grew anxious. "Oh,

you got the test results back already. Find anything interesting?"

Test results? What test results? Suddenly a cold fist seemed to squeeze Joe's throat. Was Emmylou sick? Suddenly the television ER vision of Dr. Hartnett holding a frantic woman's hand wasn't so ridiculous. The hand he was holding was Em's.

"I don't know whether he used the hot springs water or well water. I'll ask Olive and Lydia, maybe one of them will know."

Joe scratched his head. This conversation made no sense at all. If she were sick, she'd hardly be discussing hot springs versus regular water. Maybe it was something to do with one of the aunts.

"What else was in it?" she asked.

After a pause, she continued, "And you're absolutely sure there was nothing that could have been dangerous"—her voice lowered, but not enough—"or caused stomach upset?"

Finally she said, "Thanks, Gord. That's a big relief. No, I won't forget. I'll ask them. Yes. You, too. You're coming to the town meeting, aren't you? Okay. See you there."

Emmylou didn't return to his bed for more early-morning rolling around, he noted sourly, but made to walk right past his open door.

"Hey," he called.

She popped her head in the door looking rather pink about the face and definitely guilty.

Even as he told himself to stick a sock in it and not make an ass of himself, he said, "Are you sleeping with Gordon Hartnett?"

She looked at him for a steady second or two. "Not anymore," she said finally.

Then he was right. He knew it. Throwing the bedclothes aside, he rolled out of bed naked and stalked across the room to face her. "But you have slept with him."

She didn't appear defiant or embarrassed or guilty or anything. "Yes."

This was none of his business, so why was he feeling so irate? "When did it end?" he demanded, feeling like a demented stalker rather than a rational man who lived a very modern lifestyle.

She crossed her arms over her chest in a defensive move he'd never seen her display before. "When he fell in love with someone else and got married."

"Oh." His anger was gone as suddenly as it had appeared and he felt only compassion. "I'm sorry, honey. But he wouldn't have been right for you."

He advanced on her, ready to pull her into his arms, but she pushed her arms out in front to forestall his advance. "Gord and I had a very convenient affair. That's all it ever was or could be. He found the woman he wanted to spend his life with, so of course we ended things. It was as simple as that. It was just sex. Just like—"

"Don't say it!" he snapped, cutting her off. "Don't you dare try and tell me that what's going on between us is 'just sex.' "

"What is it then?" she asked softly before turning and walking down the hall.

"Em," he said, following her.

Lydia emerged at that moment from another room with a basket of folded towels, and glanced at him, standing there naked. "Yep, just like I figured. Nice package."

Bare-assed, mortified, and feeling an atavistic urge to go plow Dr. Hartnett's nose down his throat, Joe retreated smartly into his room and showed everyone in this house of oversexed loonies how mature he was by slamming his door.

He showered and dressed with his usual efficiency, then made a call of his own. When he got downstairs, Emmylou was in the kitchen. A batch of fresh muffins and fruit sat on the table.

"I wasn't sure whether you'd want your breakfast here or in the dining room," she said to him in the cool, professional tone she used when she greeted first-time guests.

"Neither, thanks," he said, grabbing a muffin and an apple. "I'll take it with me."

"Are you going out? What about our picnic?"

"Maybe later, if there's time. I'm seeing Dr. Hartnett this morning."

Her eyes widened. "But your appointment's not until tomorrow morning."

"I called and they were able to squeeze me in this morning."

Two spots of color flared on her cheekbones. "Any particular reason you changed your appointment?"

"Yes. I'll see you later."

He was striding out the door in seconds. What the hell was the matter with him, acting this way? He wasn't some tenth-century barbarian, but he felt like one. He must have some evolutionary memory buried in his bones or something, for he felt an almost overwhelming urge for violence, even if it was only verbal. There was a term he'd come across in an article about Vikings one time. Blood lust. That's what he had. A strong and powerful case of blood lust.

"Joe, I think we should talk about this," Em said behind him, but he didn't want to talk. Not to her.

His car had as mysteriously started to work fine as it had mysteriously stopped working less than a week earlier. He'd offered a brief word of thanks to the local mechanic when he'd been informed of this miracle.

The man had made no mention of a repair bill.

Now the car jumped to life at the turn of his key and he pulled out of the parking area in front of the Shady Lady, doing his best to ignore the lady standing in the middle of her garden staring at him with concern written all over her too-pretty-for-her-own-good face.

The drive to Hartnett's office wasn't far—nothing was in Beaverton—and unlike every other doctor's waiting room he'd ever been in, this one had no lineup.

"The doctor will be with you in just a moment," said the

kindly-looking, middle-aged receptionist, in the same tone she'd have used if she was manning the Pearly Gates.

Joe scowled and sat. One thing this waiting room had in common with others was the lack of reading material. A well-thumbed issue of *Reader's Digest* from the early nineties shared table space with a golf magazine published later the same decade.

Normally, Joe wouldn't have cared, but without his cell phone, laptop, or Palm Pilot, he was screwed.

He was halfway through a mildly interesting article called "I Am Joe's Liver," when the doctor's faithful handmaiden told him rapturously that he might go in now. As she ushered him into one examining room, a pretty, obviously pregnant woman emerged from the other.

Dr. Hartnett walked out of another door, his office maybe, nodded to Joe, and kissed the pregnant woman. On the lips.

At a gentle push from the doctor's receptionist, Joe went into the examining room. Hartnett came in a few seconds later. "Well, Joe," he said with a friendly smile. "I'm glad you decided to stay. How's it going?"

Joe glared at him. "Do you fuck all your female patients?"

The smile disappeared from Hartnett's face and he leaned back against the doorjamb and crossed his arms. "That woman is my wife."

God, didn't that sound like the punchline to some stupid old joke.

"And Emmylou?" His posture must have mirrored the doctor's, he realized. He'd crossed his own arms and was leaning against the windowsill of the only window in the small room.

"Ah, so that's what this is about," the doctor said, loosening his stance and glancing around the room. There was a tiny counter with doctor paraphernalia, an examining table with fresh paper laid over it, and one chair.

Joe didn't say anything, just glared.

"Did Emmylou tell you about us?"

"I asked her after I heard the two of you on the phone this morning."

"I see. And you're upset that she and I used to be . . . close?"

"I'm upset that you goddam hurt her."

Hartnett glanced up sharply, a crease marring his noble brow. "She told you I hurt her?"

"No. She said you two ended things when you met your wife. But I'm not stupid. I've been with a lot of women. I know when one's been hurt."

"And what symptoms is Emmylou showing?"

Joe found himself leaning onto the newly papered examining table, so the stiff paper crackled. "She's cool about sex. Casual. Her attitude is more like a guy's."

Hartnett nodded. "And you think I made her like that?"

"Didn't you?"

"No. Emmylou is who she is. She and I—well, I'm not proud of it. It was convenient for both of us. Frankly, I thought I was too busy as a doctor and research scientist to ever go the love and family route." He smiled slightly, more as though he couldn't help himself than that he actually wanted to smile. "Then I met Terri."

There was silence for a moment. Joe hadn't nearly finished, but he wasn't entirely sure what he wanted to say next.

Hartnett spoke next. "So I take it you and Emmylou . . . ?"

"Yes."

"I can see that it might have been disconcerting for you to discover that she and I—"

"Disconcerting, my ass. I wanted to knock your teeth down your throat."

Hartnett, far from looking terrified at the prospect, seemed curious. "Why?"

"Because you . . . because I . . ."

"Love her?"

Joe felt as though he were the one who'd had his teeth

knocked down his throat. Love? Who'd said anything about love?

Love Emmylou? But if he loved Emmylou, that meant changing everything he'd ever believed about himself, and probably everything he'd planned for his future.

But then wasn't he questioning that already?

"You can take that know-it-all smirk off your face, doc. It could never work for Em and me."

"Why not?"

"Because I live in New York and she lives here."

"Mmm. I used to live in Boston. It's easier than you'd think to move here."

"Yeah, well, that isn't even the biggest problem." It wasn't, now he stopped to consider. "I'm here to put together a land deal so that one of my clients can build a factory."

"Yes, I know. I'm opposed, by the way."

"Why am I not surprised?"

"Oh, not for the reasons you probably think. I don't oppose progress, but I would oppose any activity that affects the groundwater in the area. The water has unique properties. It's extraordinary."

"Yeah, yeah. You mentioned that before, and how nobody gets sick here. Except me." And that reminded him of the other thing he wanted to know. "So what was that about on the phone with Em this morning? She said something about something causing someone stomach trouble. I got the feeling she was talking about me."

"I can't tell you what we were discussing. I'm sorry."

"But it was about me."

"Maybe you should ask Emmylou."

"Yes, I will."

"Going back to your conflict with Emmylou over the factory, I don't see that as insurmountable. If you love each other, you can respect each other's opinions about things you don't agree on. Maybe there's a way you can both be happy?"

"I don't see it," he grumbled.

"Give yourselves some credit. Two years ago I wouldn't have believed I could settle in a place like this and be happy for life, and I certainly didn't plan to get married anytime soon or start a family." He shook his head. "Now look at me."

"Yeah, well, I have another problem." He could not believe he was about to do this. "I can't sleep if there's a woman in the room. We make love, we're all done, and I lay there wide awake until she leaves, or I leave."

"Really?" Gord didn't appear shocked or even very surprised, merely interested.

"I don't know why I'm bothering to tell you this, you're not a shrink."

"No. And I take it you haven't seen one?"

"God, no. It's a quirk, not insanity."

"Right. Sure." He sat in the single chair, and Joe, barely realizing he was doing so, jumped up and sat on the scrinchy paper on top of the examining table. His feet dangled in space and there was nowhere to lean his back.

"I don't have formal psychiatric training, but I do have a psych major. From the little I know of you, I'd say you have control issues."

"Control? I always assumed it was some kind of sleep disorder."

"No, you didn't."

No, he hadn't.

"When you sleep, you are vulnerable. You've got no control over what's happening in your room. Whether you're drooling on your pillow or crying out for mommy in your sleep. Right?"

"I suppose."

"So for you being vulnerable with a woman is a pretty big deal, I'm guessing. A bigger deal than for most of us."

"What do you suggest?"

"You could try sleeping pills for a few nights so you get

used to sleeping with a woman, then your psyche might cut you some slack."

"No drugs. Any other ideas?"

"Yes. I think you should see someone. A therapist, when you get home. If you're trying to solve this yourself, all I can suggest is that you start figuring out what terrifies you so much about being vulnerable."

"Do you think a person can be very relaxed about sex but terrified of love?"

"Yes." He said it the way a less professional doctor might have said, *Duh*. "To paraphrase the old comedian, sex is easy. Love is hard."

Joe hauled himself off the examining table. "Thanks for seeing me."

"No problem." The doctor rose and came closer. "While you're here, how's your stomach?"

"Oh, it's great. No more pain."

"Good. You can take those antacids I prescribed if you're planning on eating a heavy meal, otherwise eat sensibly, go easy on the booze and spicy food, and you'll be fine."

"Can I have coffee?"

"If you must."

"I've been drinking raspberry tea for a week. Believe me, I must."

Hartnett finished his exam, made some notes in Joe's file, and they shook hands. "Come back if you get any more symptoms or have questions."

"I will. Sorry if I was out of line earlier."

"Don't worry about it. Love makes people crazy."

When he emerged into the waiting room, Emmylou was sitting, flipping through the same *Reader's Digest* he'd perused earlier. He felt a kick of delight at the sight of her. "Hi, what are you doing here?"

"I thought I might have to break up a fistfight," she said, looking worried. "Is Gord all right?"

"Just the fact that you appreciate I could kick his ass if I

wanted to makes this a great day. He's fine. I met his wife."
Sort of.

"You know you're psychotic, don't you?"

"Only around you," he assured her, a little afraid that that
had turned out to be true this morning. God, what an idiot.

And how much more, how ten thousand times more of an
idiot had he been not to recognize his own feelings? Maybe
he wasn't in love with Em yet, but he was awfully damn close.

Too close to call.

"Are you okay?" she asked.

"I'm ready for a picnic."

"How's your stomach?"

"I am allowed to have coffee again."

"Oh, happy day," she said, and took his hand.

Chapter 24

They rode through fields of wildflowers and past farms where cows stared at them from big, vacant brown eyes before going back to grazing. The wind was fresh, and when it dropped, the still air was warm on his back. The horses plodded contentedly along, trotted when urged—trying to go any faster would have been cruel—and seemed to be enjoying the day as much as the riders.

Naturally, Emmylou had chosen their route carefully to showcase the organic, unspoiled beauty of the area. And because she was smart, she kept her mouth shut and never once mentioned that the area was bound to lose some of its charm when it was torn up to make cat litter.

She felt the land itself rebuked Joe every step of the way.

After about an hour's ride, they came to a wooded area that ran beside a slow-flowing river. "I thought we'd have our picnic here and let the horses have a drink and a rest," she said over her shoulder, then dismounted from Lucky.

"Well done, my trusty steed," Joe said as he patted the flanks of his black horse, Bruiser. The horse looked down at him and then snorted as though he did not appreciate the sarcasm.

Emmylou took off the saddlebag, looped her reins around the pommel, and then let Lucky head for the river for a drink. Watching her, Joe said, "Shouldn't we tie them up?"

"Where do you think they're going to go?"

"Right," he said, patting the big black gelding once more. "I guess their race is already run. They can nap while we eat lunch."

Bruiser clopped his way to the river and he and Lucky stood side by side drinking. From Lucky's saddlebag, Emmylou retrieved the blanket she'd put in there along with the sandwiches, lemonade, fruit, and cookies.

As she laid out the blanket on a grassy patch near the river, shaded from any chance visitors along the path by a thatch of trees, she caught Joe's eyes on her and knew he'd clued in to exactly what was on her mind.

Not a word was spoken, but she saw the way his gaze grew more intense, dropping knowingly to her chest. Her nipples tingled and the sensation spread. Some wayward tendrils of hair blew into her face and she felt each silky strand against her skin.

Very deliberately, she reached out and smoothed the blanket against the springy grass, as though she were smoothing sheets onto a bed. It was made of polar fleece in a dark green pattern with cranberry and mustard colored designs on it. The fabric felt soft against her fingertips.

She glanced up. He hadn't moved, but lounged against a tree as though perfectly content to stay there for a while.

"Don't you want your picnic?" she asked, surprised at how husky her voice sounded. He hadn't even touched her, but she felt warm all over.

His voice, that clipped, no-wasted-words voice spoke at last. "Yes. I want my picnic."

"Then come over here."

He didn't move. "I want you naked first."

The spark that crackled between them should have caused a forest fire.

"Naked," she repeated in a strangled tone.

"That's right. Bare-assed naked."

He ought to smoke; a cigarette would have been the perfect prop for him standing there like a gambler sizing up the property he'd just won. Like he ought to take a long drag, so the tip of the cigarette would glow deep red before he blew out a lazy stream of smoke that would obscure the eyes gazing at her with such intensity.

She swallowed. She wasn't used to playing games where sex was concerned. She felt out of her element, and suddenly vulnerable. Excited. "You want me to strip?"

"That would be the quickest way to get naked."

"Where . . . where do you want me to start?"

He pondered that for a moment, then said, "Shoes and socks."

Sensible. She eased off her boots. They weren't real riding boots, but the horses didn't seem to care. Joe's gaze on her was so intent that even revealing her feet to him felt shockingly erotic. When she pulled off her socks, the air caressed her overheated toes and she wriggled them in the grass.

She settled herself in the middle of the blanket, staring up and across at Joe, who still lounged, his back against a sturdy tree trunk about six feet away. "Now what?"

She was wearing an old Levi's denim shirt that snapped up the front, but since she'd had sex on her mind ever since she dreamed up this picnic, she wore a lacy periwinkle blue bra and a scrap of matching periwinkle lace that passed as panties.

He debated for a moment. "Shirt."

The snap of the first fastening was startlingly loud in her ears. She felt Joe's attention, every atom of his being focused on watching her bare herself. She slid her fingers slowly, slowly to the second snap, and the third when she eased the shirt open enough that he could glimpse her periwinkle-supported cleavage.

A sound came from his general direction; it could have been a soft curse, or merely a groan of barely contained lust. Her breathing quickened as she felt him watching her, felt the air cool on her hot skin, watched her breasts rise and fall. She was so sensitive that the denim sliding against the silky bra cup made her nipples tingle.

Another snap, and another. Her belly was bared, and finally she flicked open the last fastening. The shirt fell away from her as she sat straighter and, with her gaze holding Joe's, snapped the fastenings at her wrists. She rolled her shoulders and let the fabric slide.

Leaves shushed above her in the canopy of trees, the river gurgled, and somewhere a bird called.

The lace and elastic and underwire felt like a prison for her breasts suddenly, so she reached behind her and undid the hooks, then slipped the straps over her arms, holding the cups coyly in place until she was done.

Joe might have looked casual lounging against his tree, but she felt the strain he imposed on himself to remain still and watch.

She tossed the bra to the blanket and let her breasts spill free.

He stared at her breasts as though he'd never seen them before, then his gaze moved down, clearly waiting for her to shuck her jeans. Instead, she leaned back on her arms and lifted her face to the breeze. A shaft of sunlight filtered through the canopy of leaves and she shifted until she felt the warmth on her face. She moved her legs so her feet were shoulder-width apart and flat on the blanket, her knees raised. The air brushed her unfettered breasts and she felt the points stiffen.

"You're killing me," Joe said softly.

"I know."

She raised her hands over her head and stretched, lengthening the muscles in her back and breathing in deep so her breasts hiked, then, feeling his restraint close to breaking, she unbuttoned the fly of her jeans. She wriggled out of them and slid them off, then resumed her position so she reclined in nothing but a bit of periwinkle lace and a whole lot of heat.

She gazed at him. She was trembling and she heard her own breathing.

"I said naked," he reminded her softly.

It was all she could do not to moan. She lay flat on her back, knees raised, and eased the panties down her legs, making sure to give him the maximum view as she did so.

When she tossed the foolish scrap of lace behind her, she felt enervated, curiously exhausted, and yet pulsingly alive as she lay back and waited.

She gazed up at the shifting patterns of the greenery above her, and beyond that a scraping of cloud against the blue bowl of sky.

She didn't hear him approach over the noises of nature and her own heart, so she jumped, startled, when she felt his hands on her thighs, pushing them apart.

A quick panting breath in and out. He pushed her wider still so she felt open to the sky and the trees and the water rushing by, so all her needy self was open. His hair brushed the soft skin of her inner thigh as he shifted her hips. She was boneless, compliant, and then she felt the warmth of sunlight between her legs and realized he'd exposed her even more completely.

She felt his eyes on her; he was so close, his breath stirred her curls and wafted over her hot, wet, intimate flesh.

Her hands fisted, and she found she was grabbing the soft blanket, open and needy and waiting, and then suddenly he was there, his mouth there, his tongue inside her, all the way inside her with no teasing first, no preparation, and the shock of it, and the amazing way he made her feel, had her crying out. Not all the way, not yet, but oh, she was so close. As though he knew, he stayed clear of her hot button, licking his way around the opening to her body, nibbling lightly, and then when she was so desperate her hips were dancing with him, trying to lead, and he was teasing her, giving her almost but not quite what she wanted, he suddenly grabbed her hips and put his mouth right exactly where she wanted it. He sucked her lightly, the way he'd learned she liked it, and his tongue danced over her clit with perfect rhythm and pressure.

Her climax started deep and she rode it, letting it build until everything, every part of her, every nerve ending, every emotion, all of it concentrated in that one central spot, and then exploded.

Her legs were wrapped around his neck and she was thrusting against his mouth; he was loving her, taking her impossibly high, and even as she cried out, "Yes," somewhere in her a voice panicked and cried, *No!*

Even when the climax subsided, she felt empty, achingly empty, and without a word he grabbed a condom, unzipped his jeans and yanked them down, then crawled on top of her and plunged inside.

He was kissing her, thrusting inside her, loving her; she tasted her own passion, felt the gorgeous hardness of his ready-to-burst arousal, and sensed that the pounding of his heart matched the rhythm of her own.

The buttons of his shirt scratched her but she still pressed him closer. She felt the waistband of his jeans and the swinging belt when she wrapped her legs around him; she grabbed his naked butt with one hand, reached for his balls with the other, wanting all of him.

His breathing was loud in her ear, or maybe that was hers. Impossible to tell where one of them left off and the other began.

He stroked hard and deep until the empty, needy places in her filled to overflowing and she cried out again, clenching him to her everywhere.

His body stiffened and the world seemed to stop for a second, then he spilled into her.

She closed her eyes against a rush of tenderness so intense it frightened her. "Joe, I . . ." She opened her eyes, feeling like she needed to be open everywhere so she could say the words that burned in her throat like tears.

But when she opened her eyes, she started to laugh.

Joe pulled his head off her shoulder long enough to stare

down at her in some indignation. "What is so damned funny?"

She couldn't even speak, she could only point. He turned, and staring back at him were the two horses, their brown eyes big and unblinking. Lucky was chewing and had a hunk of green grass hanging out of her mouth, but Bruiser just stared, obviously wondering what all the noise was.

He turned back and the laughter died. They looked into each other's eyes and she saw more than she was ready to face.

Just as she shifted her gaze, he said, "Em, I—"

"I know, you're starving," she said overbrightly. "Roll your fine self off me and I'll feed you."

For a second she thought he was going to resist, then he let it go and rolled off her. She put her clothes back on while he straightened himself up and led the horses back to the riverside.

Joe loved her, and he'd been going to tell her; she knew it as well as she knew that she loved him.

But what was the point torturing themselves and increasing each other's inevitable pain?

She slapped the wrapped sandwiches onto the blanket. The man couldn't even sleep in the same room as her, he lived in New York, and he wanted to destroy the very life she loved.

She hadn't even seen it coming. One minute he was this major sexy but hopeless workaholic, and now he was the only man she'd ever loved.

They ate, but there was so much they couldn't talk about: the future of Beaverton, her future, his future, the fact that they loved each other and it was hopeless. It wasn't like there was a single huge pink elephant in the middle of the picnic blanket that they were both trying to avoid mentioning, but a herd of the bloody things. All trumpeting and stamping around.

Somehow they got through lunch, but all she could think was that this was probably the one and only picnic they'd ever enjoy together.

She didn't even know when he was going back to New York. He'd had the all-clear from Gord, but he hadn't said anything about leaving. Obviously he'd stay for the town meeting, then what? She wondered, as they folded the picnic blanket, when they were going to make love and she'd know that it was the last time.

She ached at the thought.

"Are you okay?" Joe asked suddenly, grabbing her shoulders while she hugged the folded blanket against her chest.

No, she wanted to wail. *I'm so far from okay I'll need a road map and a guide to find my way back there.*

"Yes, of course." She turned to pack their things back in the saddlebag, then she mounted Lucky.

Joe talked softly to the large gelding he was about to mount, and Emmylou wondered if he were apologizing that he was about to climb on the old horse's back. Or maybe he was going to ask its permission first. She tried to stop herself from going weak at the knees but still her kneecaps turned to jelly.

The way home seemed a lot quicker than the way out and she suspected they'd both urged their horses on.

When they'd returned to Amy's, Joe helped put the horses away, and Amy said, "Well?"

"I don't know. I've tried to make him see how special this place is, but honestly, I think we're in trouble."

"It's not Beaverton I'm worried about, it's you," her friend said. "I've known you a long time. With this guy, it's different."

"Maybe. But once he's back in Manhattan, and I'm out here . . ." Emmylou shrugged.

Amy looked as though she had more to say, then seemed

to change her mind. "Anytime you want to come and talk, the kettle's always on."

There wasn't time for more. Joe was back. When they were settled in his rental car, he said, "How about we drive to the next town and I buy you dinner somewhere decent?"

That's when she knew. "You're leaving, aren't you?"

"Day after tomorrow. I need to go to the town meeting tomorrow night, and then I've booked a flight out Friday."

She swallowed over the lump in her throat. Nodded. "I'll miss you."

"Em, I can't make any promises. I don't know how to work this out, but you have to know I—"

"Don't say it," she stopped him in a panic. "Please don't say it." She felt tears forming and she forced them back.

He touched her arm lightly. "Let's have dinner tonight. A swanky night out like lovers do."

She smiled at him, loving him so much and wishing things could be different. "I can't tonight. I've got guests checking in."

"Really? Who?"

"I don't know. A couple. Lydia took the booking yesterday when I was out."

"Well, their timing sucks. I want to take you for a night on the town."

"I'll have to take a rain check."

"Come to New York," he said suddenly.

"Pardon?"

"We'll have our night on the town in New York, one of the best night-on-the-town cities in the world."

"You want me to come to New York for one night?"

"No. Stay as long as you like."

"I can't."

"That's it? You can't? Look, I'll send you a ticket, pick you up at the airport, we'll—"

"We'll only make it harder on ourselves. It's best this way."

For a second he looked as though he were going to argue, then he simply pulled her into his arms and hugged her hard. "I am going to miss you like hell," he said.

She nodded. "Me, too."

Chapter 25

"Our new guests must be here," she said as they pulled into the Shady Lady's parking area and she noticed an unfamiliar rental car.

She'd prepared the Yellow Room earlier for them. It was the second nicest after the Blue Room. This one also had a queen-sized bed and a small balcony overlooking the garden, but there was no fireplace. She had hoped they'd arrive later in the afternoon. Olive and Lydia could check the new guests in—but they could be a bit of a surprise to the unwary.

She hurried up the path and discovered that everything was not running as smoothly as she might have hoped. She heard a male voice raised in anger and broke into a trot. What on earth could have gone wrong already?

Two men stood in the entrance foyer, and Olive was obviously trying to calm them down. Her cheeks flamed with the color of a woman on high blood pressure medication. Emmylou had no idea what was going on but she was already feeling angry and defensive. Olive was an old woman. How dare they upset her? One of the men turned and glared at her as she entered. He was a big, barrel-chested guy with a lot of curly black hair and a humorless mouth.

The other was skinny and balding.

"Oh, Emmylou, thank God you're here," Olive said. "There seems to be a problem with the booking."

"I see." She eased behind the counter and squeezed Olive's shoulder. "What seems to be the trouble?"

"We need two rooms. Preferably in a real hotel."

Oh, goodie.

She plastered a cool smile on her lips. The sooner she could get rid of them the better. They wanted a real hotel? Great. Let them drive an hour and find it.

"As you can see, the Shady Lady is a bed and breakfast. I'll give you a map to the closest real hotel. It's in the next town."

"How far is it?" the skinny guy asked her as though she might have personally moved the Hilton as far away from them as possible.

"It's about an hour's drive. You'll need to get back onto the highway and turn—"

"That's too far, Milt."

"Well, I'm not staying in this flophouse."

She slapped her pen down on the desk, not even caring that it spat ink onto the antique surface. She was about to let them have it and good when Joe walked in. Both men turned around and stared.

"Joe?"

"We heard you were in the hospital or something."

"I was. I'm out."

"You look healthy enough to return a damned phone call."

Joe shot a quick glance at Emmylou. "My phone's . . . missing."

Her mood had plummeted when she found out Joe was leaving Friday, and she wouldn't have thought it could go any lower, but apparently there was an emotional subbasement she hadn't even known she possessed. These guys had to be the cat litter people. And they didn't look like there was a hope they could be dissuaded from destroying the town. They looked like the kind of guys who got a kick out of razing paradise for their own profit.

The larger one spoke up. "We came to see the place for ourselves. You staying here?"

"Yes."

A grunt. "We'd better stay here, too."

"Really, I think you'll be more comfortable at the Hilton," she broke in.

"Obviously," the obnoxious larger man said, as though she were stupid to have pointed that out. "But we're staying here."

He turned back to Joe and his tone lightened a little. "Are you feeling well enough to have a meeting? We want to know what the hell you've been doing down here. What's the progress?"

Imperceptibly, she felt Joe changing back into the driven man she'd tried so hard to save. His eyes cooled to pewter, his jaw tightened. "Emmylou? Would it be all right if we borrowed your office for an hour or so?"

She wanted to say no. Hell, no. But what was the point? "Yes, of course."

"Hey, Joe?" the skinny one said.

"Yes?"

"You might want to get the leaves out of your hair before we meet. Both you and the lady."

She felt her annoyance mount. She smiled at the two men. "Please don't think rolling in the hay comes with your room rental. Joe is a special case."

There was a moment of stunned silence, then the big guy guffawed and slapped Joe on the back. "Let's see what else you've been doing down here."

"We'll meet in half an hour."

She signed the two men in and escorted them to their rooms—the yellow room was freshly cleaned and had fresh flowers—she gave the skinny one that she liked least the green room they usually saved for kids. It had twin beds and a doll's house in the corner.

Then she slipped into the parlor.

Her great-grandmother stared down at her with her usual expression, but Emmylou still felt her disapproval. Surely her great-grandmother would never have given up so easily. But Em knew she was beaten. With Joe she had a fighting chance, with the boor brothers, she didn't think so.

With the ease of practice she opened the safe and removed Joe's laptop, his cell phone, and his Palm pilot, then she took them to his room.

She heard the shower running in his bathroom, so she left the things on the bed and slipped out again.

She didn't see him again that day. She heard male voices coming from the office when she came down later, after spending a good hour on her books upstairs in her room. With so much to depress her today, the state of the Shady Lady's finances barely registered.

The men went out to dinner, where she had no idea, so she and Olive and Lydia spent a quiet evening eating food from the gastric diet menu. Their conversation was desultory. Even the house felt different, as though an occupying army were staying with them against their will.

"Did Dr. Hartnett give Joe a clean bill of health?" Olive asked after a few minutes of silence.

"Yes. Yes, he did."

"That's good."

"Oh, that reminds me, the doctor wanted to know if you remember whether Emmet Beaver used local water in his cordial?"

Olive screwed up her face trying to remember. "I think it was the water from the hot springs. He swore by that stuff. Do you remember, Lydia?"

"I remember what it did for a body, not what went into making the stuff." She sighed dreamily and gazed off into the distance, an irritating habit she had developed since she'd hooked up with her old flame.

"I know everything he used was found locally. I'll dig

through his old papers and see what I can find," said Olive. She'd become the unofficial guardian of Dr. Beaver's papers since no one else had ever shown the least interest in the job.

"Thanks, Olive."

"When's Joe leaving?"

"Friday."

Olive reached out and grabbed her hand. "I'm sorry, honey."

She nodded.

"You should go with him," Lydia said.

"I don't think so." She rose suddenly and excused herself. She loved the aunts, but right now she felt too raw to discuss the Joe scenario.

She felt too raw to do much of anything, so she washed dishes and cleaned her kitchen until it shone, and then took herself up to her bedroom. A long bath helped the stiffness in her legs from the riding, and the herbal scent she'd thrown into the hot water soothed her a little.

There had never been only Joe, she had to remember that. Always she'd known that he was merely the agent for a big company and that Beaverton and its odd collection of citizens might end up having to face corporate Goliath with a pretty feeble slingshot.

Even though Joe had never slept all night in her bed, she still missed him. She hugged a pillow against her belly and wished things could have turned out differently. Still, she was a practical woman and she knew that even the pain of her first experience with love would ease over time.

Keep busy, she reminded herself. And since she and her town were about to stage the fight of their lives, she didn't think keeping busy was going to be a problem.

She woke suddenly in the pitch black not certain what had woken her. She felt another presence in the room. Was it the cat?

The bed shifted, and it was too big a shift for the cat. Then she turned her head and smelled him. The soap and skin scent of Joe, a scent that had her reaching for him blindly. She pulled him against her and noticed he was fully clothed. He kissed her, then put his mouth close to her ear and whispered, "I've got an idea. I've convinced the Gellmans to come to the town meeting tomorrow night. I need you to take care of a few things beforehand."

"Do you think it will work?" she asked when he'd explained what he wanted her to do.

"Yes."

"But what you're planning is—"

"I know. Shut up."

Then he kissed her, so she decided that shutting up was a very good idea. She helped him undress in the dark, then stripped off her cotton nightgown.

They made love slowly, sweetly, and she marveled that the sex got better each time. More intense, more emotional. Love would do that, she supposed.

When he came, deep inside her body, she rose to meet him, clutching him to her. "I love you," he cried out.

"I love you, too," she finally admitted aloud. The words were a little shaky, but they were there. "And you were right about me. I'm scared to death." In her experience, men didn't stay. Joe would be no different except it would hurt more when he left.

"Don't be," he whispered in the dark. "We'll figure this out."

Because she didn't want him leaving her when they had so little time left, she said, "Let's make love all night."

By way of a reply, he took one of her nipples into his mouth.

Joe woke alone.

Even before his eyes opened, he was reaching for Emmylou, only to receive a *brrrrp* of annoyance when he hit not warm, naked woman but the furry back of Mae West.

"How did you get in here?" he asked the feline who was

sitting on Emmylou's bed regarding him through slitted green eyes. "And what did you do with my woman?"

Mae West was staring him as though he were being very stupid. Something was different, he knew, but what?

He stretched out and yawned, conscious that he'd had the best sleep he'd enjoyed in months, and then his jaw locked in the wide-open position as it hit him. He'd slept with Emmylou. Really, truly, literally *slept* in the bed of the woman he loved.

Joe had a second shock when he checked the clock on Em's bedside table. Eight thirty-five? No. Damn old place. Nothing worked efficiently, including the clocks. He picked up his Rolex. It was guaranteed accurate to the millisecond. It informed him, with Swiss precision, that the time was in fact eight thirty-five and twenty-three—no, twenty-four—seconds.

Blinking stupidly at the thing for another three and three-quarter seconds, he finally accepted that not only had he fallen asleep with a woman in his bed, but he'd slept much later than normal.

He looked around at the former madam's quarters and started to laugh. Old Emmet and his crazed ideas about this place were true. He'd been healed by the most talented Intimate Healer of them all.

Chapter 26

The bingo hall was more than usually stuffy. Every person in town seemed to be there, but probably about two hundred people in total packed the hall. Every chair and bench seat was taken, and the back of the hall and around the edges were packed.

Emmylou had done her best; the rest was up to Joe, the townspeople, the unpleasant men from the cat litter company, and most of all, fate.

There was a restive feeling something like she remembered before big concerts in her college days, when the anxious crowd of fans waited for the band to mount the stage.

Of course, most of the restlessness in this venue was caused by anxiety. There was a sudden hush from where she sat near the main entrance, and she watched the Gellman brothers enter, pause when they saw the size of the crowd, and then make for the stage. Joe came in behind them. He touched her shoulder in passing, giving it a reassuring squeeze, then followed to the stage.

Emmylou rested her hand on her shoulder where the imprint of his touch still lingered.

The microphone made an ear-piercing shriek as Joe pulled it to his mouth. "Good evening," he said. "Most of you have seen me around here the last couple of weeks. I'm Joe Montcrief. I'm here to tell you about an exciting project we're thinking about implementing in the immediate area of Beaverton. Something that will bring jobs and prosperity to this area. These gentlemen with me are Milton and Eric Gellman. They're going to tell you what they're planning and then we'll take questions. Now I'd like to introduce Mr. Eric Gellman."

He passed over the microphone and the thin brother rose and took his place. "Thank you, Joe," he said. "Now, we know this area is depressed and your incomes are paltry."

Oh, great. Start by insulting them, that was going to work. Sheesh. Around her she felt hackles rising. These were people who didn't take to patronizing well. As Joe knew.

Across the sea of heads she saw that Joe was looking in her direction, and she could have sworn he winked at her. She kept her gaze on him for another five minutes while the thin man rambled on about how bad the economy was in this area, then Joe nodded. It looked to anyone else as though he was agreeing with Gellman, but it was her signal. She pushed *Send* on his cell phone.

Beneath the table her foot started to tap. Was there any chance at all that his plan was going to work?

Another minute went by, the longest sixty seconds of her life, and then she heard a woman shrieking. Everyone in the vicinity of the main entrance turned their heads, and at the front Gellman paused in midsentence and then continued. "What we have in mind is job creation, a boost to your starving economy, a—"

He fell silent when the shriek turned to a scream and Geraldine Mullet burst into the bingo hall as though bayonets were at her back. She looked fabulous in one of Olive's old gowns, a heavy red velvet with a full skirt. Emmylou had no idea where they'd found the bonnet, but she was pretty sure she recognized part of her straw sun hat, which had been sacrificed to make a not bad imitation of something Vivien Leigh might have worn in *Gone with the Wind*.

The beeswax candle was certainly one of the good ones she kept for Christmas, and it looked very authentic in the brass-handled candleholder that had belonged to Emmet Beaver. The flame flickered alarmingly in Geraldine's trembling hand. She waited a moment until everyone had seen her, then rushed to the stage and put one hand to her heaving bosom.

"They're here!" she cried. "Those damned Yankees are here. They won't take Tara. I won't let them!"

Emmylou tore her eyes away to look at the thin Gellman brother who was gaping at Geraldine.

After a dramatic pause, Geraldine shouted, "I'll burn this place before I'll let them take it!"

She waved the candle around a bit and Olive yelled "Fire," and elbowed Harold Beasman sharply in the ribs. He'd been half dozing but at the magic word "fire," he rose. Olive handed him the red plastic fireman's hat that she'd put in her bag. He took it, shoved it on his balding head, and said in a remarkably commanding tone, "Don't worry about a thing, folks. Everything's under control."

"What is this insane old biddy doing?" the thin Gellman brother said, obviously forgetting he was still standing at the microphone. His words boomed out across the crowd. "Put that damned candle out," he ordered.

Everyone in town might agree that Geraldine was an insane old biddy, but they liked her and you didn't go around name-calling in Beaverton and get away with it.

Geraldine obviously didn't like it, either, because she reached into the pocket of her dress and pulled out a heavy-looking gun that had to be an authentic Civil War piece. It was big and wooden and bulky in her hand, but it looked awfully impressive as she waved it in Gellman's direction. "Stay away from me, you damned Union cur or I'll shoot you like the dog you are."

A lot of people rose, heading for the exits, standing on top of tables, and yelling theatrically. The other Gellman brother was on his feet now, and would have run for the exit if the steps leading to the stage weren't clogged with people who'd crowded closer for a better look.

There was no garden hose in the auditorium, and Harold Beasman soon realized this, glancing around in a puzzled way while Geraldine Mullet waved her blunderbuss and the candle with amazing dexterity.

Joe nudged the ersatz fireman and pointed to the big fire extinguisher on the wall. "Hang on, folks," Harold said, and ran for it, then came at Geraldine from behind, shooting a stream of white that hit her, the candle, both Gellmans, the podium, and a great deal of the floor.

Geraldine shrieked even louder and turned on him, but he was having the time of his life. The candle was snuffed, but he continued to spray everything in sight, including the crowd at the bottom of the steps. They backed up in a hurry, which left the thick Gellman room to bolt. He ran for the stairs, slipped in the fire-retardant foam, and, reaching for anything to stop his fall, grabbed the microphone stand. The thunk as it and Gellman hit the floor was magnified throughout the hall, along with a very ripe curse.

This was great stuff. Emmylou felt like applauding.

But the best was yet to come.

She heard the sound of hooves thundering outside and then Napoleon rode in on his black stallion. People backed away to clear a path, and he trotted forward a few paces then stopped, surveyed the melee, and pulled out a trumpet to blow a loud report.

"I will have order from my army," he shouted. Then he blew his trumpet again. The noise was deafening.

"General Lasalle, you will take your troops outside." He bowed graciously to Madame Dior, who rose nobly to the occasion and marched everyone who'd been sitting at her table out of the hall in orderly formation.

His strategy was simple but brilliant. Table by table, almost like at a big banquet when tables numbers were called,

Helmut Scholl aka Napoleon called on people he knew to lead their neighbors out of the hall. Emmylou was called on to exit behind Ernie, who was standing in for Marshall Ney.

Soon everyone stood outside the bingo hall looking at Napoleon. Including Emmylou. She'd never seen the man so commanding. Helmut really should have gone for a life in the military, she thought.

Geraldine Mullet stalked out of the place. Instead of the candlestick or the old-model gun, she held Harold Beasman's fireman hat in one hand and Harold's ear in the other, by which she was dragging him. "My dress is ruined," she cried. "You're nothing but a damned Yankee."

"Madame," Napoleon said. Geraldine Mullet looked up at him. "My Josephine." He smiled down at her and held out his hand. "Come, my empress. We will depart this place."

Geraldine dropped the hat and poor Harold's ear and tottered forward. "Oh yes, Rhett. Take me away from here."

Joe ran forward and knelt with his hands cupped so Geraldine could place her foot there, and then he hoisted her up to settle sideways in Napoleon's lap.

It was a mishmash of historical time periods and Hollywood endings, but as an exit it was superb. The black stallion tossed its head and Helmut circled Geraldine's waist with his arm.

With a brisk nod to the gaping crowd, he turned the horse and they cantered away.

"Did you plan that ending?" Joe asked Emmylou softly.

She sighed deeply, watching the horse disappear from view. "I couldn't have dreamed up anything so perfect," she said, hazarding a pretty shrewd guess that Geraldine Mullet was soon going to appear in Empire-waist dresses and hang on Napoleon's arm. In fact, she thought, they made a pretty cute couple.

"Why didn't you just tell us this town was full of kooks?" Milt Gellman said to Joe over a beer at Ernie's tavern. The place was packed, but they had a corner to themselves, and it was clear that as soon as they left the real celebration would begin. "We wasted a bunch of time and money on this site for nothing." He groaned. "Shit, I gotta get back and see my chiropractor. My lumbar is definitely out. I should sue those crackpots."

"They don't have any money," Joe reminded him.

"Right. And they're sure as shit not getting any of ours."

"So you definitely don't want to proceed on this?"

"What, are you hard of hearing? I never want to set foot in this place again. Bunch of weirdos." He groaned again and rubbed his lower back. "We're heading out tonight. I can't stand this place. We'll spend the night in Spokane and fly out tomorrow. You coming?"

"No. I've . . . got some things to wrap up."

"Yeah, well, when you get back to New York we'll start looking for another location for a plant. And not in a nut farm."

"You'll want to get on your way pretty soon," Joe said, thinking Ernie's would be rocking the minute they left.

The thin Gellman drove them back to the Shady Lady. "I'll go settle the bill." He left, and Milt looked at Joe and said, "Goddamn bed and breakfast. Doesn't even have a porter."

"Right. Let me carry your bags down to the car for you. Save your back."

He didn't even glance Emmylou's way as he passed her in the foyer, where she was chatting pleasantly to Eric Gellman while he signed his charge card slip.

Joe put the bags in the Gellmans' rental car and shook hands with them both before watching them drive away.

He walked slowly back to the Shady Lady. Emmylou walked around from behind the desk. "Well? Are they gone?"

He nodded.

"Are they ever coming back?"

He shook his head.

"Wa-hoo!" she cried. "We did it!"

She ran forward into his arms and he spun her around, then stopped to kiss her long and hard.

Holding that sweet, sweet body in his arms gave him some ideas on exactly how he wanted to celebrate the crash of a big deal. Not caring in the slightest that the aunts were looking on, he picked up his woman and showed her exactly how the Rhett and Scarlett climbing the stairs thing was done.

When he kicked her door shut behind them, he carried her to her bed and laid her gently down. "I fell asleep last night in your bed," he said, still hardly able to believe it.

"I know." She smiled up at him, her eyes telling him she knew exactly what that meant to him.

"You cured me."

"You saved Beaverton."

"I need to make love to you so badly I hurt."

For answer, she attacked his belt buckle, and when she had them both naked, she climbed on top of him and took them both for a ride.

While he thrust up into her, he knew he wasn't leaving. Not this woman. What he was going to do he hadn't figured out yet, but he knew he was going to be the man who proved to Emmylou that the right man stayed.

By the time they'd recovered their breath, cars were arriving and townspeople showing up at the door. Within the hour all the major players in the town meeting farce were assembled in Emmylou's parlor.

"Tea?" Emmylou asked the assembled company.

"Or scotch?" Joe asked, flourishing the Johnny Walker Black Label that the Gellman brothers had left behind unopened.

When the beverages of choice were dished out, Emmylou raised her scotch glass and said, "I'd like to make a toast. To all of us for saving our town."

"Those awful men did have a point, though," said Olive, "about the local economy not exactly thriving."

"But we're all getting by. We're all happy."

"Sure, but it's hard for the young people. They mostly leave. It sure would be nice to have something for them to do around here."

Dr. Hartnett nodded. "Olive's right. Plus, we may have driven off the cat litter factory, but the sanitarium still owes back taxes. That's a prime piece of property. Someday, somebody's going to buy it up."

"I've got some ideas about that," Joe said, as the obvious answer hit him like a lightning bolt.

"What now?" Lydia piped up. "A flea collar factory?" She and the old boy who'd played Tony in the town play were holding hands and mooning at each other. Her wrinkled beau laughed his head off at her joke.

Joe shook his head, but he smiled at her anyway. How could he resist? "I cannot believe I didn't see it sooner. It's perfect."

"What's perfect?" Emmylou asked. He heard the thread of hope in her voice and he hung on to it.

"Dr. Emmet Beaver's sanitarium for health, both physical and mental. You know what we call that kind of place today?"

Everyone stared at him, then Emmylou's expression changed from puzzlement to wide-eyed delight. "A spa?"

"Yes. A spa. I've got connections and investors. There are hot springs, the kind you can drink. There's the scenery, which is superb."

"So you did notice," Emmylou said.

"After you pointed out what was under my nose, yes. There's the main building, which will need some renovation but has a lot going for it." He remembered the marble baths and thought those alone would pack in the guests.

"We'll do all the usual treatments, the facials, the wraps, the specialty baths, but we'll also offer this unique location, we'll offer walking tours and trail rides. We've already got so much here to take advantage of. There's Amy's organic herbs and vegetables, the horses that are perfect for city slickers, the air's clean."

Gordon Hartnett spoke up. "I've found something in this water that I've still been unable to identify exactly, but there is no doubt in my mind that it's healthier here. People will come back again and again."

"We've got something else, too," Olive said.

"What's that?" Joe asked.

"I found the recipe for Dr. Beaver's special tonic."

"You mean the love potion? You found the recipe?" For a medical doctor, Gord sounded pretty damned excited.

"If we get started right away, we can have a batch ready for my birthday," Lydia said. "Under the O, orgy!" Then she looked at her old boyfriend sitting next to her with his eyebrows raised. "Oh, what the hell," she said. "We can play strip bingo. Just the two of us."

Gord whispered to his wife, who nodded and said, "If you want a local investor, Joe, count me in."

"Me, too," said Aunt Olive.

Joe blinked, saw Emmylou was also showing signs of shock. "What do you mean?" Emmylou asked her. "You've got money to invest?"

"Honey, your great-grandfather was a very smart man. You know all his theories about electricity?"

"Yes."

Olive nodded smugly. "In his will he left me and Lydia a thousand shares of stock in General Electric. I've never sold a single one. Didn't have any reason to. But Emmet would sure love this."

"I can't believe—"

"I've got my thousand, as well," Lydia piped in.

"Why didn't you ever say anything?"

The two old women looked at each other. "You've got a thousand, too."

"What?"

"Your grandmother left them to us for you." The old woman grinned. "Do you have any idea what those shares are worth now? With all the times the shares have split, and the dividends that we've reinvested—well, it's a small fortune."

After the way she'd been stretching pennies lately, she was having trouble taking in the news. And also, she wasn't pleased to have been kept in the dark. "But why in trust?"

"Patrice wanted you to have something to fall back on if you ever needed a financial cushion. She was worried you'd do something stupid if you had the shares too soon."

"Well, that's ridiculous. I'm not foolish with money."

"What would you have done with it?"

"Well, I'd have, I'd have . . ." Joe watched as Emmylou sent her aunts a rueful look. "I'd have paid off the back taxes on Emmet's property."

They nodded in unison. "Your gran wanted you to be able to leave if this town ever died, which, let's face it, it came close to doing."

"But now?"

"Now we pay off the taxes and let's build ourselves a spa."

They all turned to Joe, who was still trying to absorb the fact that so many of these fruitcakes were crazy like foxes. "What do we do now, Joe?"

"Now, you let me do what I do best. I'll put this deal together."

"From New York?" Emmylou asked, looking at her drink instead of him.

"No, Em. From right here."

She glanced up quickly and he saw the hope leap into her eyes.

"This is where I belong."

Olive snorted. "You mean you're crazy, too?"

"No," Joe said, still looking at Emmylou. "I was crazy before. Now I know that following your dream is more important than making more money or bringing in more business.

I know that people are more important than gain and that good friends and loved ones are the true riches."

"Oh, Joe," Emmylou said, and she rose from her chair and walked straight over to him. She kissed him, and he knew in that moment that the craziest thing he'd ever done was also the sanest.

Triple your pleasure with
3 BRIDES FOR 3 BAD BOYS
by Lucy Monroe,
available next month from Brava . . .

Anticipation thrummed through Carter Sloane's body. Soon he would know the answer to a very important question, a question that had been plaguing him for over four years.

Would Daisy Jackson's lips taste as good as they looked?

Impatiently, he increased his pace as he approached her office. The building was pretty much deserted, and he'd made sure it was so. He'd even sent security off the floor. He didn't want any witnesses for what he was hoping would take place. A kiss that would prove the desire went both ways.

Sweat broke out at his temples, and he tugged at the collar of his custom-tailored shirt that suddenly felt too tight. Thinking about Daisy made his blood so hot, it boiled in his veins.

His torment had been working for Sloane Electronics since she was eighteen. Not that he'd met her that early on. If he had, he wondered if he would ever have ended up engaged to Phoebe. Starting in clerical, Daisy had worked her way to an important behind-the-scenes position in marketing.

She was much too shy to thrive on the sales team, or even in a position where she had to present her ideas to upper management. He found that endearing.

He'd met her over four years ago when she'd first moved into the marketing department, and he had fallen in instant lust. She was the main reason he'd left Phoebe practically standing at the altar. If he could feel such strong sexual attraction to another woman, he had no business marrying Phoebe. He had been convinced he carried his father's curse when it came to relationships and women.

But four long years of wanting the same woman, dreaming about her and finally getting to the point where he wasn't even interested in sex with other women, had taught him something about himself.

He had a helluva lot more staying power than his father. He might not be any more capable of real love, but he *could* do the fidelity thing.

Now he just had to convince Daisy she wanted to do it with him.

He was almost positive that her hormones were as affected as his. She blushed when their eyes met, and whenever he came close, her breathing got erratic. All definite signs the attraction was mutual, but he had to find out for sure.

Right now. He couldn't wait any longer.

It was after six P.M., but he knew she'd still be in her office. She had no social life. He'd asked around and discovered she never dated. Which shocked the hell out of him. Were the men around her blind or just stupid? His little Daisy was ripe for the plucking, and he was the lucky guy who was going to savor her sweet fruit.

He stepped into her office, and sure enough she was busy typing away at the computer. His nostrils flared just like an animal in heat scenting his mate as her vanilla perfume reached out and surrounded him.

"Don't you ever go home?"

She jumped and spun her chair around to face him.

Her black hair flew like a silk cloud around her face, and her almond-shaped brown eyes went wide like a Japanese animated cartoon. "*Mr. Sloane.*"

He took a step farther into the room and noticed with interest how she scooted back in her chair, even though the desk was an effective barrier between them. "Call me Carter."

He couldn't picture himself coming inside her as she screamed *Mr. Sloane* in his ear.

"I-I don't feel comfortable calling the owner of the company by his first name."

He watched her luscious lips move and form the words. Their natural raspberry fullness just begged to be kissed. Why didn't other men react to the sensuality she exuded? Her lack of a social life was inexplicable to him, even taking into account her shyness. But he'd been in the room when she was exuding subtle mating signals, of which he was sure she was oblivious, and so were the men working with her.

He'd noticed, though, and they made him nuts.

She made a nervous movement with her hands as his silence stretched, and his libido went into attack and conquer mode. It had been way too long. If his experiment failed, he didn't know what he was going to do.

It could not fail.

She had to want him, too.

No way could this much desire be one-sided.

"I'm the owner, aren't I?"

She nodded, her pink tongue darting out to lick her lips and then retreating in a game of erotic peek-a-boo he was positive she did not intend, and he had to stifle a groan.

"I don't mind you calling me Carter. In fact, I prefer it."

"But . . ."

"Daisy, even your admin calls me Carter. I think you're the only person in the company besides old Mrs. Berger in the cafeteria that calls me Mr. Sloane."

She sighed, as if it really mattered. "All right . . . Carter."

He didn't know why, but he felt like he'd won a major concession. "Good. Now, I have a question for you."

She sat up straighter, scooting her chair forward, and clasped her hands on top of her desk. "Yes?"

"Have you ever felt sexually harassed here?"

Her dark brown eyes opened wide, and her lips parted, but nothing came out, not even a huff of air.

She was taking so long to answer, he was beginning to wonder if there was some guy working for him that he was going to have to fire. "Have you?"

Finally, she shook her head. "Uh . . . no."

"Good."

She knocked some papers off her desk and bent to pick them up, sending a CD-Rom in its case flying to the floor as well. She gathered the papers and dropped them in an untidy heap on her desk with the CD-Rom on top. Her cheeks were now as berry pink as her lips.

"Mr. Slo— I mean, Carter, why did you ask me that?"

He moved around her desk, stalking her and hoping like hell her nerves were due to reciprocal attraction to the boss and not fear. "It's important."

She leaned back in her chair, away from him. "But why?"

"If you don't want to do anything, you don't have to."

"That's good." She was looking at him as though he'd gone nuts, and the truth was, he had.

His nuts were controlling his brain, and it wasn't doing his powers of conversation any good. While he could schmooze company presidents, man-woman communication was not his thing, and right now he felt like a rookie manager giving his first presentation to the board of directors.

He gave up on the subtle approach and decided on blunt honesty. "Daisy, I want to kiss you, but I don't want you to feel pressured into letting me because I own the company you work for."

She squeaked like a startled mouse, and then shook her head, sending that gorgeous black silk cloud into motion again.

Disappointment took his heart in its grip and squeezed. Had he been wrong about her reaction to him? Or was she afraid of it, and how far could he push it without going into the realms of harassment? Not very damned far.

She gaped at him. *"What?"*

He took another step toward her, finding it more and more difficult to rein in the primitive urges she brought out in him. "I want to kiss you."

"Now?"

That was definitely better than *no*. "Yes."

"I-I . . ."

He forced down the desire to just pick her right up out of that small black office chair and devour her lips. "You don't have to let me if you don't want to. Your job is not on the line. I won't hold it against you if you say no." But his balls were going to turn blue and fall off if that happened.

"I promise," he said for good measure. This had to be absolutely voluntary on her part, or it wasn't happening.

She tucked her shiny black hair behind one ear in a nervous gesture. It rippled over her shoulder, and he wanted to touch it. *Bad.*

"You really want to kiss me?"

"Yes."

"Now?" she repeated, and it was all he could do not to shout the affirmative.

"Yes, now." His voice came out like some kind of animal growl, and he hoped like Hades he hadn't scared her.

She stood up and closed all but two feet of the distance left between them.

He had long arms, and they were itching to reach out so he could grab her. It took more concentration than he felt he could spare to stop from doing it.

"My job doesn't depend on this?"

"No." More growling. In a minute he was going to start howling like a wolf at a full moon.

Moons made him think of backsides, naked backsides. Carter came closer to losing it than he had since he was fifteen and necking with his girlfriend when she let him cop a feel under her blouse for the first time.

"Is that why you asked me about the um . . . the sexual harassment thing? Did you think I felt pressured sexually by you?"

"Not yet." He hadn't pressured her at all. He'd been extremely careful not to.

"But now you want to kiss me." She seemed to be having a really hard time taking it in.

He closed the distance between them and laid his hands on her shoulders. Her small bones felt fragile under his fingers. "I want to kiss you, and I need you to either say yes or tell me to take a hike in something like two seconds."

Her head tilted back so she could see him. She didn't look scared. She didn't look intimidated. She just looked confused, and at that very moment that wasn't a whole lot better than the other two. He needed to have his lips on hers in the worst way.

"Do you want to use your tongue?" She asked it like she'd ask if he wanted a mint, and it took him a second to grasp the meaning of the words.

When he did, his knees about buckled. "Yes. I'm going to want to use my tongue."

She bit her lip and stared at him for a second. "Oh."

"Is that a problem?"

"I don't like using tongues."

It was his turn to stare. Not like tongues? No. She couldn't possibly have said that. He wanted to use his tongue in a lot more places than her mouth.

"I'll make you like it."

"If I don't, will you stop?"

"Stop kissing you?"

"Stop putting your tongue in my mouth."

His knees did buckle, and he pivoted to fall back against her desk. He leaned on the edge and pulled her between his legs, so her body was one inch from rubbing up against the biggest, baddest erection he'd ever had.

"I'll stop if you don't like it."

"How will you know? I can't talk with—"

He couldn't bear to hear her say it again. "Hit my shoulder. I'll stop if you hit my shoulder."

"Okay."

His hands gripped convulsively on her shoulders. "Did you just say I could kiss you?"

"Only if you stop using your tongue if I tap your shoulder."

"I promise." But he was going to do everything in his power to make her like it.

Like it hot? Here's an advance look at
OUT OF CONTROL
by Shannon McKenna,
coming in April 2005 from Brava . . .

San Cataldo, California

A poke in the eye, that's how it felt.

Mag Callahan curled white-knuckled hands around the mug of lukewarm coffee that she kept forgetting to drink. She stared, blank-eyed, at the Zip-Loc bag lying on her kitchen table. It contained the evidence that she had extracted from her own unmade bed a half an hour before, with the help of a pair of tweezers.

Item number 1: Black lace thong panties. She, Mag, favored pastels that weren't such a harsh contrast to her fair skin. Item number 2: Three strands of very long, straight, dark hair. She, Mag, had short, curly, red hair.

Her mind reeled and fought the unwanted information. Craig, her boyfriend, had been uncommunicative and paranoid lately, but she'd chalked it up to that pesky Y chromosome of his, plus his job stress, and his struggle to start up his own consulting business. It never occurred to her that he would ever . . . dear God.

Her own house. Her own *bed*. That pig.

The blank shock began to tingle and go red around the edges as it transformed inevitably into fury. She'd been so nice to him. Letting him stay in her house rent-free while he bug-swept and remodeled his own place. Lending him money, quite a bit of it. Co-signing his business loans. She'd bent over backward to be supportive, accommodating, womanly. Trying to lighten up on her standard ball-breaker routine, which consisted of scaring boyfriend after boyfriend into hiding because of her strong opinions. She'd wanted so badly to make it work this time. She'd tried so hard, and this is what she got for her pains. Shafted. Again.

She bumped the edge of the table as she got up, knocking over her coffee. She leaped back just in time to keep it from splattering over the cream linen outfit she'd changed into for her lunch date with Craig.

She'd come home early from her weekend conference on purpose to pretty herself up for their date, having fooled herself into thinking that Craig was only twitchy because he was about to broach the subject of—drum roll, please—the Future of Their Relationship. She'd even gone so far as to fantasize a sappy Kodak moment: Craig, bashfully passing her a ring box over dessert. Herself, opening it. A gasp of happy awe. Violins swelling as she melted into tears. How stupid.

Fury roared up like gasoline dumped on a fire. She had to do something active, right now. Like blow up his car, maybe. Craig's favorite coffee mug was the first object to present itself, sitting smugly in the sink beside another dirty mug, from which the mystery tart had no doubt sipped her own coffee this morning. Why, would you look at that. A trace of coral lipstick was smeared along the mug's edge

Mag flung them across the room. Crash, tinkle. The noise relieved her feelings, but now she had a coffee splatter on her kitchen wall to remind her of this glorious moment forever. Smooth move, Mag.

She rummaged under the sink for a garbage bag, muttering. She was going to delete that lying bastard from her house.

She started with the spare room, which Craig had commandeered as his office. In the bag went his laptop, modem, and mouse, his ergonomic keyboard. Mail, trade magazines, floppy disks and data-storage CDs clattered in after it. A sealed box that she found in the back of one of the desk drawers hit the bottom of the bag with a rattling thud.

Onward. She dragged the bag into the hall. It had been stupid to start with the heaviest stuff first, but it was too late now. Next stop, hall closet. Costly suits, dress shirts, belts, ties, shoes, and loafers. On to the bedroom, to the drawers she'd cleared out for his casual wear. His hypoallergenic silicone pillow. His alarm clock. His special dental floss. Every item she tossed made her anger burn hotter. Scum.

That was it. Nothing left to dump. She knotted the top of the bag.

It was now too heavy to lift. She had to drag it, bumpity-thud out the door, over the deck, down the stairs, across the narrow, pebbly beach of Parson's Lake. The wooden passageway that led to her floating dock wobbled perilously as she jerked the stone-heavy thing along.

She heaved it over the edge of the dock with a grunt. Glug, glug, some pitiful bubbles, and down it sank, out of sight. Craig could take a bracing November dip and do a salvage job if he so chose.

She could breathe a bit better now, but she knew from experience that the health benefits of childish, vindictive behavior were very short-term. She'd crash and burn again soon if she didn't stay in constant motion. Work was the only thing that could save her now. She grabbed her purse, jumped into the car and headed downtown to her office.

Dougie, her receptionist, looked up with startled eyes when she charged through the glass double doors of Callahan Web Weaving. "Wait. Hold on a second. She just walked in the door," he said into the phone. He pushed a button. "Mag? What are you doing here? I thought you were coming in this afternoon, after you had lunch with—"

"Change of plans," she said crisply. "I have better things to do."

Dougie looked bewildered. "But Craig's on line two. He

wants to know why you're late for your lunch date. Says he has to talk to you. Urgently. As soon as possible. A matter of life and death, he says."

Mag rolled her eyes as she marched into her office. "So what else is new, Dougie? Isn't everything that has to do with Craig's precious convenience a matter of life and death?"

Dougie followed her. "He, uh, sounds really flipped out, Mag."

Come to think of it, it would be more classy, dignified, and above all, final if she looked him in the eye while she dumped him. Plus, she could throw the panties bag right into his face if he had the gall to deny it. That would be satisfying. Closure and all that good stuff.

She smiled reassuringly into Dougie's anxious eyes. "Tell Craig I'm on my way. And after this, don't accept any more calls from him. Don't even bother to take messages. For Craig Caruso, I am in a meeting, for the rest of eternity. Is that clear?"

Dougie blinked through his glasses, owl-like. "You OK, Mag?"

The smile on her face was a warlike mask. "Fine. I'm great, actually. This won't take long. I'm certainly not going to eat with him."

"Want me to order in lunch for you, then? Your usual?"

She hesitated, doubting she'd have much appetite, but poor Dougie was so anxious to help. "Sure, that would be nice." She patted him on the shoulder. "You're a sweetie-pie. I don't deserve you."

"I'll order carrot cake and a double skim latte, too. You're gonna need it," Dougie said, scurrying back to his beeping phone.

Mag checked the mirror inside her coat closet, freshened her lipstick and made sure her coppery red do was artfully mussed, not wisping dorkily, as it tended to do if she didn't gel the living bejesus out of it. One should try to look elegant when telling a parasitical user to go to hell and fry. She thought about mascara, and decided against it. She cried easily: when she was hurt, when she was pissed, and today she was both. Putting on mascara was like spitting in the face of the gods.

She grabbed her purse, uncomfortably aware, as always, of the automatic pistol that shared the space inside with wallet, keys, and lipstick. A gift from Craig, after she'd gotten mugged months ago. A pointless gift, since she'd never been able to bring herself to load the thing, and had no license to carry concealed. Craig had insisted that she keep it in her purse, along with a clip of ammunition. And she'd gone along with it, in her efforts to be sweet and grateful and accommodating. Hah.

If she were a different woman, she'd make him regret that gift. She'd wave it around at him, scare him out of his wits. But that kind of tantrum just wasn't her style. Neither were guns. She'd give it back to him today. It was illegal, it was scary, it made her purse too heavy, and besides, today was all about streamlining, dumping excess baggage.

Emotional feng shui. Sploosh, straight into the lake.

By the time she got to her car, the unseasonable late autumn heat made sweat trickle between her shoulder blades. She felt rumpled, flushed and emotional. Frazzled Working Girl was not the look she wanted for this encounter. Indifferent Ice Queen was more like it. She cranked up the air conditioning to chill down to Ice Queen temperatures and pulled out into traffic, the density of which gave her way too much time to think about what a painful pattern this was in her love life.

Used and shafted by charming jerks. Over and over. She was almost thirty years old, for God's sake. She should have outgrown this tedious, self-destructive crap by now. She should be hitting her stride.

Maybe she should get her head shrunk. What a joy. Pick out the most icky element of her personality, and pay someone scads of money to help her dwell on it. Bleah. Introspection had never been her thing.

She parked her car outside the newly renovated brick warehouse that housed Craig's new studio and braced herself against seeing Craig's assistant bouncing up to chirp a greeting. Mandi was her name. Probably dotted the "i" with a heart. Nothing behind those big brown eyes but bubbles and foam. She had long dark hair, too. Fancy that.

But there was no one to be seen in the studio. Odd. Maybe Craig and Mandi had been overcome with passion in the back office. She set her teeth and marched through the place. Her heels clicked loudly on the tile. The silence made the sharp sounds echo and swell.

The door to Craig's office was ajar. She clicked her heels louder. *Go for it. Burn your bridges, Mag, it's what you're best at.*

And finally, here is a portion of Lori Foster's
next bestselling novel JAMIE.
Available from Zebra Books in June 2005.

The relentless rain came down, accompanied by ground-rattling thunder and great flashes of lightning. Jamie liked storms . . . but not this one. This time he felt more than the turbulence of the weather. The air crackled with electricity—and good intentions. Determination. Resolve.

They hunted him. Well meaning, but destructive all the same. He had only himself to blame. He'd allowed them to become friendly. He hadn't been aloof enough, had interfered too many times. But God, what other choices did he have? Watch them suffer? Feel their pain?

No, he couldn't. He had enough of his own pain to deal with.

Sitting on the plank floor, his back to a wall, his knees drawn up, he stared out at the darkness. Not a single lamp glowed in his home. The fireplace remained cool and empty. A chill skated up his spine, and he laid his forehead to his knees, trying to block them out, wanting to pray that they wouldn't find him, but unable to summon the right words in the midst of so many feelings bombarding him.

Then it dawned on him. His head shot up, his black eyes unseeing. *Not just the townsfolk.* No, someone else crept up his mountain. Someone else wanted him.

Without conscious decision, he came to his feet and padded barefoot across the cold floor. No locks protected his doors;

he didn't need them. He shoved the heavy wood open and moved out to the covered porch. Rain immediately blew in against him, soaking his shirt and jeans, collecting in his beard and long hair until he looked, felt, like a drowned rat.

Something vaguely close to excitement stirred in his chest, accelerating his heartbeat, making his blood sing. He lifted his nose to the wind, let his heavy eyelids drift shut . . . and he knew. He saw the first visitor, alone, a stranger. A woman. Seeking him out. *Needing* him.

This he could do.

Half furious and half thrilled for the distraction, he stepped inside the house and shoved his feet into rubber boots. Foregoing a jacket, sensing the limitations of his time frame, Jamie stepped off the porch and into the pouring rain.

Storms were different in the woods, with leaves acting as a canopy, muffling the patter of the rain, absorbing the moisture. Once, long ago, he had hoped they might absorb some of the emotions that assaulted him. But they hadn't. Even from such a distance, high up the mountain in the thick of the trees where no one ever ventured, he'd still gotten to know the townsfolk; first the children, then the others.

And they'd gotten to know him.

Despite his efforts to the contrary, they were starting to care. They didn't know that their caring could destroy him, could strip away the last piece of self-respect he had. And he couldn't tell them.

Twice as dark as it'd be in the open, Jamie made his way cautiously away from his home, down an invisible trail known only to him. He walked and walked, mud caked up to his knees, his clothes so wet they were useless. Pausing beside a large tree that disappeared into the sky, he looked down the hillside.

Clint Evans, the new sheriff who'd listened to Jamie's dire warnings without much disbelief, picked his way tirelessly up the hillside. Jamie narrowed his eyes, knowing this was Julie's doing, that she wanted him at her wedding.

He would have gone. To make sure everything stayed safe.

To keep watch. She didn't need to send her hulking new lover after him. He should be pleased it wasn't Joe, because Joe wouldn't give up, no matter what. Worse, it could have been Alyx, Joe's sister, who surprised him once when she'd gotten too close for Jamie to send her away. She'd actually been in his home, and damn her, she wanted in his heart. She wanted his friendship. They all did.

Jamie closed his eyes and concentrated on breathing, concentrated on feeling the other intruder. His eyes snapped open, and he lifted a hand to shield his vision from the downpour. There, farther up the hill from Clint, she shivered and shook, miserable clear to her bones, tears mixing with the rain and mud on her face.

Jamie felt . . . something. He didn't know what. Odd, because it was only people he cared about that he couldn't read clearly. When he cared, emotional reactions mixed with his truer senses, muddling his readings.

Maybe *she* didn't know what she felt, so how could *he* know?

Dismissing Clint from his mind, already knowing what Clint would see and what he'd do, Jamie pushed away from the tree. The woman wore no hat and her hair was plastered to her skull. A redhead, Jamie thought, although with her hair soaked it looked dark enough to be brown. He didn't have to survey her to know of her pale skin sprinkled with a few freckles, or her blue eyes, now bloodshot. Her face, more plain than otherwise, served as a nice deception to her body.

She had incredible breasts and a small waist. Her legs were long and shapely, and she had an ass that would excite many men—if they noticed. But her quiet demeanor and ordinary appearance put them off. As she wanted. She hid—just as Jamie did.

They had that in common.

Holding tight to a skinny tree, she tried and failed to take a few more steps up the mountain. Her feet gained no purchase in the slick mud, and she fell forward with a gasp that got her a mouthful of mud. Moaning, she rolled to her back and just laid there, more tears coming as she labored for breath.

Jamie picked his way toward her, and with each step he took in a sense of alarm that expanded until her fear and worry and pain became his own. She hurt. Fever robbed her of strength. Her lungs labored and her eyes burned.

Before Jamie could get to her, before he could warn her not to move, she tried to stand again. She got upright, then one foot slipped out from under her and her arms floundered in the air—and she fell back. Hard.

She didn't roll down the hill.

The rock kept her from doing so.

In seconds, Jamie reached her. He touched her cheek and knew the fever wasn't that bad. Sick, yes, but not so sick that he had to worry. The bump on her head . . . that worried him. He patted her cheeks, unwilling to speak, knowing that Clint drew nearer, and he simply couldn't deal with them both right now.

Tipping a leaf to gather the moisture off it, Jamie wiped some of the mud from her face. Her hair spiked up in front when he pushed it away from her eyes. He tapped her cheeks again, smoothed his thumb along her cheekbone, and her eyes opened. As he already knew, they were blue—deep, dark blue, like a sky at midnight. At first vague, her gaze sharpened the moment her eyes met his.

Jamie half-expected hysterics, which was absurd given he should have known exactly what she'd do. But still, her reaction surprised him. Her eyes widened, then her lashes sank down and she said, "Jamie Creed. Thank God."